ACCLAIM FOR KATHLEEN FULLER

"These are light stories perfect for fans of the genre that will . . . bring some warmth and romance to readers."

—THE PARKERSBURG NEWS AND SENTINEL ON AMISH GENERATIONS

"Fuller cements her reputation a top practitioner of Amish fiction with this moving, perceptive collection."

—PUBLISHERS WEEKLY ON AMISH GENERATIONS

"A warm romance that will tug at the hearts of readers, this is a new favorite."

—THE PARKERSBURG NEWS & SENTINEL ON THE TEACHER'S BRIDE

"Fuller's appealing Amish romance deals with some serious issues, including depression, yet it also offers funny and endearing moments."

—BOOKLIST ON THE TEACHER'S BRIDE

"Kathleen Fuller's The Teacher's Bride is a heartwarming story of unexpected romance woven with fun and engaging characters who come to life on every page. Once you open the book, you won't put it down until you've reached the end."

—AMY CLIPSTON, BESTSELLING AUTHOR OF A SEAT BY THE HEARTH

"Kathy Fuller's characters leap off the page with subtle power as she uses both wit and wisdom to entertain! Refreshingly honest and charming, Kathy's writing reflects a master's touch when it comes to intricate plotting and a satisfying and inspirational ending full of good cheer!"

—KELLY LONG, AUTHOR OF THE PATCH OF HEAVEN SERIES, ON THE TEACHER'S BRIDE

"Kathleen Fuller is a master storyteller and fans will absolutely fall in love with Ruby and Christian in *The Teacher's Bride*."

—RUTH REID, BESTSELLING AUTHOR OF *A MIRACLE OF HOPE*

"*The Teacher's Bride* features characters who know what it's like to be different, to not fit in. What they don't know is that's what makes them so loveable. Kathleen Fuller has written a sweet, oftentimes humorous, romance that reminds readers that the perfect match might be right in front of their noses. She handles the difficult topic of depression with a deft touch. Readers of Amish fiction won't want to miss this delightful story."

—KELLY IRVIN, BESTSELLING AUTHOR OF
THE EVERY AMISH SEASON SERIES

"Kathleen Fuller is a talented and a gifted author, and she doesn't disappoint in *The Teacher's Bride*. The story will captivate you from the first page to the last with Ruby, Christian, and engaging characters. You'll laugh, gasp, and wonder what will happen next. You won't want to miss reading this heartwarming Amish story of mishaps, faith, love, forgiveness, and friendship."

—MOLLY JEBBER, SPEAKER AND AWARD-WINNING AUTHOR OF *GRACE'S FORGIVENESS* AND THE AMISH KEEPSAKE POCKET QUILT SERIES

"Enthusiasts of Fuller's sweet Amish romances will savor this new anthology."

—*LIBRARY JOURNAL* ON *AN AMISH FAMILY*

"These four sweet stories are full of hope and promise along with misunderstandings and reconciliation. True love does prevail, but not without prayer, introspection, and humility. A must-read for fans of Amish romance."

—*RT BOOK REVIEWS*, 4 STARS, ON *AN AMISH FAMILY*

"The incredibly engaging Amish Letters series continues with a third story of perseverance and devotion, making it difficult to put down . . . Fuller skillfully knits together the lives within a changing, faithful community that has suffered its share of challenges."

—*RT Book Reviews*, 4 ¹/₂ stars, on *Words from the Heart*

"Fuller's inspirational tale portrays complex characters facing real-world problems and finding love where they least expected or wanted it to be."

—*Booklist*, starred review, on *A Reluctant Bride*

"Fuller has an amazing capacity for creating damaged characters and giving insights into their brokenness. One of the better voices in the Amish fiction genre."

—*CBA Retailers + Resources* on *A Reluctant Bride*

"This promising series debut from Fuller is edgier than most Amish novels, dealing with difficult and dark issues and featuring well-drawn characters who are tougher than the usual gentle souls found in this genre. Recommended for Amish fiction fans who might like a different flavor."

—*Library Journal* on *A Reluctant Bride*

"Sadie and Aden's love is both sweet and hard-won, and Aden's patience is touching as he wrestles not only with Sadie's dilemma, but his own abusive past. Birch Creek is weighed down by the Troyer family's dark secrets, and readers will be interested to see how secondary characters' lives unfold as the series continues."

—*RT Book Reviews*, 4 stars, on *A Reluctant Bride*

"Kathleen Fuller's *A Reluctant Bride* tells the story of two Amish families whose lives have collided through tragedy. Sadie Schrock's stoic resolve will touch and inspire Fuller's fans, as will the story's concluding triumph of redemption."

—SUZANNE WOODS FISHER, BESTSELLING
AUTHOR OF *ANNA'S CROSSING*

"Kathleen Fuller's *A Reluctant Bride* is a beautiful story of faith, hope, and second chances. Her characters and descriptions are captivating, bringing the story to life with the turn of every page."

—AMY CLIPSTON, BESTSELLING AUTHOR OF
A SEAT BY THE HEARTH

"The latest offering in the Middlefield Family series is a sweet love story, with perfectly crafted characters. Fuller's Amish novels are written with the utmost respect for their way of living. Readers are given a glimpse of what it is like to live the simple life."

—*RT BOOK REVIEWS*, 4 STARS, ON *LETTERS TO KATIE*

"Fuller's second Amish series entry is a sweet romance with a strong sense of place that will attract readers of Wanda Brunstetter and Cindy Woodsmall."

—*LIBRARY JOURNAL* ON *FAITHFUL TO LAURA*

"Well-drawn characters and a homespun feel will make this Amish romance a sure bet for fans of Beverly Lewis and Jerry S. Eicher."

—*LIBRARY JOURNAL* ON *TREASURING EMMA*

"*Treasuring Emma* is a heartwarming story filled with real-life situations and well-developed characters. I rooted for Emma and Adam until the very last page. Fans of Amish fiction and those seeking an endearing romance will enjoy this love story. Highly recommended."

—BETH WISEMAN, BESTSELLING AUTHOR OF *HER BROTHER'S
KEEPER* AND THE DAUGHTERS OF THE PROMISE SERIES

"*Treasuring Emma* is a charming, emotionally layered story of the value of friendship in love and discovering the truth of the heart. A true treasure of a read!"

THE FARMER'S BRIDE

The Middlefield Family Novels

Treasuring Emma

Faithful to Laura

Letters to Katie

The Hearts of Middlefield Novels

A Man of His Word

An Honest Love

A Hand to Hold

Story Collections

An Amish Family

Amish Generations

Stories

A Miracle for Miriam included in *An Amish Christmas*

A Place of His Own included in *An Amish Gathering*

What the Heart Sees included in *An Amish Love*

A Perfect Match included in *An Amish Wedding*

Flowers for Rachael included in *An Amish Garden*

A Gift for Anne Marie included in
An Amish Second Christmas

A Heart Full of Love included in *An Amish Cradle*

A Bid for Love included in *An Amish Market*

A Quiet Love included in *An Amish Harvest*

Building Faith included in *An Amish Home*

Lakeside Love included in *An Amish Summer*

What Love Built included in *An Amish Homecoming*

THE FARMER'S BRIDE

AMISH BRIDES OF BIRCH CREEK

Kathleen Fuller

 ZONDERVAN®

ZONDERVAN

The Farmer's Bride

Copyright © 2019 by Kathleen Fuller

This title is also available as a Zondervan e-book.

Requests for information should be addressed to:
Zondervan, *3900 Sparks Dr. SE, Grand Rapids, Michigan 49546*

ISBN 978-0-310-35512-0 (trade paper)
ISBN 978-0-310-35513-7 (ebook)
ISBN 978-0-310-36385-9 (mass market)

Library of Congress Cataloging-in-Publication
CIP data available upon request.

Printed in the United States of America

21 22 23 24 25 / LSC / 5 4 3 2 1

To James. I love you.

Glossary

ab im kopp: crazy, crazy in the head

aenti: aunt

appeditlich: delicious

boppli/bopplin: baby/babies

bruder: brother

bu/buwe: boy/boys

daed: father

danki: thank you

dawdi haus: a small house built onto or near the main house
for grandparents to live in

Dietsch: Amish language

dochder: daughter

familye: family

frau: woman, Mrs.

geh: go

grossdochder: granddaughter

grossmammi/grossmutter: grandmother

grossohn: grandson

grossvatter: grandfather

gut: good

gute morgen: good morning

gute nacht: good night

haus: house

Herr: Mr.

kaffee: coffee

kapp: white hat worn by Amish women
kinn/kinner: child/children
lieb: love
maedel: girl/young woman
mamm: mom
mann: Amish man
mei: my
morgen: morning
mudder: mother
nee: no
nix: nothing
onkel: uncle
schee: pretty/handsome
schoolhaus: schoolhouse
schwester/schwesters: sister/sisters
sehr: very
seltsam: weird
sohn/sohns: son/sons
vatter: father
ya: yes
yer/yers: your/yours
yerself: yourself
yung: young

CHAPTER 1

Martha Detweiler dashed into her house, slammed the front door behind her, and leaned against it. She closed her eyes. *Not again.*

Her mother came into the living room, wiping her hands on a kitchen towel. "Goodness, Martha. What's all this racket?"

"Ruby's having a scavenger hunt this Saturday."

"Oh?" *Mamm* tucked the towel into the band of her apron, which was dotted with a few globs of the strawberry jam she was making. "That's nice."

"Nice?" Martha slumped against the door. "How can you say that when she invited other people!"

"You can't have a scavenger hunt with just two people," her mother said, referring to Ruby and her husband, Chris.

Martha snuck a peek through the curtains covering the front window. "Oh *nee*," she whispered.

"What in the world has gotten into you?" *Mamm* looked over Martha's shoulder. "Where are all those *yung* men going?"

"Here." She turned to *Mamm*, her eyes widening. "They're coming here. I think they all want to ask me to the scavenger hunt."

Mamm turned pale. "All of them? At the same time?"

Martha nodded. "Yes. I think so." Then she shook her head. "I-I don't know."

Mamm looked out the window again, and then she grabbed Martha by the hand and practically dragged her into the kitchen.

"*Geh*," she said, shooing her out the back door. "I'll make sure the *buwe* don't follow you."

Martha nodded her thanks before taking off, running through the neighbors' backyard. Fortunately, they weren't home, or for sure they would wonder why she was flying by. Making a quick decision to flee to Cevilla's house—the boys weren't likely to look for her there—she snuck across another backyard, this one behind a large house that had been empty since her family moved here nearly two years ago. Out of the corner of her eye, she saw a figure walking out the back door. Was someone living there now? She hadn't known the house was for sale.

She shook off the thought as she zipped through a small field. She glanced at the road behind her. Seeing the five young men turning into her driveway, she picked up her speed.

When she turned the corner at the end of the road, she slowed down, then stopped, her chest heaving. She gasped for air. There had to be a better way to avoid the single men of Birch Creek.

When she finally caught her breath, she walked to the end of the street where Cevilla lived and imagined her mother giving Ira, Zeke, Zeb, Owen, and Samuel an explanation for her absence—or at least for her unavailability. Her body perspired from a mix of the heavy summer humidity, running faster than she had in years, and a good dose of guilt. She shouldn't have let her mother deal with the boys. It wasn't *her* responsibility to fudge the truth on her daughter's behalf.

But what else could she do? Since Ruby had married Christian last year, and Christian's sister, Selah, had moved back to New

York, Martha was the only single young woman in a district full of young single men. And for some reason, lately they all had courting fever. She wasn't even sure that was a thing, but it didn't matter. She couldn't go anywhere, except maybe to her job, without having one of them approach her for a date. Their overzealous attention even squashed her interest in Zeb, whom she had kind of liked up until a few months ago and might have gone out with if he'd asked. Now she just wanted them all to leave her alone, not compete for her attention.

I just want a simple life, Lord. Is that too much to ask?

She knocked on Cevilla's front door. Cevilla's *English* friend, Richard, answered. "Hi, Martha," he said, looking a little surprised.

Martha looked over her shoulder. So far no one was following her, which meant her mother had been successful in keeping them from sniffing out her trail. When she looked back at Richard, Cevilla stood next to him.

"What brings you by?" Richard asked.

"*Bu* trouble," Cevilla said, then motioned for her to come in.

Martha quickly stepped inside, wondering how Cevilla knew. Then again, the octogenarian seemed to have a sixth sense about everything.

"Get the dominoes," Cevilla said to Richard, pointing at a cabinet on the other side of the room. "I'll make the tea."

Looking confused, Richard gave Martha a small smile before heading to the cabinet. Martha followed Cevilla to the kitchen.

"I'm sorry I'm imposing," Martha said, standing in the doorway.

"Nonsense." Cevilla began filling her teakettle with water. "Just sit down and tell me what happened."

Martha dropped into a chair at the table and explained how Ruby had invited every *single*, unattached young person in the district to her house for a scavenger hunt, with Martha the only single woman. "I had just gone out for a walk when I saw Ira, Zeb, Zeke, Owen, Samuel—"

"Oh dear," Cevilla said, now sitting across from her.

"—all heading toward *mei haus*. I ran back inside." She looked down at her lap. "That sounds cowardly, doesn't it?"

"It sounds like they took you off guard—in a group."

She lifted her eyes and looked at Cevilla again. "They did. But I shouldn't have been surprised. This isn't the first time several of them have asked me for a date, or to take me home from a singing, or even just tried to talk to me. When I saw them all coming at once, I panicked."

Cevilla nodded as Richard walked in. The teakettle started to whistle, and Cevilla moved to get up. "Stay put," he said, and then set the dominoes on the table. "I'll get the tea too."

Martha didn't miss the softness in Cevilla's eyes as she looked at her friend, giving him a small nod. It tugged at Martha's heart. They had an unusual relationship for many reasons—their advanced age, the fact he was *English*, and the fact that after six decades apart they'd reunited. He'd even moved from California and now lived in a small house next to hers. Everyone could see they were in love.

Love. Martha let out a small sigh.

It wasn't that she didn't appreciate romance or didn't want to fall in love. She wanted to date and someday to be in a relationship. She just didn't want to be coerced into going out with someone. She didn't want to be chased just because she was the only woman available.

Cevilla opened the tin box of dominoes and started placing

the pieces on the table. "Many a young woman would love to be in *yer* shoes, Martha."

"They can have my shoes," Martha muttered.

Richard poured the hot water into a plastic pitcher, where Cevilla had placed several teabags. As he went to the gas-powered fridge freezer to get ice, Martha helped Cevilla turn over the dominoes. "I'm sorry about this," Martha said.

"No need to be sorry." Richard pulled out an ice cube tray. "We love a rousing game of dominoes, don't we, Cevilla?"

"That we do."

Martha's emotions started to settle a bit. She loved playing dominoes too. She loved any type of game, indoors or out-doors, and playing dominoes with Cevilla and Richard would help keep her mind off her problems, at least for the short-term.

"Care to shuffle?" Cevilla said to Martha.

Martha nodded, and after Richard put glasses of iced tea in front of the women, they started a game of chicken foot. Richard immediately shot ahead.

"I don't know why we let him play," Cevilla grumped as she wrote down his most recent score, a whopping three points.

"Because I'm charming." Richard took a sip of his tea.

"Don't flatter yourself." But she smiled. "It's because we need three players to make this game worth playing." Cevilla put down her pencil and looked at Martha. "Feeling better, sweetie?"

"*Ya.*" She leaned back in her chair and watched Richard shuffle the dominoes. "I can't keep doing this, though."

"You're not that far behind Richard," Cevilla said.

"Not the dominoes."

Cevilla nodded, her gaze growing soft. "I know. And it's all right. We'll just have to figure out a plan B, that's all."

"When was there a plan A?" Richard asked.

"There wasn't." Cevilla raised an indignant gray eyebrow. "I just think plan B sounds better."

Martha didn't care what they called it, as long as it worked. She couldn't continue to literally run away from her problems.

Richard sniffed. "I don't know why you don't tell those fellas you're not interested."

Both Cevilla and Martha gaped at Richard. "It's not that easy," Cevilla said.

"Sure it is. Men like it when women are straightforward." He started choosing his dominoes. "To the point is best."

"I can't tell them I'm not interested in marriage," Martha said. "That would be a lie."

"And we don't lie, do we, Martha?" Cevilla lifted her chin.

Richard frowned. "Isn't your mother lying to those young men right now?"

"Fudging," Cevilla corrected. "And it's only temporary."

"Until you come up with plan B." Richard shook his head. "I never will understand women."

Martha didn't say anything as she grabbed nine dominoes. Richard wouldn't understand, of course. He was *English*. He was also a man, and while they might claim to like women to be straightforward, that wasn't always the case. She'd told Ira and Owen she wasn't interested in dating anyone, but they seemed to take that as a challenge, and she couldn't shake off the feeling that they considered her a prize to be won. She'd never be that.

"Tell me more about the scavenger hunt," Cevilla said, standing her dominoes on their sides. "Is this another of Ruby Ropp's harebrained ideas?"

"It's not harebrained." Martha checked her dominoes and saw that she had a double three. She put it in the middle of the table. "I think it sounds like fun. She said she wanted to do something different from supper and volleyball." Martha would have been happy to play volleyball, but the scavenger hunt intrigued her.

"What is Ruby planning to do?" Richard asked.

"I have no idea." She'd been speaking English since she arrived, since she knew Richard knew only a few words of *Dietsch*. Cevilla always spoke English when she was with him.

"Chris will keep her in line." Cevilla placed a four/three domino next to the double three. "He seems to have a grounding effect on her. They make a lovely couple."

Martha thought so, too, even though she had at one time thought Chris Ropp was interested in her. But now she could see that had been her imagination. His heart had always belonged to Ruby, even when he didn't know it. "I'm sure whatever she decides to do, everyone will have a good time," Martha said.

"Will you?"

She glanced up at Richard's question. He was looking at her with his kind eyes, the wrinkles around his cheeks more pronounced as he smiled gently. She liked him, and it was obvious he and Cevilla adored each other. They had fallen in love later in life, but Martha enjoyed the youthfulness of their interaction. She had lived in lots of communities, but she had never encountered a couple like them. Perhaps they were unique, which was why no one raised an eyebrow about their relationship. That, and Cevilla would never stand for it.

"I'll try to have a good time," Martha said. Somehow she would dodge the men's advances. Or maybe by Saturday they would have given up on her. Hopefully.

"You've been approached by every single young man in Birch Creek?" Richard asked.

Martha nodded. "Except for one."

"Who?" Cevilla said, her brow lifting behind her silver-rimmed glasses.

"Seth Yoder."

"Who does that *yung mann* think he is?" Cevilla slipped into *Dietsch*. "Does he believe he's better than you?"

"Cevilla." Richard put his hand on hers. "I don't know exactly what you said, but I can see that flash in your eyes."

"What flash?"

"The one that tells me your blood pressure is on the rise."

"My blood pressure is perfectly fine. I'm just confused as to why Seth hasn't asked Martha out on a date yet."

"Maybe he doesn't want to." Martha added another domino to the game. She frowned. She hadn't thought about Seth not paying attention to her until Richard asked that question. And while she didn't want to be vain, why *hadn't* he'd shown any interest?

"Or he already has a girl," Richard said. "Pass." He picked up another domino, scowled, and added it to the group in front of him.

"I'm sure he doesn't," Cevilla said.

"How can you be so sure?"

"Because I know Mary Yoder, and she can't keep a secret. She would have told her sister-in-law Carolyn, or Naomi, or Rhoda. Probably all three. Eventually that tidbit of information would get back to me." She lifted her chin again. "Nothing goes on in this community that I don't know about."

Martha didn't doubt that. "It doesn't matter anyway," she said. "I'm grateful he isn't interested in me. That's one less man I have to say no to."

Cevilla snapped her fingers. "That's it."

"What?" Martha and Richard said at the same time.

"You need to say yes to Seth."

Martha stilled. "He hasn't asked me anything yet."

"No, he hasn't." Cevilla leaned forward, the indignant flash in her eyes replaced with a crafty one. "But he will."

"Is this plan B?" Richard said, his expression wary.

"It's the best plan B there is." Cevilla laughed. "I'm surprised I didn't think of this before."

"I don't understand," Martha said.

Cevilla sat back in her chair and smiled. "You won't have to worry about those boys soon enough. By this time next week, everyone will know you're dating Seth Yoder."

. . .

Seth tossed a bale of hay down from the loft in the barn and then wiped the sweat from his brow before grabbing another one. This summer had been hot, humid, and long. He turned and looked at the full hayloft, and gratitude filled him. Not long ago the loft had been empty, the family had been down to one cow, and the crops had failed for the third year in a row. He'd been twelve at the time, still a kid, but old enough to notice his father's stressed, worried face and his mother's constant hand-wringing.

He grabbed another bale. How things had changed. His father was now the bishop of Birch Creek and had been for several years. Any strain he saw on *Daed*'s face came from his bishop duties, not worrying about how he would feed his family over the winter. His mother was her bright, joking self, and his older sisters, Ivy and Karen, were happily married with families and businesses of their own. Seth and his younger brothers, Ira and

Judah, worked hard on the farm, and not only was the hayloft filled to bursting but they had sizable herds of Angus cows, goats, and pigs, as well as chickens. Judah wanted a dog, but their father had put his foot down, a decision Seth agreed with. "We have enough animals to take care of," Seth pointed out. Their father nodded in agreement.

Yes, life was good. Great, even. Except for one thing.

Seth hated farming.

He tossed the bale to the barn floor. *Hate* was too strong a word, and a term the Amish frowned on using anyway. Hate in the heart only led to bitterness, bad choices, and separation from God. But he'd be hard-pressed to find an equivalent for how he felt about farming. Unlike his father and Ira, Seth didn't feel connected to the land, and he didn't find peace raising animals. He hated—no, intensely disliked—working outside from dawn to dusk. He'd rather be pursuing a passion for woodworking he'd secretly harbored but had found less and less time for as the farm became more successful. But he couldn't make money woodworking—at least not yet—and he would never again live in poverty the way he had as a child.

Seth slid down the ladder, landing softly on the ground. His attitude toward farming had nothing to do with his physical fitness. Out of all his brothers, he was the most athletic, and he and Ira were about equal in strength. He picked up two of the bales, one in each hand, and carried them to the cart outside the barn. His horse, Pinto, was already harnessed and ready to go, dragging one front hoof against the gravel driveway. "Easy, *bu*," Seth said as he tossed the hay into the cart. "Just two more and we'll be ready to *geh*."

He was carrying out the last two bales when he saw Ira trudging up the driveway. Over the past year his brother had shot up at least four inches and was now taller than Seth. He'd kept his stocky build, though. He ate like a horse, but all that food had transformed to muscle. "What's got you so down?" Seth said, dropping the bales into the cart.

"*Nix.*" Ira put his hands in his pockets, but he didn't look at Seth.

"That's not true." Seth brushed off his hands and went to Ira. "You look like you lost *yer* best friend."

Ira shook his head. "Not exactly." He blew out a breath and looked at the cart. "Where are you headed?"

"Cevilla's. I told her I'd bring her some of *Mamm*'s gooseberry jam. I also want to check on her and her friend Richard, to see if they need anything."

"Hard to believe a rich *English mann* like him is fitting into our community so easily."

"I'm sure Cevilla keeps him in line."

Ira looked at the hay in the cart. "What are you doing with those?"

"Dropping them off at *Aenti* Carolyn's on the way home. We had some extra bales." Seth climbed up onto the bench seat. "Want to come with me?"

Ira shook his head. "*Nee.* I told *Daed* I would hoe the cornfield before the weeds take over. They seem to love the heat and humidity." He pulled his hands out of his pockets and headed for the second barn, where they kept their farming implements.

"See you later," Seth called out. When Ira didn't turn around, Seth shrugged. Clearly something was on his brother's mind, but if he didn't want to talk about it, Seth wasn't going to press him.

A short while later he arrived at Cevilla's. He parked the cart near the barn, made sure Pinto was secure, and picked up the small box of jelly jars his mother had packed. When he knocked on the front door, Cevilla answered it immediately, as if she'd been standing on the other side. She looked a bit surprised.

"Oh, Seth. I can't believe I forgot you were coming today." Then she smiled. "*Yer* timing is perfect. Well, a little less than perfect. It would have been better if you'd been here a few minutes earlier—"

"Are you going to invite the boy in?" Richard showed up next to her, opened the screen door wider, and then held out his hand. "Hello, Seth."

Seth shook his hand, still surprised by the strong grip the old man had. "Hi, Richard."

"Richard's right. Where are my manners? Come in, Seth. Have a glass of tea and a butterscotch cookie. Carolyn dropped a few off the other day, fresh from her bakery. Richard's allowed only one. He has to watch his sugar because of his diabetes."

Richard rolled his eyes. "I'm sure Seth isn't interested in my medical issues."

Seth wasn't sure what to say about that. Seemed like all the older people he knew talked about their aches and pains, and he didn't expect Cevilla and Richard to be any different. "Thanks for the invitation, but I just came to drop these off." He held up the box. "I can put them in the kitchen for you."

"How nice," Richard said. "Thank you for bringing those by. I've developed a love for gooseberry jam, thanks to Cevilla and your mother. Are you sure I can't pay you?"

Cevilla put her hand on his arm. Then she looked up at him. "This is our way, remember?"

Nodding, Richard looked at Seth. "Thank you."

"No problem." He stepped inside the house and headed for

the kitchen. He'd been here several times over the years, and the house was so small he knew it by heart.

"Can you wait for a few minutes before you leave?" Cevilla said, following him. "I won't take up much of your time."

"Sure." He had a few minutes to spare, and truth be told, he didn't mind visiting with Cevilla and Richard for a little bit, even though he did have to finish his errands and get back to the farm. Richard was a nice guy, and, of course, Seth never knew what Cevilla would say next. He was up for a little entertainment.

He set the jars on the counter. In the past, extra bales of hay would have been brought for Cevilla, too, but she had to give up driving her horse and buggy. His father had always made sure Cevilla was taken care of. "Do you need me to do anything around here?" he asked.

"We're fine," Cevilla said, as Richard went to the opposite counter. He picked up a knife and started chopping carrots. "Cevilla's making vegetable stew for supper tonight," he said. "I hope you don't mind if I finish the prep work while you two talk."

"Not at all," Seth said.

Cevilla sat down at the table and pointed to the chair next to her with her cane. "Have a seat, Seth."

Seth sat down, clasping his hands loosely in his lap. He squirmed a little as Cevilla looked him up and down. That was unexpected. "*Ya*," she said, her voice barely above a whisper. "I don't know why I didn't think of this before."

"About what?"

"You just missed Martha." She sat back in her chair and leaned her cane against the table.

He nodded, frowning a little. "Uh, okay."

"She's going through a hard time, poor thing." Cevilla clucked her tongue. "She could really use your help."

"Me?" Seth lifted one brow. He knew Martha, but not all that well. She'd moved to Birch Creek about two years ago, he thought, and he hadn't had much interaction with her. He'd stopped going to singings last year to devote his free time to his woodcarving. Overcoming his surprise at Cevilla's comment, he switched gears. He was always willing to help. "What can I do?"

"Date her."

"Cevilla." Richard turned around. "You're being rather blunt, don't you think?"

Seth agreed, and he would have said so if he wasn't so shocked.

"Oh, all right." Cevilla let out a sigh. "Martha is having a bit of boy trouble, for lack of a better term. Perhaps you already knew that, though."

"Um, *nee*." He didn't pay attention to other folks' social lives, so he had no idea what Cevilla was talking about.

"To make a long story short, she needs a boyfriend."

"Now, wait a minute," Seth blurted. "I'm not interested in dating."

"Oh, I know that." Seth was about to ask her how she was privy to his personal business, but she kept on talking. "I don't mean you have to really date her. Just make it look like you are to the other single men. They're bothering her. Just be her friend. Take her home from church a couple of times. Everyone will get the message."

"The wrong message." Seth stood. "I'm sorry, Cevilla, but I don't want people thinking Martha and I are an item."

"It's only for a little while." Cevilla waved her hand. "Just long enough so the rest of the boys will leave her alone. Then you can break up with her."

"Oh brother," Richard mumbled. When Seth turned and looked at him, he held up his hand. "I tried to stop her."

Seth couldn't believe this was happening. "I've got to get back to the farm," he said, heading for the back door, the quickest way to escape. "I'm sorry I can't help you with this . . . this—"

"Plan B." Cevilla gave him a curt nod. Then she frowned. "I'm sorry, Seth. I didn't mean to make you uncomfortable."

"Too late for that." Richard went back to chopping the carrots.

"I'm not . . . uncomfortable." But he was exactly that. Why in the world did she think this was a good idea or that he'd even agree to such a thing? "I'm sorry Martha's in a pickle, but I just can't help her."

"I see that now." Cevilla slowly got up from the chair. "Thank you for hearing me out."

He gave her a look, making sure she wasn't mad at him. When she finally smiled, he felt relieved.

"Thanks again for the jam." Cevilla shooed him toward the door, the exact opposite of her behavior when he'd arrived. "Tell your folks I said hello."

"I will." As soon as Cevilla opened the door, he went outside, and she shut the door behind him.

He took off his hat and scratched his head. That was the strangest conversation he'd ever had. Him dating Martha Detweiler. Talk about out of the blue. The thought hadn't crossed his mind. Not that she wasn't attractive. He had to admit she was. But he wasn't interested in her or in dating. He'd finally convinced his mother to leave him alone on that subject after two years of her applying pressure for him to find someone. It had been her idea for him to ask out Ruby after he accidentally bloodied her nose with their screen door last year. He agreed, but only because he felt he owed her one.

When he arrived at her house, though, Chris was there, acting strange, as usual. He'd noticed there was something going on between them, even if they didn't know it yet, and he'd jumped at the chance to make his escape. He hadn't thought about asking anyone out since—anyone being Martha, since she was the only valid candidate.

No, there wasn't room in his life for Martha, or any other woman. He was fine being single and focusing on the farm . . . and his secret passion. That was all he needed and wanted.

. . .

"That poor kid," Richard said as he picked up an onion from the bowl near the sink and started chopping.

Cevilla sat back down at the table, still smiling. Plan B was in motion. She would have been shocked if Seth had agreed to pretend to date Martha. First, it was deceptive, and she knew it. Second, she'd been keeping an eye on him lately. He hadn't been staying for fellowship after church, and when she and Richard had supper at the bishop's house last month, he'd left right after they'd eaten, saying he had some business to take care of. Something was going on with him, that she was sure of. She had a sixth sense when it came to these things, just like the sixth sense she had when it came to matchmaking. Or would that be a seventh sense? Anyway, she'd at least planted the seed in Seth's mind, and since she knew he was a kind and generous young man, she was certain he would be thinking about Martha's plight. Fairly certain, anyway.

"Uh-oh."

Cevilla looked up at Richard, his back to her. "What?" Had he cut his finger? She'd told him he didn't have to help her in the kitchen, but he insisted. And she hadn't put up too much of a fuss. She liked working with him there. And being with him. She really loved this man. Only one thing was keeping them apart—a big thing.

"You're quiet," he said with a faint smile. "That doesn't bode well."

"Very funny." She got up, the bones in her back creaking. She didn't want to admit it, but she was slowing down, faster than she wanted to. But she wouldn't let a few aches and pains and uncooperative body parts stop her. She started washing her hands. "I'm just thinking, that's all."

"About what you put that unsuspecting boy through?" Richard added the onions to the chopped carrots.

"I didn't put him through anything. I asked him a simple question."

"That question made him look like a jackrabbit in a trap." Richard turned to her. "I think this might be a situation where you should mind your own business."

"Poppycock. This is exactly a situation where I should interfere." She lifted her stewpot from a cabinet.

"At least you're calling it what it is—interference."

"With good motives."

His expression softened. "You always have good motives. You really care about your community."

"I do." Oh bother, she was getting teary. But she didn't like to see Martha, who normally was self-assured and sweet, afraid to leave her house. And when she mentioned that Seth wasn't pursuing her, the lightbulb had gone off in Cevilla's head. Martha and Seth were perfect for each other. They were both kind, generous, hardworking young people. That could be said for all the young people in Birch Creek, but she couldn't get it out of her mind that these two were meant for each other. It would just take a little nudging on her part to make them realize it.

"I don't suppose you're going to change your mind about this," Richard said.

"Nope." She filled a pitcher with water and carried it to the stewpot, now sitting on the stove. She poured the water into the pot, longing for the days when she didn't have a cane, when she could carry a full stewpot of water from the sink without thinking about it. But she'd adapted, and although it would take another pitcher to fill the pot three-quarters of the way, this was reality. "It's been a while since I've done some matchmaking. My record is two out of two, I'll have you know."

Richard nodded. "All right. If you have confidence, I have confidence too. I just ask one thing."

"Anything."

"Keep me out of your shenanigans." He put his hand over his chest. "My heart can't take it."

Cevilla laughed, and he hugged her. She was happy, and she wanted that happiness for Martha and Seth. If she had anything to do with it, they *would* have it.

CHAPTER 2

"Ya, Loren. I think this place will do nicely."

Nina Stoll rubbed her nose with the back of her hand as her grandmother perused the outside of the property her father had bought nearly a month ago. This was their first time to see it. When he'd returned from Ohio and said he'd found the perfect place to open a small inn, Nina had hoped it was just a whim. But after seeing *Grossmammi*'s approval of the house, small barn, and grounds today, Nina's hopes were dashed. She couldn't see anything wrong with the place, either, which made her certain they wouldn't move back to the only home she'd ever known.

Her brother, Levi, came from around the back of the house. "Nice big field back there," he said, pushing his glasses farther up the bridge of his nose. "The barn needs some work, but it shouldn't take too long to get it into shape."

"The property has been abandoned for quite some time. An *English familye* used to live here, according to the real estate agent." Her father stroked his chin. A widower of many years, he'd shaved off his beard long ago. "We won't have to add any electrical for the guests, which is a plus. We'll build a small *haus* for ourselves in *nee* time. With a little elbow grease, we'll have a nice little inn on our hands, and a new place to live."

"This was an excellent decision." *Grossmammi* stood next to her son. She was short, a bit wide, and strong. Much like Nina herself. More than once she'd been compared to her grandmother, at least physically. Personality-wise . . . That was another matter.

"What do you think, Nina?" *Daed* turned to her with an expectant look.

She threaded her fingers together, wishing she could tell him the truth. She wasn't okay with leaving Wisconsin. Her life had been fine the way it was. She'd had her favorite fishing hole, the huge oak tree in front of the house she still climbed whenever she thought her grandmother wouldn't catch her, a seasonal job at the bait shop near Orchard Lake, and, of course, her friends. So what if they were all male? *And married. Don't forget that part.* She couldn't spend time with them the way she had when they were all growing up together, but she was fine with that. She didn't mind being alone, as long as she wasn't stuck inside tending a house.

Or an inn. This property didn't even have a decent climbing tree on it.

"Nina?"

She blinked and looked at her father. Instead of telling him what was in her heart, she said, "It's . . . nice."

Daed looked at her a bit longer. She could tell he didn't believe her, but fortunately he didn't question her further. He turned to Levi and *Grossmammi*. "As I told you, the bottom floor of the inn is livable for us while we renovate. Levi, you're in charge of repairing the barn and getting the front and back yards into shape. Nina, you and *Mamm* will work on the inside of the inn, alongside the workers I've hired."

"And what do *you* plan to do?" *Grossmammi* asked, tapping

her foot twice. Delilah Stoll didn't like being bossed around by her son or anyone else. Not that anyone dared.

"Start on our *haus*, *Mudder*." He gave her a long-suffering look. "*Mei* hope is that we can open the inn in four months. I want our *haus* to be finished sooner than that."

Nina rubbed her nose again. Was it too late to go back home? They had extended family in Wisconsin. She could move in with her cousin Fannie, or even get a full-time job and live by herself. She'd prefer that anyway. Fannie was nice, but she, like her grandmother, had been urging her to give up her tomboy-ish ways. "How will you ever get a husband if you can barely do laundry?" she'd asked one day when Nina had stopped by for what turned out to be a regrettable visit.

"I do laundry just fine." She'd plopped down on one of the kitchen chairs. Fannie was peeling potatoes for the potato salad she was making for lunch after church the next day.

"*Yer Grossmammi* does the laundry." Fannie pointed the paring knife at her and then resumed peeling.

"She makes me get out *mei* own stains." Nina glanced down at her light-green dress. Faded grass stains were still visible on its skirt, but she didn't care. It was clean enough for her.

Fannie sighed. "You're twenty-two years old, Nina. When are you going to start thinking about marriage and a *familye*?"

Never. Well, not exactly never, but she didn't want to get married anytime soon. Then she'd really be stuck in a house doing chores and taking care of *kinner*. That didn't appeal to her at all. She still had living to do. She rubbed her nose yet again.

"Stop that," *Grossmammi* said. "It's not ladylike."

Nina put her hands behind her back. Her grandmother had been trying to mold her into a respectable Amish woman for years. That hadn't worked out too well.

Neither would moving back to Wisconsin. She could see that. Once her father made a decision, he didn't change his mind, and he did need her help. A lot of work had to be done. Perhaps after the inn was ready, she could leave. She'd miss her brother, father, and even her grandmother, despite their tense relationship. But at least she'd be home. A knot of homesickness tightened in her stomach.

"You look a bit peaked." *Grossmammi* walked up to her. "You also picked at *yer* breakfast this morning before we left the hotel. Usually you have a hearty appetite." She glanced at Nina's hips. "A little too hearty, sometimes. What's wrong with you?"

Nina shook her head, unfazed by her grandmother's directness, although she didn't miss the irony that her plump grandmother was mentioning Nina's appetite. Nina didn't care that she was on the stout side. A little extra weight had never interfered with her job, her fishing, or her other activities. "*Nix*," she said, hoping *Grossmammi* wouldn't pick up on the fib. "I'm fine."

"*Gut.* Because we need all hands on deck for this business to be successful." *Grossmammi* crossed her arms over her chest and looked around the property again. "This place has potential."

"I agree." Levi sauntered up to them. He tilted back his straw hat and once more pushed his glasses up. "I think we can make a *geh* of this, especially since no other inns are nearby."

Of course Levi would be optimistic. His glass was always half-full and sometimes overflowing.

"Which means we don't have to worry about competition." *Daed* pulled out his cell phone, a new purchase for the move to Birch Creek, where the district allowed phones for business. He'd never had a phone back home. He'd always worked construction—as had Levi—and he'd never been his own boss. This new venture had given him renewed energy.

Nina kicked at a pebble in the driveway. From what she could tell, the rest of her family would have an easy time with the transition, but she wasn't sure about the fancy technology, or about the inn, or about being so far from the familiar. But she was sure she wouldn't let down *Daed*. He was a good man, and a great father, and if this was what he wanted, she would support him.

Her father flipped open the phone. Nina had seen some *English* people with larger phones with screens and touching them all the time, but her father had purchased a simpler model. "Hello?" he said into the phone after punching in some numbers. "This is Loren Stoll. We're ready to go back to the hotel . . . That's fine, thank you." He snapped the cover shut and slipped the phone into his pocket. "The taxi will be here in fifteen minutes."

"Does this mean I get a phone too?" Levi asked with a half grin.

"Maybe." *Daed* smiled.

"I think you're both foolish for wanting that . . . thing." *Grossmammi* sniffed. "No *gut* can come of it."

"It's just for business, *Mudder*." *Daed* let out a sigh, and Nina could tell he'd had this conversation with *Grossmammi* before. "It's impossible nowadays to conduct business without it. You want us to succeed, *ya*?"

"If it's God's will, he'll make it happen—with or without a highfalutin phone." She turned and went up the four steps to the expansive front porch. She started walking its length, testing the wood planks. She motioned to *Daed*. "All these will need to be replaced."

"Not all of them."

She gave him a stern look. "*All* of them."

Daed grimaced and went to her. "This board is perfectly fine, *Mudder*."

"It doesn't match the rest of them."

While her father and grandmother bickered, Nina looked around the property again. Despite the lack of climbing trees, she had to admit the place was pretty. It had lots of decorative trees, as if the former residents had chopped down all the stately ones and replaced them with fancier ones. It was a nice touch.

"You going to be okay with all this?"

She looked at Levi, who now stood next to her. A bead of sweat dripped down the side of his face. Was it always so hot in Ohio? "*Ya*," she said, staring at the road in front of her.

"Why don't I believe you?" He moved to stand in front of her. "We all need this change, Nina. *Daed* was miserable working construction. *Grossmammi* needs a new challenge now that we're older and she can't boss us around."

"She bosses us plenty."

"Not as much as she used to."

Nina nodded. Their grandmother had moved in with them years ago, after their mother died. Lately she seemed at loose ends, other than her attempts to fundamentally change Nina's personality. "What about you, Levi? Why do you need a change?"

His expression grew uncharacteristically serious. "Change is always *gut*. For everyone. Don't want to get stuck in a rut, do you?" Then he grinned. "It will be all right. The moving van is coming this afternoon, and you'll feel better once you're surrounded by *yer* own things. And when we're done with the work around here, I'll help you find a fishing hole. *Daed* says

Birch Creek has plenty of ponds, and I'm sure we'll find a *gut* one." He glanced over his shoulder. "Guess I better *geh* referee. *Daed* knows *Grossmammi*'s right. He just doesn't want to admit it."

As her brother went to mediate between her father and grandmother, Nina looked up at the sky. Levi's offer was nice, but for the first time in her life she didn't care about fishing. What kind of community was Birch Creek? Were the people nice? She wasn't a social butterfly, but she didn't want to live in a district in conflict. She'd heard stories from other family members who lived in Michigan, about their district splitting into two different ones, each with their own set of rules. She hoped nothing like that was going on here.

Then again, if Birch Creek was a difficult place to live, maybe her father would change his mind. He didn't like conflict either, although her grandmother had never shied away from it. If the Birch Creek community had problems, perhaps *Daed* would sell this place and move them all back to Wisconsin. It was selfish of her to want that, but she couldn't stop hoping it would happen.

. . .

Seth pulled his buggy up to Hezekiah Detweiler's optics shop and then tied Pinto to a hitching post. "Be back in a minute," he said, patting the horse on his flank. Pinto bobbed his head as if acknowledging his words. Seth grabbed the antique clock from the front buggy seat and headed inside.

A bell rang above the front door as he opened it. The shop in the single-story building on Hezekiah's property had been open a little over a year, ever since Hezekiah and his family moved in next door to the Detweilers. Hezekiah was Martha's uncle. This was the first time Seth had needed to come here, where Hezekiah repaired clocks, sold binoculars, and did a little optician work.

After half a minute or so, Martha appeared from the back of the shop and stood behind a counter. "Hi, Seth."

He'd been distracted lately, but how could he have forgotten that Martha worked here? Especially since Cevilla's request hadn't been too far from his mind since their conversation two days ago. He was still a little annoyed that she'd asked him to spend time with Martha. Not that there was anything wrong with her, because there wasn't. He looked at her for a moment. She had clear blue eyes and light-blond hair peeking out from underneath her prayer *kapp*, and her skin looked unblemished, except for the freckle on the side of her nose. Hmm, he'd never noticed that before.

"May I help you?"

"Oh, right." If he was a braver man he'd have a few words for Cevilla for messing with his head, but he knew better than that. Time to get down to business. "*Mamm* wondered if Hezekiah could repair this clock. It's pretty special to her." He placed the clock on the counter.

"It *is* pretty." Martha examined it, her eyes sparkling as she looked over the piece.

It was an impressive clock, the fanciest thing his parents owned. *Mamm* had seen it in his sister Ivy's antique shop a month ago and had purchased it, taking advantage of the family discount, of course. Though *Daed* had thought it was too flashy for display in the living room, *Mamm* insisted that it stay on a shelf there, where everyone could enjoy it.

"What's wrong with it?" Martha asked, looking at him.

"It stopped working last week. That's all she told me. I don't know much about clocks and watches."

"I'm sure *mei onkel* will get it fixed up for you." She picked up a pad and pencil and started to write. "When do you need it?"

"It's not a rush job, but it's a favorite of *Mamm*'s, so the sooner the better."

Martha nodded as she scribbled more on the pad, then she set it and her pencil back on the counter and tore off the top sheet of paper. "I'll let *Onkel* know." She picked up the clock and put it on a shelf behind her, sliding the paper under it. A couple of binoculars, three pocket watches, and another mantel clock were on the shelf.

"Looks like you're busy," Seth said.

"*Ya.*" She tilted her head at him, and her expression suddenly changed, her eyes sparkling a little more. "Do you have, um, anything else to ask me?"

"Huh?"

"Anything . . . else?" Her brow lifted.

"Um . . . I guess you'll let me know when it's ready?"

Her shoulders slumped a bit. "*Ya.* We'll let you know."

"All right, then." He gave her a nod and walked out of the shop. He untied Pinto and got into the buggy. Something was niggling at him. Martha's eyes weren't as bright when he left as they'd been when he arrived. It was almost as if she were . . . disappointed. Nah, that couldn't be it. What would she have to be disappointed about? It wasn't as if she was expecting him to ask her out, like Cevilla wanted him to. Surely the woman wouldn't have talked to Martha about this plan B of hers before she knew if he'd go along with it. Would she?

He gripped the reins, and Pinto whinnied. Apparently, he'd pulled on them without realizing it. "Sorry," he said absently.

A sinking feeling came over him. What was Cevilla up to? Whatever it was, he wasn't playing along. He made his own decisions when it came to his personal life, thank you very much. *If* he dated anyone, it would be because he wanted to, not because of someone else's meddling. Cevilla would have to accept that.

. . .

Martha leaned against the counter and sighed. Cevilla had been wrong. When she stopped by the shop yesterday, she'd said she'd seen Seth, and that plan B was in motion. Martha had been stunned, and more than a bit embarrassed that Cevilla had said anything to him. But the old woman had insisted everything would work out fine—for everyone. "No need to fret," she'd said, patting Martha's hand. "You'll see."

Although she'd felt a little comforted by Cevilla's words, she'd almost pretended she wasn't there when Seth came into the shop. When she was back in the office, she often peeked around its door before going out, just to see what kind of customer had come in. It had taken a few deep breaths for her to calm her nerves, plus a reminder that being nervous about Seth Yoder was ridiculous to begin with. She had little feeling toward him one way or the other, but ever since Cevilla's plan B conversation, the man had been on her mind. *Thanks a lot, Cevilla.*

She was sure Seth wasn't dropping off his mother's clock as a ruse, though. The clock did need repairing. Still, she'd wondered enough about plan B that she'd blurted out that question to Seth, and immediately regretted it. He looked confused, which meant that whatever Cevilla had said to him hadn't made an impact on him. Maybe she'd been too subtle? Either that, or how he'd reacted to Cevilla's suggestion—as in, declining to be involved—hadn't made an impact on *her*.

She bent forward and put her elbow on the counter, then her cheek in her hand. This was more of an emotional roller coaster than dealing with her overeager suitors, and she'd never thought she'd say that. She wished she'd never said anything to Cevilla, or to her mother. She was an adult. She should have handled this alone. Richard was right—being straightforward was a lot better than going along with Cevilla's confusing plans. But how could she be straightforward without hurting anyone?

"Did the bell ring a little while ago?" Her uncle walked up beside her, his work glasses perched on top of his head. They were regular glasses with magnifiers on the lenses so he could see the small parts of the items he repaired.

"Seth Yoder dropped that off." She waved at the shelf behind her.

"The clock?"

"*Ya.*"

"This is a beautiful piece." He took it off the shelf. "Very old, probably nineteenth century." He turned it over in his hands. "Can't wait to see what secrets you're keeping," he said to the clock.

Martha was used to her uncle talking to the items he repaired. She thought it was rather sweet. He seemed oddly affectionate toward them and took great care and time with the repairs. But even his kindly nature didn't keep her from letting out a long sigh.

"Something wrong?" He put the clock back on the shelf.

She shook her head and straightened. "*Nee.*" She turned to him and smiled. "What do you need help with today?"

The best way to get her mind off her troubles was to do some work.

"I thought I'd show you what the inside of a pair of binoculars looks like."

"Oh. Sounds . . . interesting." Not really, but she did like to learn new things, and thinking about binoculars would be better than thinking about Seth Yoder.

"It is. It's amazing how sophisticated this pair is." Hezekiah started for his workroom at the back of the shop, still talking. "I'm really impressed with how far the technology has come along in the past decade or so."

Martha followed, forcing her thoughts toward binoculars and away from Seth. She had to do something about her problem, and she would stay away from any social events until she had a solution. That included the scavenger hunt, although she'd have to figure out how to break it to Ruby that she wouldn't attend. And she would have a talk with Cevilla for sure. Martha was walking away from plan B, as well as from singings and socials and any other activity that had even a whiff of romantic possibilities. Cevilla would have to find someone else's love life to meddle in.

After supper that evening, Martha was in the living room, reading one of her uncle's books on the history of binoculars. It was more interesting than she'd thought it would be, and he'd been happy to loan her the small book. "You do like to learn new things, don't you?" he'd said. "*Yer mamm* told me you learned how to tie nautical knots two weeks ago."

She had, although she wasn't sure if she'd ever need to use that bit of obscure knowledge. But she'd seen the book in the library in a display of fishing and boating books, and now she could make a rolling hitch in nothing flat.

A knock sounded on the door, and her father lifted his head from the seed catalog he was reading. His trade was carpentry, but now that *Mamm* had put her foot down about moving again, he'd mentioned he might want to help plant a larger garden in the spring. "I'll get it," Martha told him. *Mamm* nodded from her chair near the gas lamp. She was darning a pair of *Daed*'s socks. Two battery-operated fans were on the coffee table, cooling the room to a more comfortable temperature.

Martha opened the door, and Ruby blew right by her. "I don't know what I'm going to do," she said, her voice sounding close to a wail.

"About what?" Martha asked as she shut the door.

"The scavenger hunt." She started to pace. "I realize I'm not the best at planning things—except for *mei* lesson plans, of course—but I really dropped the ball this time." She blew out a breath but didn't slow down. "Of course, Christian has had reservations about *mei* pulling it off all along, which has only made me want to prove him wrong. Now I think he might be right." She halted, then looked to the right. Her mouth dropped open. "Oh. Hi, John and Regina. I didn't see you guys there."

Mamm lifted her hand in a short wave, then resumed her darning. *Daed* gave Ruby a nod and went back to reading the catalog, as if Ruby Ropp bursting into their house in a frenzy was a frequent occurrence.

"Why don't we get some iced tea and sit outside?" Martha said. It was still warm and muggy, but it was cooler on the patio than in the kitchen. They'd also have more privacy out there.

Ruby looked at her, relief on her face as if Martha had already solved her problem, whatever that was. "That sounds wonderful."

A short while later they were seated on the plastic chairs on the back patio. The iced tea was refreshing, and Ruby had calmed down. Martha turned to her. "Now, what's the problem with the scavenger hunt?"

"There's *nix* to scavenge!" Ruby took another sip of her iced tea and then set it on the patio table. Droplets of condensation were already settling on the glass. "I thought it would be easy to come up with items everyone could hunt. But every time I think about it, I draw a blank. The only idea I had was to have everyone hunt for different kinds of leaves and bring them back to the *haus*. But Christian said that sounded more like something for *mei* students than for adults."

Martha wasn't surprised Ruby's thoughts had gone in that direction. She and her husband, Chris, were the district's schoolteachers. Ruby taught kindergarten through third grade, and Christian taught the older students up through eighth grade. Last year was Ruby's first year to teach, and from all accounts she had done an excellent job. But she had to agree with Chris—collecting leaves sounded like something children would do.

"The hunt is in two days. What am I going to do?" Ruby rubbed the back of her neck.

"Maybe you should just have a supper after all."

"Christian said the same thing. But what fun is that?" Ruby sighed. "How many singings and frolics and suppers and volleyball games can we have? I want to do something different." She looked away. "I should have thought this through before inviting everyone, though."

Martha suddenly had an idea. "What about instead of a scavenger hunt, you have a treasure hunt? You could divide everyone into teams, and they can collect clues. Whoever finds and follows all the clues and then finds the 'treasure' wins something."

"Like a pie?"

"A pie would be *gut*."

Ruby tilted her head, and Martha could see her mulling over the idea. "That could be fun. I'll have to put *mei* own spin on it, of course."

"Of course." Martha smiled. She usually wasn't the one to think of things like this, and it made her feel good to help Ruby. Not to mention this was a prime opportunity to let her know she wasn't going to be there. "Ruby, I have something to tell you—"

"Do you mind coming over early to help me? This is *yer* idea, after all. I can't pull it off without you."

Martha paused. She should have told Ruby she wasn't going before she had her idea. Ruby's eyes filled with pleading, and Martha didn't want to disappoint her. *Be straightforward and tell her the truth.* "Maybe—"

"Wonderful!" Ruby clasped her hands together. "I feel so much better about this already. We're going to have a great time."

Martha fell back in her chair. Why couldn't she just say no? Her life would be so much easier if she weren't afraid of that simple word.

Ruby started throwing out ideas for the hunt, and by the time she left, they had the evening planned, except for a few details. After Ruby left, Martha drank the last of her tea and watched the sun dip below the horizon, streaking the sky with beautiful lavender, rose, and peach colors. Normally she would feel peace watching the placid scene, but peace had eluded her lately. And now she had to go to Ruby's on Saturday.

"Great," she muttered. Although the treasure hunt did sound like fun. Maybe it wouldn't be as bad as she thought. Maybe she didn't have to dread going. She could just help Ruby, who'd be in charge, and then work in the kitchen preparing supper or something. She hadn't promised she'd take part in the hunt. Readying the food didn't sound like as much fun as the hunt, but she couldn't put herself in proximity to any single male. *Desperate times.*

She sighed and stared into her empty glass. How did everything get so complicated so quickly? She really wished Selah were here. She missed her friend. A visit to New York might be in order. But with the business load at work growing, she couldn't take the time off. Her uncle needed someone available to take orders while he was working. Besides, wouldn't that still be running away from her problems? She needed to stop doing that. She'd never been a coward before, but lately she was acting like one.

CHAPTER 3

O n Saturday Martha arrived early to help Ruby set up. Ruby talked nonstop, barely giving her a chance to get a word in edgewise. The Ropps didn't live too far from Martha and her family. Behind their house was a wooded area, thick with oak and maple trees. Several other houses were on the street, including the abandoned one Martha had run past on her way to Cevilla's, where she'd seen someone come out the back door. She'd also noticed a buggy there today when she'd walked over.

Chris was outside placing the last of the clues. Martha had helped Ruby hide some of them the evening before. All in all, it should be a good hunt. Too bad Martha wasn't participating.

When she was able to interject into Ruby's string of chatter, she asked, "Did somebody move into that *haus* down the street?"

Ruby nodded as she made fruit punch. "*Ya*, on Tuesday. But they've kept to themselves. I went over yesterday and introduced myself. Their last name is Stoll, and they're from Wisconsin. Oddly enough, that's all the information I got out of the woman who answered the door. Delilah is her name, I think. She looks to be in her late sixties, but I'm never a *gut* judge of age. She didn't even invite me inside."

"She doesn't sound very friendly."

"Or she was busy with unpacking." Ruby shrugged. "I'm curious, though. They're building a separate *haus* in the back, but it seems too big for a *dawdi haus*. And they've already started building an addition on the main *haus* too. I saw Sol Troyer there yesterday. It's already the largest *haus* in Birch Creek, but I guess they have a large *familye*. Maybe not all of them have arrived."

It sounded to Martha a little like Ruby had been watching them, although Martha knew it was from curiosity and not nosiness—and there was a difference.

"I did see two *yung* people there, a male and female," Ruby added. "They looked to be around our age."

"Did you invite them to the hunt?" Maybe the woman was single. Wouldn't that be an unexpected answer to prayer.

She shook her head. "I thought I'd wait until Christian and I got to know them better. I didn't want them to be overwhelmed so soon after moving in."

Martha nodded. Ruby was the only one who called her husband Christian, his given name. Selah had explained that until Chris moved to Birch Creek, he'd always been called Christian. But Martha couldn't see him as anything but Chris.

The outside door opened, and Chris walked into the kitchen. He went straight for the sink to fill a glass with water. "All the clues are planted," he said, then took a long drink.

"*Danki*, Christian." Ruby turned to Martha. "Do you mind putting the cookies on this plate and taking them to the table in the living room?" She glanced at the clock on the wall. "The guests should be arriving soon."

Dread formed in her belly at Ruby's words. She'd managed not to think about the single men on the guest list all day, but now they would be here in a few minutes. She hurriedly placed several monster cookies on the plate Ruby had set out. Then she took a deep breath. "Fun," she whispered. "This is all going to be fun."

She carried the plate toward the living room, where Chris had set up a long table for the food and drinks. While everyone was out looking for clues, Ruby would set out the sandwiches, potato salad, macaroni salad, pickles, chow chow, and home-made potato chips for supper, along with brownies and pie for dessert. Martha had seen all the food in the kitchen, and at first thought it looked like too much. Then she remembered how many men would be eating. Maybe there wasn't enough.

When Martha entered the living room carrying the cook-ies, she saw Leanna and Roman Raber. She set the cookies on the table and headed for Leanna just as the front door opened again. Before she could talk to her, more guests streamed inside—Phoebe and Jalon Chupp, Ivy and Noah Schlabach, Karen and Adam Chupp, and Joanna and Andrew Beiler, along with the single men—Zeb, Zeke, Owen, and Ira. Samuel, the youngest of the group, hadn't arrived yet. Martha tried to duck back into the kitchen, but she made the mistake of making eye contact with Zeke. He immediately strode toward her, a deter-mined look on his face.

Her stomach twisted, and she looked for a place to hide. There wasn't one.

"Glad to see you here, Martha." He smiled at her, his teeth slightly crooked, but it didn't make him unattractive. To her, all the men were nice-looking, in their own unique ways. But that didn't mean she wanted to date them.

"I stopped at *yer haus* the other day," he said. "*Yer mudder* said you weren't home."

"I was there too." Ira joined them, but not before he gave

Zeke a sharp look. He moved closer to Martha, and she had to crane her neck to look at his face. It wasn't that long ago that he was shorter than Seth, and now he was the tallest man in Birch Creek. "She said she didn't know where you'd gone. Is that right?" Was Ira suspicious?

"*Ya*," she said quietly, guilt about leaving her mother to fight her battles washing over her. After all the fuss she'd made over running from the boys, she'd had to go back to her mother and explain why she was going to the hunt after all. "I promised I'd help Ruby," she'd said.

Mamm wiped the last crumbs from the table before looking at Martha. "I'm confused. I thought you didn't want to date any of those *buwe*. Clearly, they're bothering you."

"I don't want to date them. And they're not bothering me . . . too much."

Setting down her cloth, *Mamm* went to her. "You're not still thinking about Paul, are you?"

Her heart hitched. She tried not to think about him at all, but sometimes the painful memories wouldn't stay where they belonged. "Of course not."

"*Gut*. Paul is in the past, *dochder*. You don't need to use him as an excuse in the present."

An excuse? Was that what she was doing? Using what happened between her and Paul so she didn't have to go through that with anyone else?

"Would you like to get some ice cream next week?" Zeke asked.

"Or *geh* on a buggy ride?" Ira queried.

"I'll show you *mei* new horse," Zeb said, joining the group.

"Not before I show her our new cow," Owen said, moving to stand next to his brother.

Martha took a step backward, almost knocking over a chair in the process. She glanced around to see where Ruby was, or Phoebe, or Joanna, or anyone else who could intervene. But Ruby had disappeared somewhere, and the other women were busy talking. Maybe if she yelled for help—

"I asked her first," Zeke said, lifting his chin and eyeing the other men.

"Did she say *ya*?" Zeb asked, his gaze challenging.

"Not yet—"

"Then it's free game," Ira added. Owen nodded, and soon the men were arguing with each other, ignoring Martha.

This was her chance. She slipped out of the room to the kitchen. Thankfully it was empty. She looked at the back door. No, she wasn't going to run away this time. She had to figure this out for herself. She was going to set them straight, no matter how difficult that would be.

But Paul's words came to her mind. *You ruined* mei *life.*

"Martha?" Zeb called out, sounding as though he was close to the kitchen. "You in there?"

Panicked, she flew out the door and dashed into the woods.

. . .

Seth wiped the sweat from his face in the small woodshop. He felt like he was working inside an oven, but he didn't care. He couldn't wait to get to his shop today. The wood had been calling to him. When he was younger, he used to whittle on occasion, but woodcarving was different. Much more satisfying. This was his passion, what he dreamed about doing not just as a hobby but to make a living. But he wasn't anywhere close to being skilled enough to do that yet. It took time and practice,

and lately his practice times had been too few and far between
for his liking, especially since he'd stopped sneaking in here on
Sundays. The guilt had gotten to him a few months ago. Not
that he wasn't still tempted to work on the Sabbath. Mighty
tempted.

The moment he'd stepped into the shop, he immediately relaxed. He never would have thought a hot, dusty shed in the
middle of the woods would become his sanctuary. He never
would have thought he needed one. But he did.

He applied a #3 gouge to the wood, creating a curlicue shape
at the end of the piece of cherry wood. He still needed improvement at this particular skill. Lots of improvement, from the
looks of the wobbly curlicue he'd just made. He dug into the
wood again, sweat dripping into his eyes. Although the shed
was in a shady part of the woods, the summer heat filled the
inside. But the heat and sweat didn't bother him when he was
working. He grabbed a terry cloth headband and slipped it
over his hair. He probably looked ridiculous, but at least it kept
the droplets out of his eyes.

He was about to make another curlicue when the door flew
open. He dropped the gouge as Martha Detweiler rushed inside and then shut the door behind her. She closed her eyes and
whispered, "Not again. You said you wouldn't do this again."

Seth gaped. "Martha?"

She opened her eyes and whipped her head toward him. Her
eyes grew wide. "I-I didn't know anyone was in here."

Her chest heaved as she gasped for breath, and blotches of
perspiration showed on her dress, as if she'd been running a
long distance. He went to his lunch cooler and got out one of
the extra cans of pop he'd packed. "Here," he said, handing it
to her.

She grabbed the can and popped the top, then took a long swallow. "*Danki*," she said, offering it back to him. She wiped her forehead with the back of her other hand.

"Keep it." He eyed her as she took another drink. "Were you running?"

She nodded.

"From what?"

Her cheeks reddened to a deeper hue, which he thought was impressive, considering how red and sweaty her face already was. "Men," she said.

"Men?" His brow raised. He hadn't expected that answer. "Any men in particular?"

"*All* of them." She leaned against the door and looked at him, then at the wood and tools on his workbench. "What's all that?"

"None of *yer* business." He moved to stand in front of the workbench. He might sound rude, but at least he wasn't bursting into other people's workshops uninvited.

"I'm sorry. I didn't mean to be nosy." But even as she was talking, she was looking around the shop. Wood, tools, sandpaper, and sawdust were strewn everywhere. "It looks like I interrupted something."

"You did." He wanted to ask her to leave, but not until he was sure she was okay. "Are you in danger?"

She let out a bitter laugh. "Hardly."

"Then why are you running?"

She lifted her gaze to his, meeting his eyes. "Because I'm a coward."

The determined look on her face was anything but cowardly. "I doubt that," he said.

She glanced around again. "May I stay here for a while? I need a place to hide."

He tilted his head. Maybe she was afraid. "What's going on, Martha?"

"Ruby's hunt."

He nodded. He'd been invited but declined. He didn't want to give up the opportunity to work in the shop. "The hunt is scary?"

Her eyes grew big again as she nodded. "Very."

Her overreaction made him laugh. "How can a game like that—prepared by Ruby Ropp, *nee* less—be scary?"

"You have *nee* idea." She frowned, her shoulders slumping slightly. "I'm sorry," she said again. "I didn't mean to bother you." She set the empty can on the metal shelving unit near the shed's entrance. "I appreciate the drink. I'll let you get back to whatever you were doing." She turned and started to open the door.

"Wait." He walked over and stood in front of her. "I'm sorry. You're obviously bothered by Ruby's gathering. I didn't mean to make light of that."

Her expression softened. "*Danki*," she said, this time her voice sounding softer. And for some reason, sweeter. He looked down at her. He was several inches taller than she, and even though the light wasn't very bright in this part of the shed, he could see her blue eyes, which he had to admit were kind of pretty. He hadn't paid too much attention to Martha over the past year, mostly because he knew his best friend, Zeke, liked her. Zeke would be at the hunt, along with all the other young men in the community. For some reason he remembered what Cevilla had said to him the other day. *Boy trouble.* He put two and two together and said, "Are the guys bothering you?"

"Not . . . yet." She sighed and averted her gaze. "I just feel uncomfortable with all the attention."

"I see." And he did, at least a little. He'd never thought about what it must be like to have suitors when you didn't want them, and by the way Martha was behaving, he concluded Cevilla had been right. Martha didn't want suitors. But that wasn't his problem. Like he told Cevilla, he didn't want to be involved.

He looked at her again. She was rubbing her finger against the doorframe, looking deep in thought—and still pretty off-kilter. Against his better judgment he said, "All right. You can hide here if you want." Her eyes brightened as he lifted his hand. "On one condition."

"What's that?"

He leaned forward, looking straight into her eyes and making sure she understood how serious he was. "You don't tell a single soul about this place."

. . .

Martha was tempted to laugh, and she would have if Seth wasn't being so serious. Still, she couldn't help but make light of the situation. "What do you have here, a secret stash of gold?"

"It's more valuable than that," he murmured.

She looked up at him. He was standing closer to her than when he'd blocked her from leaving the shed. Blocked wasn't exactly the right word, but he had been in her way. Surprisingly, he'd apologized. Seth Yoder was a bit of an enigma to her, since he seemed to be keeping more and more to himself lately. Not that she had paid much attention to him, at least not until he'd come into the shop the other day.

He was nice-looking, something she couldn't deny. He wasn't wearing his hat, and his dark-brown hair, straight except for a slight curl at the ends, was covered in sawdust. He was also wearing a white headband, which made him look a little silly, but she wouldn't tell him that. His blue eyes, darker than her own, held her gaze, and she was sure he would stare at her until she gave him her promise. "I won't say anything," she said.

He nodded and took a step back. "I've got to get back to work. There's a stool in the corner if you want to sit down." He turned and went back to the workbench.

Martha glanced at the stool, which had seen better days. It was also on the opposite side of the shed from his workbench. She ignored it and followed him. "What are you making?"

"None of *yer* business." He pushed a funny-looking tool into the wood, making a curved shape.

That was the second time he'd said that, but she decided to ignore it too.

"You're a woodcarver?"

"Not exactly." He glanced over his shoulder and looked down at her, scowling a little. "Do you mind?"

She stepped back, moving to the side so she could get a better view of his work. He slid the tool into the wood, looking at her while he did. The tool suddenly became stuck in the wood, twisted out of his hand, and hit the floor.

"I told you to sit in the corner." He bent down and picked up the tool.

"Seriously? You're putting me in time-out?"

His lips formed a smirk. "Don't tempt me."

Wow, he was touchy. "I'm just watching you work."

"I don't need an audience." He turned his back to her, fully blocking her view, and began to scrape the wood again.

Martha moved away, studying the tools in the woodshop. She recognized some of them—a hand plane, several sanding blocks, an awl, and a chisel. Tools unfamiliar to her hung on the hooks on the wall. One was a knife with a long blade that curved a little upward. She lifted it and examined it, touching the tip of her finger to the blade. It immediately broke the skin. She winced and hung the tool back on the hook, then put her finger in her mouth to staunch the small amount of blood flow.

She turned and looked at Seth again, or rather mostly at his back. At this angle, though, she could see a little more. He was a well-built man, and as he ran the tool over the wood, the shavings falling to the floor, the muscles in his forearms flexed. She might not want to date anyone, but she did appreciate Seth's attractiveness. Above his head hung a bright, battery-powered lamp suspended from a hook on the ceiling. He turned the plank of wood he was working on to the other end and began carving again.

"Are you making a gift?" Martha said, unable to stop the question from flying out of her mouth.

He let out a long sigh, then looked at her. "I'm practicing."

"Practicing what?" She walked over to him again.

"Curlicues, if you must know." He gave her a curt glance. "Enough with the questions."

But she was full of questions, namely why he was working in a shed in the middle of the woods when he could have a woodshop at his home. She'd been to the Yoders' when they held services, and they had two barns, a large house, and plenty of land where they farmed and raised their animals. Surely there was room in one of the large barns for a woodshop, or even to build one on the property. Why have this shed well over a mile away?

And what was he practicing for? From what she could tell, he was pretty good. She turned and looked at the metal shelving unit where she'd set the pop can. Next to it was a small, square-shaped block of wood. She picked it up and examined the sea-shell carving in the middle of it. She ran her fingers over the piece. The wood was smooth, including the crevices in the shell. It was a simple but beautiful piece. "Did you make this?

"You don't listen very well, do you?" He set down his tool, turned, and walked over to her. "*Ya*, I made it," he said, taking it from her. "I made everything in here." He set it back on the shelf and then bent to the cooler and offered her another can of pop. "It's hot in here."

She looked at the can. She was thirsty, and it was sweltering in the shop. What a thoughtful gesture.

"Now take this and sit on the stool." He pointed to the corner again.

So much for being thoughtful. "You're being rather bossy," she said, but she took the can from him. "Why can't I watch?"

"Because I don't want you to," he said, not looking at her. "This is *mei* shop, remember?"

"I had *nee* idea you were so cantankerous."

He looked at her again, this time smirking. "*Mei* shop. *Mei* rules."

She glanced at the stool again, then smiled. "Fine. I'll follow *yer* rules."

"Finally." He turned, mumbling something about how he hoped Ruby's hunt would end soon, and returned to his workbench.

Martha walked over to the stool, then picked it up and carried it to the end of the workbench. She sat down and sipped on the cola.

"What are you doing?" he asked, putting his hands on his hips.

"Sitting on the stool, like you told me to."

"That's not what I meant . . . Oh, forget it." He shook his head and went back to making curlicues. But Martha thought she saw the trace of a smile.

For the next half hour or so, she watched him work. She still thought he was very good. He was meticulous with each curlicue and had gone through several pieces of wood, practicing the same carving element. Martha leaned forward, taking in how he angled the tool—a gouge, he called it when she'd asked—and pushed it against the wood. "What kind of wood is that?"

"Birch," he said. "It's soft. *Gut* for practicing. We have a lot of it around here." He blew the sawdust off the wood.

Which explained the name of their community, although they had more ponds and small lakes around here than creeks. "You look like an expert already."

He turned to her. The scowl on his face since she'd parked herself at the end of his bench softened a bit. "*Danki*, but I have a long way to *geh*."

His expression made her smile. At least he was talking to her as though she was a normal human being instead of a child.

A while later, after he'd switched to another tool, she asked, "How long have you been doing this?"

"A year or so."

"What made you start?"

"I used to whittle when I was a little kid." He picked up another piece of scrap wood. "I wanted to try something a little more challenging."

"I know how to whittle."

He turned to her, holding the wood in midair. "You do?"

She nodded. "*Mei onkel* taught me one summer when we

were visiting. Not *Onkel* Hezekiah. His brother, Nehemiah. I think I was about eight or so."

Seth set down the wood and picked up the tool.

"I haven't whittled in years, though," she said. "Not since that summer. Is it at all similar to carving?"

"A little. Whittling can be anything from shaping a stick to making an object. Woodcarving is a little more elaborate. It also takes skill."

"And whittling doesn't?"

"I didn't say that." He looked at her, then, to her surprise, he handed her the tool. "Try it. You'll see what I mean."

She took the tool in her hand and examined it. It was heavier than *Onkel* Nehemiah's penknife, obviously, but it wasn't too heavy. She set her pop can on the floor and stood next to Seth.

"What is it?"

"A backbent chisel."

"What do I do with it?"

"You've been watching me. What do you think you do?"

Martha picked up the scrap wood Seth had just taken from the pile. She looked at the rectangular piece, studying its thickness the way she had seen Seth do. It wasn't the same kind of wood as the birch block he'd just finished working with. She brushed the sawdust and wood shavings off the table, then set down the wood. She placed the chisel against the corner of the rectangle.

"Hold on. You forgot one thing." He took the wood from her and put it in a small vise. "If you push too hard without securing it, that block will *geh* flying across the shop."

"You're not using the vise."

"I've had more practice than you have."

She couldn't argue with his logic, and once the wood was

secured in the vise, she slid the tool across it. A razor-thin shaving of wood appeared.

"Push harder," Seth said. "You're not going to hurt it."

Martha applied more pressure and wiggled the tool a few inches over the top of the wood. The carve was crooked, but she was pleased with her attempt. She grinned. "This is fun."

"Try it again."

She looked up at him, this time seeing a genuine smile on his face. It made him even more good-looking. He had a nice smile. He should show it more often.

A short while later she'd made six grooves in the wood. Seth released it from the vise and handed it to her. "*Yer* first creation."

The wood and her carving were filled with imperfections, but she didn't care. She had created something, and she'd had a blast doing it. She also wanted to do it again. She kept her gaze on Seth, and he continued to look at her. He frowned a bit.

"What?" she said.

"You've got sawdust on *yer* nose."

She wiped it away, not surprised. "Better?"

"*Ya.*" But his gaze had shifted from her face to the door, his frown deepening. "Do you think they're looking for you by now?"

"How long have I been here?"

Seth moved a few pieces of wood aside on the table, revealing a small battery-operated clock. "At least an hour," he said. "Maybe longer."

"Oh, I didn't realize I'd been gone that long. They probably are looking for me."

Seth suddenly put his arm around her shoulders, practically shoving her to the door. "You should hurry back. Don't want anyone to worry about you."

"Or to find *yer* woodshop."

"That too." His hand touched the doorknob, and he started to open the door.

She realized she didn't want to leave. It didn't matter to her if people were looking for her. She whirled around, nearly bumping into Seth. "I have an idea."

"You can tell me all about it another time." He pulled on the doorknob.

Martha leaned against the door, shutting it. "Teach me how to carve."

He stepped back, his expression filled with surprise. "Why would I do that?"

Hmm. He had a point. Just because he'd let her carve a little bit didn't mean he was interested in showing her more. "Because I asked you to?"

"Then the answer is *nee*."

She should have expected that. He was obviously in a hurry for her to leave too. Her mind searched for a reason he might agree to. And one came. Before she thought it completely through, she said, "I'll keep *yer* secret if you do."

CHAPTER 4

S eth looked down at Martha, stunned. Was this woman with the sweet smile trying to coerce him? "You realize that sounds like blackmail, don't you?"

Apparent guilt replaced her smile. She brought her hand up to her mouth. "It does?" She shook her head vehemently. "I'm sorry. I didn't mean it to be. I just wanted to learn . . ." Martha glanced at the floor. "I'm so sorry."

"It's all right," he said quietly. And it was, now that he knew she wasn't being coercive on purpose. He doubted she had a manipulative bone in her body. "You really want to learn how to carve that badly?"

She looked up and nodded. "But I understand if you don't want to teach me. Especially after what I just said."

"It's not that . . ." This was becoming more than he'd bargained for when he decided to let her try carving. He couldn't help himself when he saw how eagerly she was watching his every move, excitement in her eyes. It was almost contagious. Next thing he knew he'd handed her the chisel. But that didn't mean he wanted to teach her. Or let her come back to the shop. This was his place, after all, and he wasn't interested in sharing. "I don't have time to teach you." He expected her to protest and come up with some other half-thought-out excuse to get him to agree. Instead, she nodded.

"I understand. And I really am sorry for trying to blackmail you."

"Blackmail is a little strong, but *yer* apology is accepted."

"*Danki.*" She turned and faced the door. But when she touched the doorknob, his hand shot out and covered hers.

"Wait." Good grief, what was he doing? He'd wanted her to go, and she was going. Why did he stop her? Because for some incomprehensible reason, at that moment he didn't want to disappoint Martha Detweiler. "Maybe we can work something out," his mouth said, as if it were disengaged from his brain.

"Really?" She turned and looked up at him, the brightness back in her eyes.

He found himself nodding and sighing. "*Ya.* Really."

"Oh, *danki.*" She was grinning like a cat that had licked the best of the cream in the bowl. A cute cat, at that. "How about tomorrow, bright and early?"

"Tomorrow's Sunday." There was no way he was going to meet her here on a Sunday. He had vowed not to break the Sabbath anymore, even if that meant he went a week or more without engaging in his hobby. His faith was more important than woodcarving.

"Oh goodness, you're right. How did I forget that? Then Monday? We're usually done with supper by six. What about you?"

"It depends." He scratched the back of his neck. He was already feeling regret. *I'm a nitwit for doing this. A complete nitwit.* "I'm not sure I'll be free." If he put her off long enough, maybe she'd forget about it.

"All right." Her smile dimmed, but she still looked happy. "Tuesday, then."

"Why Tuesday?"

"Why not?"

He didn't have an answer for that, and his brain had already started to twinge with a headache. Clearly, he wasn't getting out of this. Then again, he was the one who had agreed to teach her. *Nitwit.* "Fine," he said, lamenting his weak resolve. "We'll meet here on Tuesday. After supper."

She took a step toward him, and for a minute he thought she was going to hug him. But she kept her distance. "Don't worry, Seth. *Nee* matter what, *yer* secret is safe with me. I promise." Then she turned and dashed out the door. This time he didn't stop her.

"It better be," he muttered as he closed the door. He turned around and looked at his worktable. Wood shavings were everywhere, along with a good measure of sawdust. He walked to the table and picked up the piece of wood Martha had been working on. She'd gotten the hang of the chisel more quickly than he'd anticipated, but that didn't mean she would catch on to everything else in a timely manner. Which meant the lessons could keep stretching on and on and on . . .

He shook his head and tossed the wood into the scrap pile again. A woodpecker started to drill against the outside of the shed. That didn't help the headache just beginning to throb.

Seth yanked the headband off his head and dropped it on the table. Maybe this wouldn't be so bad. He hadn't told Martha he would give her *lessons*, just that he would show her how to carve. Considering her aptitude, he could do the basics in one session, easy. If he was lucky, she might want to forget about woodcarving altogether by next Tuesday. *It would be mighty fine with me, Lord, if Martha had a case of selective amnesia.*

As he haphazardly cleaned the shop, he thought of the proposal Cevilla had made the other day. The one he'd refused.

He let out a small chuckle. How ironic that he would end up spending time with Martha anyway, without Cevilla's interference. In a way he wished he could tell her that. But he couldn't, not without blabbing about his woodshop. And if he told Cevilla about it, he might as well rent a billboard in Cleveland and announce it to everyone. No, his secret would stay safe . . . for a long, long time.

. . .

"Martha!" Ruby hurried over to her as Martha entered the kitchen. "Where have you been? We put off the hunt because the men are out looking for you. All the *frau* are worrying on the front porch."

Martha cringed. She should have paid more attention to the time. But it seemed to fly so fast when she was at the woodshop. "I'm sorry. I went for a walk to get some fresh air."

"Without telling anyone?" Ruby crossed her arms and shook her head. "You were gone for almost two hours. We thought something had happened to you."

"Two hours?" Seth's clock must be broken. She needed to let him know. "I lost track of time."

Ruby uncrossed her arms, but her worried expression suddenly turned skeptical. "How far did you walk? Barton?"

She shook her head. They both knew Barton was too far to walk to, but Ruby's point remained. She wasn't buying Martha's story. And Martha couldn't tell her the truth, not without giving away Seth's secret. Her face heated. She couldn't believe she'd tried to blackmail him. Not on purpose, of course, but when he pointed it out to her, she realized he was right. She hadn't meant to make it sound as though she was going to spill the beans to the community. She just wanted to learn how to carve. The short while she'd done it hadn't been enough. Now she understood why Seth enjoyed it so much.

"Martha? Martha, did you hear me?"

Martha shook her head again. "*Nee*. What did you say?"

"You're acting *seltsam*. Now I don't know if we should send out some of the women to look for the men. Even Christian is out there looking." The oven went off, and Ruby moved to the stove. "I was so nervous I made more cookies." She pulled out a tray of peanut butter cookies and put them on top of the stove.

The cookies smelled sweet and peanut buttery, but Martha's mind wasn't on food. "I didn't mean to cause any trouble."

Ruby shut the oven door and looked at her. "I know. I'm just confused as to why you left in the first place. And don't tell me it was to get fresh air. The treasure hunt was being held outside. You'd get plenty of fresh air once the game started."

Martha pressed her lips together. She needed to be upfront with Ruby. She should have been upfront with her from the beginning. "I didn't want to do the hunt."

Ruby's brow lifted. "You didn't? But we planned it together."

"I know." She gripped the back of one of the kitchen chairs. "And I'm sure it would have been a lot of fun."

"*Ya*. It would have."

Martha blew out a breath. "I . . . I didn't want to be partnered with anyone. I didn't even want to come."

"Then why didn't you say that the other day?" Ruby went to her. "We could have planned something else."

"It wouldn't have mattered." She told Ruby about her problems with the single men. "They were at me as soon as they arrived this evening. I couldn't handle it."

"I had *nee* idea." Ruby's expression softened. "I should have been paying more attention."

"I didn't expect you to notice what was going on."

Chris entered the kitchen from outside. His left eyebrow raised. "There you are. Where have you—"

"Don't pester her with questions," Ruby said, brushing Christian off.

"I only made a simple inquiry."

"She took a little walk, okay? That's all you need to know."

His eyes moved from Martha to his wife. Finally, he shrugged. "I'm absolutely positive I will never understand women."

Martha would have laughed if she hadn't felt so bad for worrying everyone. Chris often looked bewildered when it came to Ruby. He was a straightforward, literal man—a little too literal, which often led to his confusion. Ruby kept him on his toes. Martha was glad Chris hadn't made any more inquiries.

"Did you see anyone heading toward the house?" Ruby asked him.

Chris shook his head. "No, but we all chose different directions for our search."

Ruby nodded. "Then the coast is clear."

His brow furrowed. "What coast? Ruby, you're acting more confusing than usual."

"I'm sorry, but it's necessary. Just *geh* with me on this." She gave him a sweet smile as she escorted Martha toward the back door. "After I tell the women you're back and okay, I'll give you a ride home. If we see . . . anyone, you can duck down on the buggy floor."

"What?" Martha and Chris said at the same time.

Ruby opened the back door, her eyes sparking with excitement. Martha suspected she was enjoying the little drama. "*Nee* worries, Martha. I'll get you home safely."

This was becoming ridiculous. She wasn't going to duck down in Ruby's buggy or anywhere else. "I'm going to stay," she told Ruby.

"Are you sure? I don't mind getting you out of here."

"Positive." She wasn't about to run away twice. Although if she hadn't left earlier, she wouldn't have found Seth's woodshop. Still, she needed to stop fleeing every time she felt uncomfortable.

Ruby closed the door. "You're a brave woman, Martha."

"Would someone please tell me what's going on?" Chris scratched his head, completely confused.

"Later." Ruby went to the stove, picked up a cookie, and thrust it into Chris's hand. "We're canceling the hunt."

He stared at the cookie and then looked at her. "We are?"

"*Ya.* When the men return, we'll have supper, and then everyone can play volleyball while Martha helps me in the kitchen. Is that all right with you, Martha?"

She nodded. Normally she'd rather play volleyball than do dishes, but she wouldn't refuse Ruby's offer of help.

"I thought you liked volleyball," Chris said. "I can assist Ruby with the dishes instead."

Ruby walked to her husband and threaded her arm through his. "Don't worry," she said, lowering her voice. "You don't have to play. The game needs a referee."

He looked relieved and nodded. "I'm capable of doing that."

Martha smiled, remembering the horseshoe match she, Ruby, Chris, and Selah had played last year. Chris might be the smartest man in Birch Creek, and the best teacher, but he was a terrible horseshoe player. Selah had told her after the game that Chris didn't like sports, and Martha had seen why. A newborn colt had more grace than Christian Ropp.

He took a bite of the cookie and smiled. "This is extremely flavorful, Ruby. I believe it's *yer* best batch yet."

She grinned, and they exchanged a sweet look.

A few minutes after all the women crowded into the kitchen to make sure Martha was all right, the men started returning from searching for her. Unlike Ruby and some of the women, who had a wary look in their eyes, they seemed to accept the excuse that she'd taken a walk and lost track of time. Men were so easy to fool sometimes.

For the rest of the evening Ruby was protective of Martha, staying close to her side.

When the volleyball game was over, and everyone was about to leave, Ruby said, "Martha, I have a quilt to show you upstairs. Christian, see our guests out. Don't wait for us," she said to everyone as she led Martha up the stairs. "See you tomorrow."

"You're not showing me a quilt," Martha said as they reached Ruby's bedroom door.

Her friend shook her head. "*Nee*. Well, I could. We have an old one that belonged to Christian's grandmother on our bed. But if you've seen one quilt, you've seen them all." She paused. "Are you okay?"

"*Ya*. And *danki* for helping me tonight." She hugged Ruby.

"You're welcome." Ruby stepped back. "I just wish I'd known sooner."

"I should have told you."

"Maybe you and I can come up with a plan to deal with those *buwe*." Ruby grinned.

Martha shook her head. "*Danki*, Ruby, but I have to handle this on *mei* own."

Later that night, after she arrived home from the Ropps', Martha pondered her predicament. So far she'd managed to involve her mother, Cevilla, Ruby, and even Seth in her dilemma, and that wasn't right. Martha decided to follow Richard's advice—from now on she would be straightforward with any man who asked her out. She would find a way to let him down easy, since she didn't want to hurt anyone's feelings. *Been there, done that*—and, according to Paul, worse. But she would have to be firm. And she would tell them the truth—she didn't have time to date now. She just couldn't tell them that was thanks to Seth Yoder. Oddly enough, she was engaging in Cevilla's plan B, even though it wasn't exactly the way the woman had wanted her to.

Yes. That's what she would do. Be firm. Tell the truth. No running away.

She set that aside and made herself a ham and cheese sandwich. She hadn't had much of an appetite tonight, but now she was hungry. Her parents were already in bed, and the house was quiet. Her thoughts shifted to woodcarving as she ate. She intended to learn all she could from Seth, even if it took her a while to accomplish it. Maybe he would be willing to share his woodshop if she bought her own tools and supplied more wood. She might bring that up to him during their first lesson.

She started to feel better. Between her job and new hobby, she wouldn't have time for dating or socializing, and she wouldn't have to say much of anything to her suitors because, except for church, she wouldn't see them. That suited her just fine.

. . .

It was almost dusk when Nina walked down the gravel drive to the mailbox. Her father had mentioned that he might pave the driveway, but that would be in the future. He had his hands full working on their new house and the inn. They were all busy. She rubbed her shoulder. It was still sore after she'd first helped with all the unpacking and cleaning and then spent the last three days pulling down old kitchen cabinets, sanding them, staining them a lighter oak color, and then, with Levi's help, hanging them back up.

The four of them had been so busy that no one had collected the mail even though the post office had been scheduled to start delivering it yesterday. She anticipated that the rusty box would be full. Her grandmother had already purchased a new metal mailbox to put in a simple new wood frame, and somehow she'd talked Sol Troyer, the carpenter helping them with the inn addition, into making the frame by Monday. *Grossmammi* never wasted time getting things done—or using any excuse to snoop around the community. She hadn't admitted to doing that, but Nina was positive she was learning as much information about Birch Creek as she could. That was her grandmother's way.

As for Nina, she hadn't ventured past their property lines, unlike Levi and her father, who had visited the bishop and introduced themselves yesterday. If *Grossmammi* had been home at the time, she would have gone with them, but she'd just left for Yoder's Bakery to purchase bread. She wouldn't be happy they were going without her, but they had invited Nina to go along with them. She had declined. She wasn't ready for that. Eventually she would meet people, but right now she wanted to keep herself at arm's length. That way she could at least pretend there was still a possibility that the rest of the family would give up this whole inn idea and move back home.

Even though it was early evening, it was still hot and humid. She pulled a handkerchief out of the pocket of her apron and wiped her forehead. She tucked it back into her pocket, then pulled open the lid to the mailbox and thrust her hand inside.

Something flew at her, and she yanked out her hand. A wasp! She swatted at it. She was fine around worms and grubs and other live bait, but she despised flying insects, especially the stinging kind. More wasps flew out. She screamed when one of them stung her arm, and she squeezed her eyes shut.

Then she felt someone strong and sturdy grab her waist and yank her away from the mailbox. "Hang on," a male voice said close to her ear.

She opened her eyes and saw that she was being dragged halfway up the front yard. When they were clear of the wasps, he released her.

"Are you okay?" he asked.

She nodded, face-to-face with a handsome man who appeared to be around her age. "I-I think so." Then the sting started to burn. "Or maybe not," she said, looking down at the bright red welt on her arm.

"For land's sake, Nina, what was all that screaming about?" *Grossmammi* marched onto the front porch, the screen door shutting behind her.

"Wasps," the man said. "She's been stung."

"Oh dear." *Grossmammi* hurried down the porch steps. Nina was always surprised at how light and quick on her feet her grandmother was. "Let me take a look at it."

The sting wasn't that bad, and she checked her arms again. Somehow, she'd been stung only once, which was a miracle considering how many wasps had flown out of the mailbox. She felt a little stupid for screeching like a wounded animal. "I'm okay, *Grossmammi*," she said, turning to the man who had saved her from a more painful experience. Her mouth dropped open. "But I don't think he is."

Grossmammi turned and sucked in a breath. "Oh *dear*."

The man winced, as if finally noticing that he was in pain. He touched the huge red bump forming above his eye. "Guess they got me too."

"Come inside right now and we'll put some ice on that," her grandmother ordered.

He shook his head, still wincing. "I don't live far from here. I'll take care of it when I get home."

"Nonsense. We'll take care of you here."

Before he could respond, her grandmother was behind him, pushing him toward the porch. "*Geh* into the kitchen and get some ice cubes," she said to Nina. "Then wrap them in a clean dish towel."

Nina nodded and did as she was told. When the man and her grandmother came into the kitchen, *Grossmammi* pointed at a chair. "Sit."

He sat down without saying a word.

Nina brought over the wrapped towel and handed it to *Grossmammi*. "I'm not the one who needs it; he is," her grandmother said. "Place it gently on his eye."

She hesitated. This wouldn't be a big deal if it was her brother or father or any of her friends back home, but she didn't know this man. She didn't want to be that close to a stranger.

"I can do it." He took the towel from her and put it against his eye, which was already swelling shut.

Nina grimaced. "I'm sorry," she said.

"It's not *yer* fault." He smiled a little, then winced. "The wasps have been a problem in this heat."

"Still, I should have been more careful—"

"He said it wasn't *yer* fault, Nina." *Grossmammi* turned to him with a sweet smile, one she reserved for special occasions. "What's *yer* name, *yung mann*?"

"Seth Yoder."

Her smile widened. "Are you related to the bishop, then?"

"*Ya*, he's *mei daed*."

"You hear that, Nina?" *Grossmammi* looked at her, clasping her hands together. "He's the bishop's *sohn*."

"That's . . . nice." The only bishop's son she'd ever known was Jonah Gruber. He had been a huge pest when he was younger, then a troublemaker when he was older. She wasn't surprised he ended up leaving the Amish. Until then, her grandmother had dropped hints that he just needed a good woman to turn him around, as though Nina was surely that woman. For some reason *Grossmammi* had always thought more highly of the bishop's family than any other. From her impressed expression as she looked at Seth, she apparently still believed that.

"Does *yer* arm hurt?" Seth pointed to her sting, looking at it with his good eye.

"It's fine."

"Here." He handed her the towel. "Put it on the sting."

This guy was nothing like Jonah. "You keep it," she said. "You need it more than I do."

"Let me get you something cold to drink, Seth," *Grossmammi* said. "Lemonade or iced tea?"

Seth stood. "Neither, but *danki*. I need to get back home. I've been gone long enough as it is."

"But *yer* eye—"

"*Mei mamm*'s got some herbs she uses for stuff like this." He cracked a tepid smile. "I've been stung plenty of times."

"But—"

"I'll walk you out," Nina said, ignoring her grandmother for once. She led Seth out the front door, glancing over her shoulder. Surprisingly, *Grossmammi* didn't follow them.

When they were on the porch, she said, "*Danki*. I would have been stung to bits if you hadn't come along."

He nodded. "I'm glad that didn't happen. I really do have to get home." He hurried down the steps and waved to her. "Nice to meet you, uh . . ."

"Nina," she called out, waving back as he half-jogged down the road. He really was in a hurry to leave. *I wonder why?*

"Nina!" *Grossmammi* yelled.

Then again, she knew exactly why. "Coming," she said, going back into the house.

"Why did you let him *geh*?" *Grossmammi* said as Nina walked into the kitchen.

She looked around the kitchen. Tools and debris were everywhere, a can with stain dripping down its sides was on the counter, and several of the floorboards were buckled. Now that she was viewing it objectively, she realized the place looked like a disaster zone except for the refurbished cabinets. Between that, her pushy grandmother, and Seth's eye being nearly swollen shut, she didn't blame him for running off. "He said he had to *geh* home."

"Humph." *Grossmammi* gave her a stern look. "You could have tried harder to convince him to stay. He's the bishop's *sohn*, after all."

Not that again. "I'm sure he'd feel more comfortable at home than here in this mess."

Her grandmother glanced around the room. "You might have a point." She looked at Nina. "How is *yer* arm?"

At least she remembered Nina had been stung too. "It's all right."

"I'll get you some ice." *Grossmammi* grabbed another dish towel off the ring it was hanging on and went straight to the cooler. She took out a few more ice cubes, wrapped them in the towel, and went to Nina. "Sit down and we'll put this on *yer* arm. I'll have Loren get rid of that nest. I told him he needed to take down that old rusty mailbox sooner than later."

Grossmammi sat down next to Nina and put the towel over the welt on her forearm. "Seth is very *schee, ya?*" *Grossmammi* said. "*Yer daed* told me about the bishop's *familye*. Said they were very nice. From what I've been able to gather, the whole community thinks highly of them."

"That's *gut*."

"And he saved you." *Grossmammi* batted her eyelashes. "You know what that means, don't you?"

"*Nee*," Nina said warily. "Other than he was at the right place at the right time." And he was willing to risk getting stung to save her from being swarmed. She admired him for that.

"It means we *must* invite him for supper." She looked at Nina, smiling. "As a thank-you for saving you."

"Can't I just write him a thank-you note?"

"You can do that too." She looked at Nina's arm, realized the towel wasn't anywhere near the sting, and placed it back over the welt. "Is this helping?" she asked.

"A bit." The redness was fading, and the sting hardly hurt at all. She must have been stung by a baby wasp.

"*Gut* thing you're not allergic. The last thing you need is to get all puffy." She stood. "I'll get some apple-cider vinegar and bandages," she said, going to one of the freshly renovated cabinets. She opened one door and got her supplies. "I'm sure we'll see Seth at the service tomorrow."

"Maybe." The swelling above his eye looked pretty serious. "I still don't think it's necessary to invite him for supper."

"Of course you wouldn't." *Grossmammi* dabbed the vinegar on the sting, which took away the rest of the pain. "However, a nice *yung* lady would do exactly that after such a daring rescue."

Sometimes her grandmother could be overdramatic. "You've been reading those Christian romance novels again, haven't you?"

Levi and their father walked into the kitchen. "What happened to you?" Levi asked.

"There's a wasp nest in the mailbox," *Grossmammi* huffed. "You should have taken care of that when I told you to, Loren."

Daed let out a long, familiar sigh. Nina knew her father had his methods of handling his mother, mainly to let her think she had her own way. "It's all right, *Daed*," she said, not wanting him to feel bad. "I'll be okay."

Levi peered at her arm. "Doesn't look too bad."

"It's not," Nina said.

"But it could have been tragic." *Grossmammi* patted her arm. "Thank goodness for Seth Yoder."

"What?" Levi asked, picking up an oatmeal cookie from the plate near the stove.

"Never mind." Nina sank back in her chair. She didn't need Levi teasing her about Seth.

Daed reached around Levi and grabbed a cookie. "When the sun goes down I'll get the mail out of there and take care of the nest. The wasps should be sluggish by then, and I'll spray some dish detergent water on them."

"Then you'll pick up our new mailbox and frame on Monday," *Grossmammi* said.

Another sigh. "*Ya, Mamm.* I will."

With a pleased smile, *Grossmammi* went to the sink, then gave Levi's hand a small pat. "You'll spoil *yer* supper."

"That's never happened," Levi said, pointing out the truth.

A short time later, Nina helped her grandmother put together a simple meal of sandwiches, chips, store-bought pickles, and prepared potato salad. After prayer and filled plates, Levi picked up a potato chip. "I'll be glad when the kitchen is put back together," he said. "I miss *yer* cooking, *Grossmammi*."

Grossmammi beamed. "I'll make you a feast, Levi."

Nina was also tired of cold meals, but it wouldn't be much longer before the kitchen was completely remodeled. Then she thought about *Grossmammi*'s supper invitation. Hopefully she would drop the idea. Having supper with Seth and her family would be nothing short of awkward. But knowing Delilah Stoll, she wouldn't care. She'd make sure Seth came for supper, even if Nina didn't want him there.

· · ·

The next morning was Sunday, and Martha prepared for church. She put on her best dress, a dark-blue one with short sleeves, then put up her hair and pinned her *kapp* in place. She never took much time to get ready, so while her parents were still getting dressed, she went outside, sat on a wicker chair on the front porch, and enjoyed the time to herself before the service. The sweet sound of twittering birds surrounded her as fluffy clouds gathered in the sky. *Thank you, Lord, for a beautiful morning. And if you don't mind, please give me the courage*

to be upfront with Zeb and Zeke and Ira and the rest of the buwe.
Amen.

Finally her parents came out of the house, and they all
loaded up in the buggy, where their horse was already hitched.
The cloudy sky grew overcast, threatening rain. She was glad
for that. It had been a dry, hot summer so far, drier than most.
She'd heard some talk among the farmers in their community.
They were worried about the lack of rainfall. Martha didn't
know much about farming, but she did know gardening, and
she was able to keep her and *Mamm*'s garden going only with
the help of a water hose. Even then her tomato plants had
looked a little wilted last night when she got home from Ruby's,
and she'd given them a long drink of water before going inside.

She closed her eyes and settled into the back of the buggy,
enjoying the peaceful morning, the sound of the horse's hooves
against the asphalt road, and the slight breeze that did little to
cool her but provided a bit of refreshment as she prepared herself for morning worship. The service was at the Yoders' house
this week.

The Yoders lived only a few streets away, so it didn't take
long for them to arrive. Her father pulled the buggy into the
side of the yard where several others were already parked.
When they came to as stop, she climbed out. A few families
lived close enough to the Yoders to walk. That included Seth's
aunt, Carolyn, and her husband, Atlee, who were already slipping into the barn. Carolyn owned the bakery down the road,
and Atlee was a cabinetmaker and carpenter. They lived in a
small house Atlee had built next to the bakery. They were an
older couple, but they didn't have any children.

She started for the barn but then saw the Bontrager boys

arrive. They lived near the Yoders and approached the property in staggered groups. Zeke and Zeb were in the lead, followed by two sets of younger brothers, then the youngest children and their parents. Thirteen children were in the family, twelve of them boys, and four of them close to her age. Zeb and Zeke, the oldest of two sets of twins, reached the edge of the Yoders' driveway first. This was her moment to stand her ground. She would walk into the service, and if either of the boys said anything to her, she would pleasantly acknowledge him, but that was all.

Her brain was willing, but her feet wouldn't move. Her stomach started to twist in knots. What if one of them—or all of them—became angry with her the way Paul was? What if they ended up hating her the way he did?

Martha ducked behind one of the buggies, disappointed in herself. Why was she such a coward?

"Hiding out again?"

Martha whirled around to see Seth standing behind her—smirking. He hadn't teased her about avoiding suitors when she'd invaded his woodshop yesterday, but she got the feeling he was now. Maybe he would have if he hadn't been so aggravated by her sudden appearance. Yet he'd showed some concern, and in the end, he'd agreed to teach her carving. She preferred the less cantankerous Seth to the mocking one she was seeing now. She didn't like being teased about this.

She opened her mouth to say something, then froze when she saw the huge red lump above his swollen eye. "Goodness, what happened to you?"

"Had a bit of a run-in with a wasp nest." He waved off her concern. "It's *nix*."

"It doesn't look like *nix*." She took a step toward him, inspecting the sting. "Does it hurt?"

"Feels better than it did yesterday."

"You probably should have stayed home."

He shook his head. "First, a wasp sting isn't an excuse to miss church. Second, church is at *mei haus*. Unlike some people, I'm not going to hide while the service is going on." He grinned.

"I'm not hiding."

He glanced around the buggy, then looked at her. "They went inside the barn."

"Who?" Martha said, feigning ignorance.

"Zeb and Zeke. That's who you're hiding from, *ya*?"

The spark of amusement in his eyes annoyed her. "I told you I'm not hiding."

"Then let's *geh* to church." There was that grin again.

"I will . . . in a minute."

His smile disappeared. "You really are afraid, aren't you?"

"I'm not afraid." She glanced away, her hands folding together. "I just don't want to upset anyone. That's all."

"But *you're* upset, like you were when you first burst into *mei* woodshop." He peered down at her. "Is that any better?"

She looked at him and nodded. "*Ya*. It is."

He regarded her for a moment. "Cevilla and I talked the other day."

Her cheeks heated, and not because it was so hot out. She was surprised he'd brought that up, considering he hadn't said anything about Cevilla when they were in the woodshop yesterday. "I guess you didn't discuss the weather."

"Nope." He pushed back his black hat as if he wanted to see her better. "She told me about *yer mann* problems."

She straightened, indignant. He made it sound like she had a contagious disease. "Excuse me, but I don't have any problems with men."

"Your behavior seems to support that idea, and that has to be why Cevilla asked me to pretend to date you."

"Cevilla should mind her own business," Martha muttered.

"Guess Cevilla has it all wrong, then? Even though you've been running away and hiding?" His grin returned. "I guess I'll have to tell her she made a mistake—"

"Nee!" She grimaced. That came out more forcefully than she'd planned, but she didn't want him talking to Cevilla again. That would make things worse.

"So you do have *mann* problems."

"Stop saying that."

He chuckled, then peered around the buggy again. "As entertaining as this conversation is, we should get to church. *Daed* doesn't like it when I'm late."

She didn't want to disappoint Freemont. He was a nice man, and a good bishop. She also didn't appreciate being Seth's morning entertainment, and she was glad to end the conversation before she was further humiliated. At some point she would have to clarify things with Seth, but it was time to go to church. Mann *problems.* What a weird way to describe her predicament.

"The coast is clear," Seth said. At her annoyed look he added, "Just helping you out."

Why was he being so irritating? "Let's *geh* already." Eager to get to church and away from Seth, she shoved past him and the buggy and headed toward the barn. She was halfway there when she heard an unfamiliar voice ring out.

"Yoo-hoo! Seth!"

She turned around to see Seth skid to a halt a few inches behind her. Marching toward them was an older woman Martha had never seen before, accompanied by a younger woman who appeared to be close to Martha's age. She trailed behind, dragging her feet. They didn't have many visitors from other communities at church services, although Ruby had said her brother, Timothy, who was the church deacon, had mentioned that more people than ever were interested in visiting Birch Creek.

"Hi," Seth said, sounding less confident than he had a minute ago.

The older woman picked up her pace and stopped in front of Seth. Martha could see she was younger than Cevilla but older than Martha's mother. The woman looked up at him, then turned to speak to the young woman next to her. "Nina," she said, waving her hand, "hurry over here. Service is starting shortly, and we need to take care of business."

The girl rolled her eyes. Curious, Martha didn't move, and neither woman acknowledged her. The young woman had a unique look about her. Stout was the first word that came to Martha's mind, and she had the thickest black eyebrows she'd ever seen. They were paired with large, round, brown eyes, and a nose that was a bit on the big side. The entire combination, while unusual, made her rather attractive, in Martha's opinion. Except right now she had a scowl on her face, as if she'd rather be anywhere than here. *How do they know Seth?*

The older woman wiped her forehead with a plain white handkerchief. Heat and humidity hung in the air like a wet wool blanket, and it had yet to rain. "I'm glad I caught you before you went into the service, Seth," she said. "I didn't have a chance to properly introduce myself and *mei grossdochder* to you yesterday." She held out her hand. "I'm Delilah Stoll, and this is . . . Nina." She introduced her granddaughter as if she were royalty.

"Nice to meet you, uh, again." He gave Martha an awkward glance. "This is Martha Detweiler."

But Delilah kept ignoring her. "Nina would like to thank you for *yer* help."

"She thanked me yesterday," Seth pointed out. "That was thanks enough."

"It was not, considering what you did for her." She nudged Nina with her elbow. "Thank the *yung mann*, Nina."

Martha wondered if something was wrong with Nina. She seemed too old to be treated like such a child.

Nina rubbed her nose, then thrust her hands behind her back. *"Danki."* Her grimace deepened. Was that because of Delilah? Or Seth? Martha wasn't sure.

"You're welcome," he said.

"Yer eye is looking a little better."

"It's healing." Seth shifted from one foot to the other. Martha had never seen him looking this uncomfortable.

"To show our gratitude, you're invited to supper this week." Delilah's smile was a bit calculating, Martha thought. The woman also reminded Martha of Cevilla, especially when Cevilla was up to something.

Seth's panicked gaze darted from Delilah to Nina. "That's not necessary."

"Of course it is." Delilah's grin widened. "We'll expect you at six sharp on Tuesday. You'll have to excuse the mess, though. We're in the process of adding on to the inn."

"The inn?" Martha asked.

As if she'd noticed Martha for the first time, Delilah looked at her. Her smile dimmed a bit. *"Ya. Mei sohn* bought the *English haus* on Parker Street, and we're converting it into a small inn."

Stoll. This was the woman Ruby introduced herself to, then. But Delilah hadn't said anything to Ruby about the home being transformed into an inn. Martha thought that was an excellent idea.

Delilah looked back at Seth. "The renovations shouldn't interfere with us having a lovely supper."

"*Grossmammi*," Nina said, "maybe we should wait until another time—"

"Nonsense. It's best to get to know everyone as soon as possible. Then we'll feel like a part of the community."

Nina opened her mouth, then pressed her lips tightly together, as if she was used to not getting very far with her grandmother.

"Seth, Nina can tell you all about her latest quilting project," Delilah gushed. "She's excellent with a needle."

"Sounds . . . fascinating."

"Trust me, it isn't," Nina grumbled.

Seth took a step back from them and shook his head. "I'm sorry, but I can't make it on Tuesday."

"Oh?" Delilah gasped as if she'd never had one of her invitations refused. "Why not?"

"*Grossmammi*," Nina hissed.

"Because . . ." He glanced at Martha, his eyes filled with pleading. He couldn't say he was busy teaching her woodworking. That would spoil his secret.

"Because?" Delilah asked again, this time looking straight at Martha.

She had to come up with something quick. Seth apparently had forgotten how to talk. "Because *mei mudder* already invited him for supper that night," she said, the words rushing out. She squeezed her eyes shut. Good gravy, of all the excuses she could have come up with, why had she given that one?

"I see." Delilah sniffed. "I didn't realize you two were together."

"We're not," Martha and Seth said at the same time. They glanced at each other before Martha added, "*Mamm* wants to thank him for helping us out the other day. Seth's such a helpful person." Oh boy, she was terrible at this. She just used the same reasoning Delilah had. Why couldn't she come up with an original thought?

"Apparently." Delilah brightened. "Wednesday will work fine as well."

Nina shook her head. "We're having the floor replaced in the kitchen, remember?"

"That's right." Delilah dabbed her damp brow again. "We'll schedule it another time, then. But we *will* have you over for supper, Seth. I promise you that. Now, I must find *mei sohn* and *grosssohn* to speak to them a moment before we *geh* inside. They've been parking our new horse and buggy." She turned and strode away.

Nina mouthed the words *I'm sorry*, then hurried after her grandmother.

Seth blew out a breath. "First time I've ever heard a supper invitation sound like a threat." He scowled and turned to her. "What do you mean I'm invited for supper at *yer haus*? I didn't help *yer* family with anything."

"I . . . I was trying to help *you*."

"Very helpful." He wiped the back of his neck with his hand. "Now what are we going to do?"

She shrugged. "Have supper at *mei haus* before going to *yer* woodshop?"

His scowl deepened. "You haven't changed *yer* mind about that, I see."

"Of course not." She lifted her chin. "Besides, *yer* only alternative is to have supper with Delilah and Nina. Want me to tell them you're free after all?"

"Woodcarving it is. And good luck explaining this to *yer mudder.*" He turned toward the barn. Everyone had already gone inside. "Great. Thanks to Ms. Matchmaker, we're late to service. I'll have fun explaining that to *Daed* later."

"How do you know she was matchmaking?"

"Because that seems to be the prime interest of grandmotherly women in Birch Creek lately."

"What do you mean?"

"I just figured it out. Cevilla's doing the same thing. She's just being a little less obvious about it." He shook his head and hurried away.

Martha frowned. Cevilla was matchmaking the two of them? Now that Seth had said the words out loud, she could see through the ruse. How had she missed it before?

She felt like this was her fault. But was it really? She hadn't asked him to help her with Cevilla's plan—her matchmaking plan, as it turned out. Cevilla had done that. And if he wasn't so weird about keeping his woodcarving a secret, she wouldn't have panicked and told Delilah he was coming to her house for supper. She hadn't even realized that Delilah was attempting to match him with Nina, but now she realized her plan had been glaring. He didn't have the right to be irritated with her. She had kept his secret. That was the important thing.

She shook her head and headed for the barn. She needed to focus on the service, not on Seth Yoder, plan B, or how she was going to tell her mother they were having company on Tuesday. Somehow her not-so-simple life had become even more complicated.

CHAPTER 5

Cevilla always sat in the front during services. When she was younger, she wanted to pay attention to the sermon and not be distracted by anyone. Now that she was older—and she wouldn't admit this to anyone—she was having a bit of trouble hearing. Her nephew, Noah, who had Meniere's disease and wore hearing aids, had offered to take her to get some. "They're comfortable once you get used to them," he'd said. But she wasn't ready for them. For some reason she felt like it was one step closer to admitting that age was creeping up on her. Noah was in his midthirties. His hearing loss was because of his disease, and while that was tragic, he was still young and vital. Her young and vital days were behind her, something she didn't like to think about.

However, sitting in the front didn't preclude her from looking over her shoulder and watching congregants come into the barn. It was one of her favorite Sunday activities. Not so long ago, Birch Creek had been a small, oppressed district. Now it was growing, and a sense of joy and peace permeated the community. She praised God daily for that. As the different families came inside and everyone settled in on their benches, the women on one side and the men on the other, she couldn't help but smile. She'd watched from the sidelines as these young couples had found their spouses and started their families, and she'd had a direct hand in her nephew Noah's relationship with his now wife, Ivy, Freemont's oldest child.

Then there were the new families that had moved in. Some were married with children, mostly young, except for a few young adults. Two of those young adults, Chris Ropp and his wife, Ruby, had met in Birch Creek and married last year. Of course, other young men were in the district, eager for a date—or on the hunt for something more permanent.

And then there were Martha and Seth. Seth had rejected her plan B, but that didn't mean Cevilla had given up on them. The more she dwelled on the coupling, the more she was sure they belonged together. She had been right about Noah and Ivy, and about Lucy and Shane, the young couple she'd matched two years ago. She was confident she was correct about Martha and Seth too. So when she saw them walking into the service together right before the singing began, with Seth darting to the men's side of the barn and Martha slipping into an empty seat next to Ruby, she couldn't help but grin. Perhaps they were both protesting too much when it came to their lack of interest in each other. *I might not have to do anything at all.*

Cevilla reached for her cane, knowing the singing would begin any minute. She looked over her shoulder one last time and saw two men, one older and one younger, both without beards, hurrying into the barn. That surprised her, since they rarely had visitors to Sunday service, although she should start expecting it with the booming growth of Birch Creek. She was about to turn to the front when she saw two women dash into the barn. One of the women was plump and short, her gray hair evident from underneath her *kapp*. Closer to her own age than not, Cevilla surmised. The young, interesting-looking girl with her must be a niece or a granddaughter.

The congregation stood, and Cevilla moved to stand, her back creaking as she did. Richard sometimes attended service with her, sitting in the back as a non-Amish guest, although today he was going to a Mennonite church. She didn't begrudge him that. He wasn't Amish, and he wasn't sure he wanted to join the church. She tried not to let that bother her. She was grateful for his companionship, but sometimes she let herself wish for more. That wouldn't happen if he didn't become Amish, and she would never pressure him to do that. That wasn't the Amish way.

Cevilla shifted her attention to the service. She concentrated on worship, then on the sermon Timothy Glick, the district minister, gave. He was a little rough around the edges, but Freemont had been as well when he first started. It was the content of the sermon that mattered to her, not the delivery system.

After church she spent her usual time chatting with everyone while maintaining an eye on Seth and Martha, who had slipped out of the barn right after the service. Separately, she noticed with a little disappointment. But maybe they were meeting up later. She'd have to figure out a way to find out what was really going on with them. Richard would probably chastise her for her nosiness, but he didn't realize the importance of the situation. His granddaughter, Meghan, had been engaged once, but now she was focused on her career as an interior decorator and had no plans for marriage. The Amish culture was different. Most of the women married, and she was one of the few exceptions. But as Martha said, she wasn't uninterested in marriage. She just didn't want to be pressured into a relationship.

As Cevilla walked out of the barn into the hot, steamy morning, she pulled out her handkerchief. The clouds had burned off, which disappointed her. She'd hoped for some rain today, but God had other plans, apparently. She couldn't remember the last time they'd had such a drought. It wasn't exactly the desert here, but the crops and gardens needed rain, that was for sure. She'd just started for the Yoders' house to offer help with setting up lunch when she spied the older woman and her niece/granddaughter/whatever their relationship was talking right outside the barn. She headed that way, pleased someone closer to her age was here for once.

"Hello," she said, hobbling toward them. She patted her brow. "Welcome. I haven't seen you two here before. Are you visiting our community?"

The woman turned to Cevilla, a look of annoyance over her face. "*Nee*, we are not. And we're having a private conversation, if you don't mind."

Cevilla bristled. She'd never been treated so rudely by someone she'd just met. And now that she was closer to the woman, she could see she was perhaps a decade or more younger than she was. *Doesn't explain her lack of manners, though.* Cevilla, who could throw out a sarcastic word or two when pushed, forced a smile. She'd had proper breeding. "I'm sorry to interrupt. "

"It's all right." The younger girl looked at her with mix of apology and defeat. "We were finished talking."

"We were not—"

"I'm Nina Stoll. This is *mei grossmutter*, Delilah. *Mei bruder*, Levi, and *daed*, Loren, are here somewhere. We moved into the community a few days ago." She looked directly at Cevilla when she talked, and she had a firm voice that was a little on the low side.

What a polite girl. Her grandmother could learn from her. "Nice to meet you. I'm Cevilla Schlabach. I've lived here a long time, so if you have any questions about the community or the area, just ask me."

Delilah nodded, then tugged at Nina's arm. "If you'll excuse us. We need to find *mei sohn* and *grosssohn*." With that, she walked away, Nina following her.

Cevilla shook her head. Perhaps Delilah was having a bad day. If so, she might have had a reason for her shortness. And even rude people have other things going on that no one knows about. No need for Cevilla to be offended. Settling into a new community wasn't easy, as Cevilla had discovered when she moved to Birch Creek, which hadn't been the most welcoming place at the time. The atmosphere was different now. "I'll invite them to supper this week," she said, shuffling toward the Yoders' home. It was the proper and hospitable thing to do. She couldn't very well expect good manners from someone else if she wasn't willing to use them herself. *Who knows, maybe Delilah Stoll and I will end up* gut *friends.*

• • •

"You didn't have to be rude to her, *Grossmammi*." Nina climbed into the hot buggy, sweat dripping down her face. It was bad enough that her grandmother had embarrassed her in front of Seth and his friend, but then she had to turn around and be impolite to Cevilla, who seemed like a nice, sweet old lady who probably had her feelings hurt. She crossed her arms as she sat in the backseat, waiting while *Daed* gave their new horse, Happy, a drink of water before they headed back home. He was a gentle animal. Unlike her grandmother.

Grossmammi gave her a curt look, but Nina saw the regret in her eyes. "Unfortunately, she interrupted us at the wrong time," she said as she climbed into the front seat of the buggy. She whirled around, her face pinched and indignant. "I wish you would just appreciate what I'm trying to do, Nina. I always have *yer* best interests at heart."

Nina refused to look at *Grossmammi*, choosing to examine her forearm instead. The wasp sting was almost invisible, unlike the swollen lump above Seth's eye. When she first saw him this morning, she felt horrible, but he seemed to be feeling all right. Then her grandmother had to shock him with the supper invitation. Nina could tell he wasn't thrilled with being invited. Not only that, but *Grossmammi* had been nosy about how he spent his time. Her grandmother was strong-willed and blunt, and she usually got her way. But this time Nina had put her foot down when the service was over, telling her she was going to uninvite Seth. At least she'd tried to tell her that.

"We will not rescind our future invitation to Seth." *Grossmammi* faced front as *Daed* and Levi got into the buggy. "That is final."

"*Yer* invitation," Nina whispered as Levi sat down next to her.

Her brother took off his hat. "Whew, it's boiling out today. Maybe we should have stayed for lunch. I saw some of the men putting their horses in the pasture. The Yoders' spread is large enough."

"I was unable to prepare anything, so we aren't staying." *Grossmammi* didn't turn around as she spoke. "Besides, the community should be reaching out to us."

"I don't see why." *Daed* chirruped to the horse and started backing out the buggy.

"We're the new ones here. That's how it works. You did enough when you visited the bishop, Loren—without me."

Nina and Levi exchanged looks, then shrugged. Levi was only a year younger than her twenty-two, and they had always been close. He fanned his red face with his hat for a few minutes, then settled back in his seat.

As they traveled home, Nina relaxed a little. Her grandmother was quiet almost the entire way, and she considered the subject dropped. But as they were turning into the driveway, she said, "Nina, I'll give you a shopping list in the morning. *Geh* to Schrock Grocery and pick up what we'll need for supper Thursday night. I should be able to use the oven by Thursday afternoon."

Nina sat straight up. "He didn't agree to come Thursday night."

"That's why I plan to re-invite him."

Nina groaned and fell back against the seat.

"There's *nee* use arguing with her," Levi said, opening one eye. How he'd managed to fall asleep in the hot buggy, Nina had no idea.

"I heard that." *Grossmammi* turned and gave Levi a hard look.

Levi grinned. "Sorry, *Grossmammi*."

"Very well. Apology accepted."

Levi had always been able to charm their grandmother, while Nina struggled just to talk to her. Nina couldn't charm anyone, and she and her grandmother seemed to have clashed more than usual since they'd arrived in Birch Creek.

As soon as her father pulled up to their barn, Nina jumped out of the buggy. The air wasn't much cooler outside than it was in the stuffy buggy, and she'd give anything to find a pond and go swimming, church dress and all. Instead she went and sat under a large shaded tree in the backyard while the rest of her family went inside the house.

She was still hot and sweaty, but at least she didn't have to listen to *Grossmammi*'s plans anymore. She knew her grandmother would do exactly what she said she would—invite Seth again and keep at him until he said yes. Nina would go to the store and pick up whatever they needed. *Grossmammi* always got her own way. Nina just wished that for once, something would go her way instead.

. . .

Bright and early Monday morning, Seth was out in the hayfield with Ira and Judah, raking in the first cut of the season. Of all the farmwork, Seth disliked this job most, especially in muggy heat like today. Though it was early, he and his brothers were dripping with sweat. But Ira and Judah were expertly and efficiently raking up the hay, not minding it a bit. As he dragged his rake across the loose hay, Seth reminded himself of the days when his father hadn't owned this field, and barely had enough money to buy hay for their one horse, much less the six horses and fifty cattle they now owned. That reminder gave him a little more energy, and by the time lunch rolled around, the hay raking was done. One thing about hard work—it sure made a man hungry.

Ira walked beside him as Judah ran toward the house. Judah was fourteen now, and with his long legs and torso he would probably outgrow Seth and their father one of these days. Maybe even Ira, although that would be a tall order, no pun intended.

"Zeb, Zeke, and Owen are going fishing at Jalon's pond Tuesday evening," Ira said. "They invited us to *geh* with them."

Seth stiffened, remembering he was expected at Martha's Tuesday night for supper. Right after church, they had quickly met up near her buggy before her parents arrived and agreed to at least keep up the ruse and go through with the impromptu invitation. Delilah seemed particularly nosy, and he didn't want her finding out they'd made up plans. After supper they would go to his woodshop, and he would show Martha how to correctly plane a rough board. That was hard work and took some muscle strength. It was also boring compared to the actual carving of the wood. He hoped that if they started with a hard, dull job, she would abandon her interest in woodcarving altogether.

But that wasn't what alarmed him now. He and Martha were supposed to go to his woodshop after supper, and it wasn't that far from the Chupps' pond. He'd thought he wouldn't have to worry about anyone finding it because it was rather deep in the woods. But Martha had found it, and Chris Ropp had found it last year, showing up at the door, then asking him about his hobbies and making notes. He still didn't know what the whole point of that was, but two people stumbling upon his woodshop was unsettling.

Usually he tried to be there when he knew not too many people would be at the pond—and since he stopped going there on Sundays, that was mostly in the evening and at night. Making his way there—and then working with Martha, no less—while his brother and friends were fishing would be cutting things close. "It's a little late in the day to be fishing, don't you think?"

"Nah." Ira took off his hat and swiped a hand through his

damp hair. "It's been so hot lately that it's better to fish at night. We probably won't catch much and will end up swimming, but that's fine by me."

It wasn't fine by Seth. He and Martha would have to wait until after dark to go to his woodshop to avoid risking exposure. Which meant he'd have to spend extra time with her at supper, which might lead to her parents getting the wrong idea. He didn't want them, or anyone, to think he and Martha were more than acquaintances. "I'll take a rain check."

"Why?"

They walked to the back patio. "I've got . . . plans."

"What kind of plans?" Ira raised a brow at him.

"Plans."

Ira stopped. "It's not like you to be secretive like this." He tilted his head to the side. "Then again, you have been making *yerself* scarce lately."

Seth froze. Ira had noticed? Which meant other people in his family might have noticed too. "I've been busy," he said, realizing too late that the excuse sounded weak.

"Doing what?"

"Stuff." He knew Ira wouldn't let this go, so he might as well admit the truth—at least partially. "Martha Detweiler invited me for supper Tuesday night. That's all." He braced for Ira teasing him about having dinner with a woman.

But Ira didn't tease him. He frowned, his eyes narrowing. "She did?"

"*Ya.*"

"Why?" Ira slammed his hat back on his head.

"I'm helping her out with something," he said, hedging. "It's *nix* serious."

"Serious enough for you to miss out on fishing."

Seth did like to fish, at least he used to. He just hadn't fished in a while, not since he'd picked up woodcarving and found that much more satisfying. "Look, I don't even want to *geh*. But she insisted, and I didn't want to hurt her feelings." There was more than a grain of truth in that. For some reason, he didn't want to hurt Martha.

Ira glowered, like he'd been forced to eat a bag of lemons. "Is this the first time she's invited you somewhere?"

Frowning, Seth nodded. Where was his brother going with this? He looked . . . angry. Which didn't make sense. Why would he be mad about Seth having a friendly supper with Martha? "*Ya*," Seth said. "The whole thing happened because of a mix-up."

"I see." Ira paused, his glare deepening. "Then you don't like her?"

"You mean am I interested in her?" He laughed. "Definitely not. That's the furthest thing from *mei* mind."

Ira's expression relaxed. He studied Seth for a minute, then gave him a smile that to Seth seemed insincere. "Too bad, then. You'll be missing out on all the fun."

"I know. I'd rather be fishing, trust me."

His brother tilted his head, his halfhearted smile disappearing. "*Ya*. So you say." He opened the back screen door. "I'm sure Judah's eating all the food by now." He disappeared into the house.

Seth rubbed the back of his sweaty neck. Nothing was going on between Ira and Martha, was there? Nah, that didn't make sense. If there was, Cevilla wouldn't have tried to get him to pretend to date her—or to be more exact, have tried to match them together—and Martha certainly wouldn't have invited Seth for supper. Besides, there was the whole issue of Martha running away from any single male in sight, and that included his brother. But he couldn't shake the feeling that Ira was still irritated. Did he like Martha? No. He would have said so. Or at least hinted about it.

Maybe they should all take a swim to cool off. He'd ask Ira and Judah if they wanted to join him for a quick dunk in the pond after lunch. They wouldn't be gone long, and the break would do them all good. Perhaps their father would even join them, like he did when they were kids. Right before their financial troubles started.

He looked around the farm, wiping the sweat off his neck. God had blessed them so much since their father had become bishop. As he did with farming, *Daed* took the position seriously and performed it with diligence. And while Seth didn't believe his family was being rewarded for their father's duties as a bishop, their good fortune had coincided with Emmanuel Troyer's disappearance. Seth didn't miss the former bishop. He'd been hard and tightfisted, and later everyone found out he'd been keeping the community fund closed to everyone, at a time when their family could have used the help. He didn't care if Emmanuel never returned.

Seth stopped his thoughts. He needed to forgive. And he had forgiven Emmanuel. He just hadn't forgotten. Through hard work and God's grace, his family now had a farm that was turning a profit, one his father was already hinting about handing down to him and Ira and Judah. Trouble was, Seth didn't want the farm. But his father's retirement was a long time off. Plenty of time for Seth to become a skilled woodcarver.

He turned and went inside, forgetting his thoughts about the farm. Eventually he'd tell his father the truth, that he would rather make a living as a woodcarver than as a farmer. What would be the point of telling him now? So far, his carvings weren't good enough to sell. He'd pursue his dream someday, though. He was just biding his time until he could.

. . .

On Monday afternoon, Martha was alone in the optics shop office when she heard the bell ringing over the front door. Her uncle had already gone to the house to eat with his wife while their children were in school, as he did every day, leaving Martha to mind the place. She didn't have a problem with that. She usually just took orders and checked out people who were picking up their repaired items. When her uncle returned, she would have her lunch break. She glanced at the clock on the wall, a simple one compared to the fancy watches and clocks *Onkel* Hezekiah often worked on. A few minutes earlier she had gone to get her lunch from the back, knowing Hezekiah would return any minute. Sometimes she went home for lunch since her house was next door, but often she enjoyed the solitude of eating outside.

She peeked out front and was surprised to see Cevilla there, dabbing her forehead with a handkerchief. "Hi," Martha said as she came out. "Would you like a cold drink?"

Cevilla nodded. "Please. It's like an oven out there. I think it's even hotter today than it was yesterday, and that was hotter than a pat of butter melting in a frying pan."

Martha had to agree. The summer had been brutal, and Cevilla looked like she was wilting. She returned to the back and picked up a bottled water from the large cooler her uncle kept well stocked during the summer. Then back with Cevilla, she twisted off the top and handed it to her. "You didn't walk here, did you?"

Cevilla shook her head. "Richard dropped me off at *yer mamm*'s a little while ago. It's been a while since I visited with her. I stayed for a quick bite, and then I stopped at *yer onkel*'s *haus*. Hezekiah caught me up on the optics business while he was eating his lunch."

Martha smiled. "He's a little obsessed with his work."

"*Nix* wrong with that, as long as God and *familye* and friends aren't ignored, and I get the impression they aren't. Anyway, I thought I'd stop by to say hello before Richard comes for me." She took a sip of the water. "And, of course, to ask what you and Seth were talking about before church."

Martha's face heated, which didn't take much since the shop was hot inside too. She should be at least a little angry with Cevilla for trying to match her and Seth with the plan B nonsense, but instead she felt embarrassed to be talking about Seth at all. "Oh? What made you think we were talking before church?"

"Because I saw you two coming into the service together."

Uh-oh. When she and Seth entered the barn at the same time, the service was just about to start, and she thought everyone was facing front. She also thought they had done a pretty good job sneaking inside. Apparently not. She almost said that she and Seth had *arrived* at the same time and that's why they walked in together, but she wasn't going to lie—especially to Cevilla. "We had a little chat. That's all."

"About what?" Cevilla's look turned sly.

Martha picked up a cloth and started dusting the glass case in front of her. They kept the most expensive items locked up there. "Neither of us thinks plan B is a *gut* idea. Seth has his own life, and I need to deal with unwanted suitors on *mei* own. Other than that, I'm not sure our conversation is any of *yer* business." She stopped dusting, fearing she'd sounded a little harsh.

Cevilla sighed. "When you're *mei* age, everything is *yer* business." She looked at Martha and smiled. "I'm sorry for prying. And if you and Seth don't want to follow through on plan B, that's *yer* choice. May I ask you one more question, though? Just a quick one?"

Martha stopped wiping. Now she felt a little guilty. In a way Cevilla did deserve to know if anything was going on, since she had been so willing to help her solve the "man issue." But she had to be careful not to reveal Seth's secret. "Of course."

"Will you let me know if you ever need a plan B?"

She nodded and smiled. "*Ya. Danki*, Cevilla, but I have everything under control." And for once she thought she truly did. At least for the most part.

"Glad to hear it." A horn honked outside the door. "That's *mei* Richard," she said. "See you later."

"Just a second. Now it's *mei* turn to ask you a question."

Cevilla looked at her, her gray eyebrows lifting with curiosity. "Ask away."

"Are you and Richard getting married anytime soon?"

Her wrinkled cheeks turned red. "Touché. Seems I'm not the only nosy one around here. But that's for me to know and you to find out." She lifted her chin and walked out the door.

Martha frowned. She hadn't meant to upset Cevilla. She was genuinely curious about her and Richard. The whole community was. He had lived in Birch Creek for nearly a year, moving from California. He'd attended church a few times, and he always accompanied Cevilla to social gatherings. He was nice, and he clearly adored Cevilla. But now she had made it clear that the status of their relationship wasn't Martha's business, and probably not anyone else's either.

A few minutes later, *Onkel* Hezekiah walked in. "*Yer aenti* Amanda made a delicious lunch," he said, rubbing his round belly. "Her roast beef sandwiches can't be beat. There's plenty left if you want some."

"*Danki*, but I brought *mei* lunch today. I thought I would eat it outside."

"Suit *yerself*. It's blazing hot, though."

"But there's also a breeze. It's bearable as long as the air is moving."

He lifted a bushy brow. "If you say so."

Martha gathered her lunch and went out the front door. A large tree with a small picnic table a few feet from it sat in front of the shop. She sat down, said a silent prayer, and then opened her paper lunch bag and pulled out a turkey and mustard sandwich, carrot sticks, and a piece of banana bread.

As she finished up the last of the banana bread, a buggy pulled into the driveway. A man about her age jumped out and tethered his horse to the post. Martha froze for a moment before she realized she didn't recognize him. Her instinct to flee settled down. She really needed to get a grip on that.

The man strolled toward the shop, pausing when he saw her. "Hello," he said, pushing back his hat. He wore silver-rimmed glasses.

"Hi." She balled up her bag and stood. "May I help you?" Technically she was still on her lunch break, but she would never ignore a customer.

"You work here?" He walked toward her as she made her way around the picnic table. Vibrant green eyes shone behind the lenses of his glasses.

Martha nodded. "This is *mei onkel*'s shop."

The man looked at the sign her uncle had made a few months ago. "It says you're an optics shop."

"We are."

"Do you repair glasses?" He took his off, squinting a bit as he showed her the break in the frame that held the right lens. "I probably need some new frames, but I don't have time to *geh* to Barton to get them. Unless you know of some place closer?"

"Where do you live?"

"Here in Birch Creek." He put his glasses back on. "Levi Stoll. *Mei familye* and I just moved here."

Martha nodded. "You're related to Nina and Delilah, *ya*? And you're converting *yer haus* into an inn?"

Levi looked surprised. "*Ya. Mei schwester* and *grossmutter*. And we're doing exactly that. How did you know?"

"I met them yesterday before church service."

He chuckled. "I bet that was interesting. *Mei grossmutter* can be a bit . . . much." He held out his hand. "And *yer* name is?"

"Martha Detweiler." She shook his hand. He had a firm handshake and a friendly expression. She could see a bit of a resemblance between him and his sister, Nina—the dark eyebrows and large nose in particular. "May I see *yer* glasses again?" When he handed them to her, she examined them more closely. The frames did look like they'd seen better days, but maybe he could do something with these. "Come inside and *mei onkel* will take a look. He can fix pretty much anything."

Levi followed her inside. After she introduced Levi, her uncle looked at the frames and gave him a nod. "It will take me a bit of time to repair them. Probably an hour. I can tighten up the screws on the frames. It also looks like one of *yer* nosepieces is about to fall off, so I'll take care of that too. Can you leave them here with me?"

Levi shook his head. "I can't see much without them. Could I make an appointment instead? Then I can come back and wait while you work on them."

"Sounds *gut*." He handed the glasses back to Levi. "Martha will set you up. Welcome to Birch Creek." He turned and went back to his workroom.

He put the glasses back on. After Martha and Levi had settled on a date and she recorded it in the appointment calendar, she gave him a reminder card. "I'm sorry we couldn't help you today."

"That's all right. I'll be careful with them until next Monday. It was nice to meet you, Martha. I'm sure I'll see you around."

She nodded, and Levi left. Hmm. That was the first easy conversation she'd had with a man her age in quite a while. Levi Stoll seemed like a nice man, and it was a relief not to have a knot of dread or frustration appear in her stomach for once.

Martha had just closed the calendar and put it under the counter when the bell over the door rung. She looked up to see Ira Yoder walk in. Uh-oh. Her pleasant feeling disappeared. Why had she thought she'd see her suitors only at church? Ira had asked her to two singings so far, plus to the ice cream shop in Barton, a popular date-night place for the *English*. At least she didn't feel bad telling him no to the ice cream, since she was lactose intolerant. That hadn't deterred him, though. Hopefully he was just here for a watch repair or to buy some binoculars. Or to see if his mother's clock was ready? Maybe he wanted to talk to her uncle for some reason. Hezekiah was so friendly that sometimes people just stopped by to visit with him, if he wasn't too busy.

Ira's normally open expression held a scowl. Dread filled her. Maybe she should have run back to the office when she saw him come in. "Hi, Ira," she said, giving him a smile. "How may I help you?"

Ira placed both of his beefy hands on the counter and leaned forward until he was too close for comfort. "Martha, we need to talk."

CHAPTER 6

I n Martha's experience, the words *need to talk* were never good ones. Her mind whirred, trying to figure out what she had done to make Ira upset—other than turn him down for the singings and ice cream. She'd done it nicely too. At least she thought she had. Then again, she'd thought she'd been nice to Paul. She took a step back from the counter. "Now?" she said, letting out a shaky chuckle. "I'm working. Can we talk later?"

He glanced around the empty shop. "You don't look that busy," he grumbled.

She threaded her fingers together. He seemed *really* upset. "Is there something wrong?"

"You tell me."

That set her nerves on edge. Paul had been like this too. She always had to guess how he felt, and most of the time she was wrong. "I can't tell you anything. You're the one who wanted to talk to me, *ya*?"

He nodded, his expression unmoving. "*Ya*." He crossed his arms over his broad chest. "What's going on between you and Seth?"

Martha pressed her lips together. Was Ira jealous? "*Nix* is going on, Ira."

"Then why did you invite him to supper?"

Had Seth told him about that? A better question was . . .

Why? Her mind scrambled, trying to come up with a reason that wouldn't require her to fib, outright lie, or reveal Seth's woodshop or Delilah's matchmaking.

"Seth said you wanted to thank him for helping you." Ira's expression softened a bit. "If you needed help, why didn't you come to me?"

"It just sort of happened," she said, which was the truth. "He was there at the right time."

A look of hurt crossed his face. "You know I like you, Martha. A lot. I had hoped we could *geh* on a date sometime. But you keep turning me down."

Ira was a nice guy—a bit pushy, she was realizing—but still nice. Yet there was no spark when she looked at him. No desire to get to know him other than as an acquaintance. That wasn't his fault; it was just how she felt. For the first time she felt sorry for him and for the other men in the community. Who else was there to pursue? Nina Stoll had newly arrived, but Martha hoped they wouldn't pounce on her. Birch Creek really needed more single females.

"Is it because of *mei bruder*?" he asked.

"*Nee.*"

"Is it Zeb? Owen? Zeke?"

"It's not any of them either," she said quietly, looking down at her shoes.

"I see." His voice was icy cold. *The way Paul's had been that day.*

"Ira," she said, measuring her words. "I—"

Two *English* customers entered the shop. Martha recognized them from last week. They had both dropped off watches to be repaired. "Excuse me," she said, relieved she'd been interrupted. As she was talking with the first customer, three more walked in the door and started looking around the shop. When

Martha looked back to Ira, she saw him disappearing out the door.

Even though she didn't have any feelings toward him, she didn't want there to be strife between them.

An hour later she had helped all the customers—all of them *English*, which surprised her. Yet the other day Carolyn Yoder had told *Mamm* she was noticing more *English* customers in her bakery. Word about Birch Creek was starting to spread.

Martha put away the calendar and filed the orders in the small flexible folder her uncle insisted on using to keep track of his work. But her mind wasn't thinking about work. What was she going to do about Ira? He was mad at her, she was sure of it. That was the exact thing she'd been trying to avoid.

She put her pencil back in the mug near the adding machine. The slogan on the mug read *Keep It Simple*. She faced it away from her. *I'm trying, Lord. I really am.* But lately her life had become far from simple.

. . .

That evening, Nina placed a bowl of macaroni salad on the table as her father and brother sat down. *Grossmammi* was already seated. Nina had made tonight's meal, at *Grossmammi*'s insistence. She didn't mind meal preparation too much, but tonight's meal, like the others, was cold and sparse—sandwiches, macaroni salad, sweet pickles, the last of the bread from the bakery, and lemonade. She sat down, and they bowed their heads in silent prayer. Then she passed the sandwiches to *Daed*.

"Did you find someone to fix glasses?" *Grossmammi* asked Levi.

He put a pile of sweet pickles, one of his favorite foods, on his plate. He could go through a jar of them in one sitting. "I did. Hezekiah Detweiler, the man who runs that optics shop we saw, said he'd fix them for me. I'll still have to get new frames in Barton, but I can do that once things settle around here."

Nina looked around the kitchen. On Wednesday the men who were installing the floors were coming, and she couldn't wait. She'd already tripped over two of the buckled boards. The new stove had been delivered today, but they hadn't finished installing it until after six. Tomorrow they would have their first homemade hot meal since they'd left Wisconsin. Nina was looking forward to it.

"I met someone else today too." Levi picked up his sandwich. "Martha Detweiler. She said she met you and Nina at church on Sunday. She works at the optics shop. Hezekiah is her *onkel*."

"Oh?" *Grossmammi* perked up as she put her napkin in her lap. "How interesting."

Levi gave her a sideways glance. "Not *that* interesting, *Grossmammi*. She is nice, though." He looked at Nina. "Maybe you can be friends."

Before Nina could answer, *Grossmammi* said, "Did she happen to mention Seth Yoder, by any chance?" She opened her sandwich and put several slices of pickles on it.

Levi looked perplexed. "*Nee*. Why would she? We were talking about *mei* glasses the whole time."

"Just wondering." She put the bread back on the sandwich, then paused, looking at her grandchildren. "*Ya*, this is all very interesting."

"*Mamm*," *Daed* said as he picked up his glass of lemonade. "I don't like that look in *yer* eye."

"What look?"

"The scheming look." *Daed* glanced at Levi and Nina before turning his attention back to his mother. "We're in the middle of a big project, trying to get our *haus* built and the inn in order. I don't need you meddling in Nina and Levi's personal lives."

"Me?" *Grossmammi* put her hand over her heart. "Meddle?" She sniffed. "I don't meddle."

"Interfere, then." Levi pushed a large scoop of macaroni salad into his mouth and kept his head down.

"Respect *yer* elders," *Grossmammi* said sharply.

Levi smirked and kept eating.

Nina added a few slices of pickle to her plate. Normally she was hungry and had a healthy appetite, something she'd inherited from *Grossmammi*. Her father and Levi were both wiry thin. But she hadn't had much of an appetite lately. She understood what both her grandmother and brother were trying to do—encouraging her to become part of the community. Levi wanted her to be more social, and *Grossmammi* wanted her to be married. Their motives were well-intentioned, but what she really wanted was to be left alone. Thankfully her father always stayed out of her business, or she'd have three people trying to orchestrate her life.

"Anyway, Nina," Levi said, after he'd swallowed, "I thought maybe you could *geh* with me to the shop next week and talk to Martha while I get *mei* glasses fixed. It would be *gut* for you to have a friend here."

Nina poked at her sandwich. She didn't want a friend. She had friends back home. That's where she wanted to be.

"I have a better idea." *Grossmammi* clapped her hands together. "What if we invite her to supper? Seth is already coming over. We could have them both over for a meal."

Nina met her brother's horrified gaze. Now it was her turn to smile. Her grandmother was about as subtle as a string of cowbells. Nina wasn't the only victim of her machinations. It was Levi's turn to be uncomfortable. "Seth never agreed to come over," she reminded *Grossmammi*.

"That's because we didn't settle on a date. Leave the details to me. Oh, I'm so looking forward to you two meeting new *friends*." She batted her eyelashes.

Nina looked at her father, silently pleading for him to intervene. But he shook his head. "Leave me out of this. Someone's got to focus on the job around here."

One of the drawbacks of her father staying out of his children's business was that he didn't spend a lot of time intervening, either, despite what he'd just said to *Grossmammi* about scheming. Nina and Levi were mostly left to deal with her on their own, the way they always had.

Levi brought up the subject of further expanding the back of the house to accommodate one more guest room, and soon he and *Daed* were discussing the prospect. Nina took a bite of her sandwich while her grandmother finished eating with gusto, not only enjoying the meal but pleased with herself. Nina sighed.

After supper she and *Grossmammi* cleaned up the kitchen while Levi and *Daed* took care of the horse and other outside chores. For some strange reason *Grossmammi* always enjoyed kitchen cleanup, and she cheerfully washed the dishes while Nina dried them. When Nina hung up the damp dishcloth to dry, Grossmammi put her hand on Nina's arm.

"I love you, *lieb*. I love you and Levi so much, and I've raised you both like *mei* own since *yer mamm* died."

Nina nodded, and guilt washed over her like dirty dishwater.

Mamm had passed away from complications of pneumonia when Nina was three, and she barely remembered her. The only mother she'd ever known was her grandmother, and although she could be difficult to deal with at times, she had always taken care of her and Levi. "I know."

"Just remember that everything I do is because of love. I want what's best for you and Levi. I always have." She patted Nina's arm again. "I think I'll head to bed early tonight. I've got a touch of a headache. That means rain, of course, and the *gut* Lord knows we need it. *Gute nacht.*"

"Gute nacht." Nina watched *Grossmammi* walk out of the kitchen. It was true that her grandmother usually got headaches before weather changes, although she couldn't predict them 100 percent. Hopefully she was right this time. They could use some rain. Even her father said so, which was something, since the dry weather had made it easier for him and Levi to work outside.

She swept the floor and returned the broom to the small closet near the kitchen. She did like some things about this house. The new stove was large and the nicest one she'd seen, and the rooms upstairs were spacious. The staircase banister had beautiful woodwork that thankfully her father wasn't going to replace. But none of that was enough to make her stop longing for home.

Maybe Levi would talk to *Grossmammi* later about the supper invitations. He could persuade her more than Nina could. The last thing she wanted was to have supper with Seth and Martha. She was sure they were fine people, and eventually she would get to know them, but she wanted to do it in her own way. Besides, nothing was worse than having her grandmother play matchmaker. She feared disaster was looming around the corner. She grimaced. Perhaps her grandmother wasn't the only overly dramatic member of the family.

. . .

During supper that evening, Seth had noticed Ira still seemed out of sorts. He was pretty sure it had to be about Martha. When he'd asked Ira to go for a swim after lunch, he'd barely acknowledged him and said he was busy, then left shortly after they'd finished eating. Seth had thought about that and their odd conversation earlier. Martha had said several of the single guys in Birch Creek were after her. Ira hadn't come to mind at the time, but now it was obvious. His brother liked her.

"Do you want more blackberry cobbler, Ira?" *Mamm* asked, holding up a square casserole dish. She plunged a large spoon into the still-warm dessert.

Ira shook his head and pushed away his dessert plate.

"Are you feeling okay?" *Mamm* plopped the full scoop back into the casserole dish.

"I'm fine." He moved back from the table and glared at Seth. "Just fine." He got up from the table and left the kitchen.

"What was all that about?" *Mamm* said. She set the cobbler on the table. Judah immediately reached for it, having polished off his first serving.

Seth shrugged but didn't look at her. His mother was perceptive, and she would know whether Seth was telling the truth. He started to get up from the table, fully intending to find Ira and reassure him that he was free to pursue Martha all he wanted. Then he stopped himself. Martha didn't want to be pursued. And for some bizarre reason, the idea of his brother and Martha together suddenly bothered him. That didn't make sense. Ira was a great guy, a good catch for any woman. And Martha was . . . Well, she was Martha.

"Seth."

He turned to see *Daed* looking at him. His father had been quiet during the meal, too, but that wasn't unusual. While he was getting wordier during his sermons, he was a man of few words at home. *"Ya, Daed?"*

"Come outside with me." His father stood.

Seth glanced at his mother. This time it was her turn to shrug. Whatever *Daed* needed to talk to him about, she wasn't in the know. "Okay." He followed his father through the back door.

Daed walked past the barn and toward the huge pasture to the back field of their property, a small plot of land he'd acquired three months ago. In a few short years he'd managed to turn this place from a dying farm to an extremely prosperous one, without the benefit of the rich gas deposits abundant in this area. Several of the families had sold their rights to the natural gas on their property to a utility company, but their land had been one of the few that didn't have any gas underground. Still, he had managed to turn everything around financially.

His father had never taken credit for his success, though. He'd simply thanked God for every blessing they had. "Been around long enough to know it might not last forever," he'd said more than once. "In a blink of an eye everything could be gone."

Seth thought about that as he walked a few steps behind his father. The idea that farming was so precarious didn't sit well with him. It was dependent on so many factors outside a farmer's control—the weather, the soil, the seed, the wildlife. It was an unpredictable way to live, and it had always made Seth a little uncomfortable. He wanted security and consistency, something he hoped woodcarving would give him once he was good enough to create items for sale.

Daed stopped at the end of the property. He faced the sunset, and Seth went to stand next to him. The sky was streaked with golden clouds that once again didn't hold a drop of rain. "Nice night," *Daed* said.

A nice night would be full of rain. He looked at the leaves on the surrounding trees. A smattering of them had turned brown at the edges, except for the oak trees, which could stand the drier conditions better. Their crops were starting to struggle, even with the water he and his brothers and father had been giving them. But nothing was better for plants than a good soaking, which they hadn't had in nearly three weeks. His *daed* didn't seem worried about that, at least not enough to mention it. "Nice night it is," Seth said. There was no need to disagree with his father over that.

Seth put his hands in his pockets and waited while his father gazed into the distance. He could tell *Daed* was gathering his thoughts, which made Seth a little nervous, but he stayed silent. Whatever his father needed to tell him, he would do so in his own time.

After a few minutes, *Daed* said, "I've been thinking a lot about the future."

Me too. But not in the way his father would ever suspect. Seth nodded.

"I've been thinking about this farm, about *yer schwesters* and *bruders.*" He turned to him. "About you."

Seth tugged at a loose thread inside his right pants pocket. "Is everything all right? You're not sick, are you?"

Daed's lips lifted in a half smile. "*Nee*, thanks be to God. I'm not. But I'm not a spring chicken either."

"You're fifty-six. That's not exactly an old buzzard."

"An old buzzard," *Daed* repeated, nodding. "I like that." He turned and faced the sunset again. "Won't be long before I'll be one."

"What are you driving at, *Daed*?" Seth didn't like beating around the bush. He was a direct man, and he expected others to be just as forthcoming. He also didn't like his growing suspicion that something was wrong.

He faced Seth. "I'm not sick. But I've been having some trouble with *mei* vision. *Mei* left eye has started to hurt some too. I haven't told *yer* mother yet. I wanted to *geh* to the doctor to find out what's happening before I say anything to her."

Seth's fingers stilled. "Did you *geh*?"

"*Ya*. He said I have glaucoma. Then he threw around some scientific words I'd never heard of and had *nee* idea what they meant. But when he bottom-lined everything, he said there's a possibility I could *geh* blind."

Seth's knees nearly buckled. His father, blind? How could he be so calm about that? "We'll pray that won't happen," he said firmly.

"Of course we will." He smiled, this one full and genuine. "But if it's God's will, I'll accept it. I can also use some medicine and eyedrops that will help slow or possibly stop the growing pressure in *mei* eyes. There's *nee* need to get bent out of shape right now. I can still see plenty well." He gave Seth a direct look. "If there's one thing I won't do, though, it's borrow trouble. I'm not worried, *sohn*. You shouldn't be either. God is in control of everything, including *mei* eyes. Knowing that gives me peace about this."

That explained his father's composure. Seth breathed out a sigh of relief. If his father wasn't panicked, Seth would follow his lead.

"I'm going to tell *yer mudder* tonight. But I'm holding off on telling Ira and Judah. Ira will jump to the worst-case scenario, and that's not what I need. Judah's a little too *yung* to have this burden to carry, especially when everything is fine right now. And *yer schwesters* are happy with their *familyes*. No need to upend everything." He clapped Seth on the shoulder. "Looks like you're the lucky one to be the first to know."

He didn't feel lucky. He felt honored that his father was sharing his burden with him. "I won't say anything to anyone. I promise."

"I know you won't." He squeezed Seth's shoulder, then let go. "I have something else to ask of you. I need to transition management of the farm over to you, in case the drops and medicine don't work and this glaucoma thing progresses quickly. Again, I don't anticipate that happening, but it's always prudent to plan. I don't want to leave you and *yer bruders* in a lurch."

Seth froze. The possibility of overseeing the farm had always been there, but he never thought it would be this soon. Or at all, if he could have entered a different vocation before his father retired. But that was far back in his mind now that he knew about his father's eye disease. "What do you need me to do?"

"I need to teach you everything I know. I've taught you *buwe* a lot of things, but you can learn more, especially from the business side. Buying livestock, knowing when it's time to expand the farm again—if it's God's will—figuring out if a purchase is a *gut* deal . . . those kinds of things, along with a few Amish secrets *mei familye* has used over generations of farming. It's a lot, Seth, and it will mean spending more time here, with me. You're *yung*, and I know you need time to *yerself* and time to be with *yer* friends. I'm sorry I'll be intruding on that."

Seth shook his head. "*Nee* worries, *Daed*, remember? I'm here for you. Whatever you need, I'll make sure you have it." For the first time he considered telling him about his woodshop. Considering what was going on, it seemed selfish to have a secret from his father. But Seth couldn't bring himself to do it, not only because he still wanted to keep that part of his life to himself until he was skilled enough to make his carvings public but because it was selfish to talk about his dreams when his father was facing possible blindness. Other than meeting with Martha on Tuesday, woodcarving would have to take a backseat.

"I figured we'd start next week," *Daed* said. "That will give me some time to plan out what I need to teach you." He shook his head. "Until I started preaching, I never realized how important it was to have an outline and a plan. Now I don't know what to do without one."

Seth nodded, a lump forming in his throat as he thought about the many nights his father spent at the kitchen table studying his Bible, making notes, and praying over his sermons. How would he do that if he lost his eyesight? How would he preach? Take care of the community? His family?

Seth clenched his fists. God wouldn't allow his father to lose his sight. *Daed* had been divinely chosen to become the bishop, a job he hadn't wanted but had fully embraced. Truth be told, Seth didn't much care for being the bishop's son. He'd never been a troublemaker, but when he was younger, he did think twice about doing anything that might reflect badly on the family. People in the community held his father in high esteem, and they weren't shy about saying it. No, it didn't make sense to him that *Daed* would go blind a few years after getting the most important position in the community. *That's not going to happen.* His father would keep his sight, and Seth would keep his promise to learn every detail about the farm and farming so *Daed* could feel at ease.

"I'm glad I can depend on you, Seth," *Daed* said.

Seth studied his father's eyes. They were gray-blue, with deep wrinkles around them from spending so much time in the sun, even with a hat. Seth couldn't tell anything was wrong with *Daed*'s eyes just by looking at them. They seemed the same as they always had, his look strong and firm. Like the man himself. But he had a disease, one that could eventually take his eyesight. Seth found that unacceptable.

CHAPTER 7

By late afternoon on Tuesday, Martha had spent the entire day restlessly watching the clock. The shop didn't have many customers, and it had taken her less than half an hour to clean the shop, which she kept almost flawless anyway. She'd brought the binocular book with her and tried to study it, but she couldn't focus. All she could think about was getting the chance to carve wood again. That, and Seth coming over for supper tonight. While she was eager to do the first thing, she wasn't looking forward to the second.

She put her elbow on the counter and leaned her chin on the heel of her hand. *Mamm* had given her a suspicious look when she explained that Seth was coming over for dinner, and Martha didn't blame her for being perplexed.

"I thought you were avoiding all the *yung* men," *Mamm* had said. She'd been in the middle of putting together a picture puzzle on the coffee table in the living room. She'd picked up three of them in Barton two weeks ago when she went exploring yard sales with Naomi Beiler and Mary Yoder. She planned to glue the puzzle to the back of a piece of cardboard when she finished it, making a nice picture for the wall.

"I *am* avoiding them." Martha had sat down, her attention

drawn to the puzzle. It was a picture of a serene-looking lake, according to the cover. Her mother had just started on it, so very few pieces were connected.

"But you've invited Seth over for supper tomorrow night," *Mamm* said.

"*Ya.*" Martha picked up a piece and placed it next to part of the finished puzzle. She turned it a quarter way and the piece fit perfectly.

"I'm confused." *Mamm* looked up, a puzzle piece in her hand. "Why aren't you avoiding Seth?"

She couldn't tell her the real reason, so she said the first thing that came to mind. "Because he's the only *mann* who's avoiding me."

"Ah." *Mamm* frowned. "I still don't understand."

Martha chuckled. "I don't either."

Mamm sat back in her chair. "Is everything all right? I've been concerned about you after what happened between you and Paul last fall."

She picked up another piece and searched for its home. "I'm okay," she said, trying not to wince at the sound of his name.

"I'd like to give that *bu* a piece of *mei* mind." *Mamm* scowled. "He had *nee* right to treat you that way."

"I hurt him." Martha set the piece down and looked at her. "He was just telling me how he felt."

"He took his pain out on you." *Mamm* shook her head. "You two weren't right for each other from the beginning. He's hot tempered and has a lot of growing up to do."

"He's twenty-six—"

"And acts like he's two sometimes." She sighed and leaned forward. "I didn't know he was going to be at Hannah's wedding.

I'd heard he moved to another community shortly after we settled here. If I had known he was still there, I wouldn't have asked you to *geh* with me."

Now Martha moved away from the counter and picked up the broom, sweeping the spotless shop floor with sharp strokes. She'd ended the conversation with her mother at that point. She didn't want to discuss Paul with her. She'd never told anyone everything he'd said to her when she'd ended their relationship. But when he'd torn her heart to pieces with his words—*You ruined* mei *life!*—she couldn't hide the tears from *Mamm* that night after the wedding. She'd given her mother a truncated version of the truth, saying that Paul had spoken to her privately after the reception and that he was still angry with her. *Mamm* had never liked Paul anyway, and her explanation had been enough to cement her mother's bad opinion about him. However, Martha couldn't forget what he'd said.

She stopped sweeping, feeling a little stupid for cleaning an already-clean floor. She shoved Paul out of her mind and thought about a better topic—woodcarving. Supper would be awkward tonight—there was no getting around that considering the circumstances that brought it about—but once Seth started teaching her how to carve, everything would be fine. She even planned to go to the library this Saturday and look up designs she could attempt when she'd developed more skill. Eventually she'd like to purchase her own set of tools, and her *daed*'s barn had plenty of room for her to set up a workstation.

Yes, she was putting the cart before the horse, but she couldn't help herself. She hadn't been this excited about learning something new since her father taught her how to train a horse when she was nine years old. It hadn't taken long before she was riding on the back of the horse standing up, having gained the animal's complete trust. She hoped learning wood-carving would be as easy.

She had just put away the broom when the bell rang over the door. Nina Stoll walked in, which was a surprise. Martha had just seen Levi yesterday. "Hi, Nina," she said, moving from behind the counter. "May I help you with something?"

"*Nee*, just looking." Nina sauntered around the store and studied the displays of simple clocks, watches, and magnifying glasses. Her face was red and sweaty, and a damp ring of perspiration sat around the collar of her dress. Had she been walking in this heat? Martha supposed she had. She didn't see a buggy outside. When Nina got to the locked case of binoculars, she stopped.

"Would you like to see any of these?" Martha asked.

Nina sighed. "*Nee*. Like I said, I'm just looking . . ." She turned to Martha. "Actually, that's not true. I'm escaping for a little while."

"Escaping what?"

"Everything." She sighed again.

Martha looked at her for a moment. She also had shadows under her eyes and a splatter of white paint on her lavender dress below the right shoulder. She glanced at Nina's black leather shoes, which were also dotted with paint. Her thick brows were knitted together, and her square shoulders were slightly slumped. She looked tired and somber.

"Would you like something to drink? I've got some pop and bottled water in the cooler. They're necessary for days like this."

"Water would be nice," Nina said, smiling a little. "It *is* hot outside."

Martha went behind the counter and opened the cooler chest on the floor. She pulled out two bottles of water and shut the lid. "It's not so bad under the tree. We can sit there for a bit, if you have time."

"I don't want to keep you from *yer* customers."

"What customers?" Martha came out from behind the counter and offered Nina her drink. "We've been slower than a river of molasses today. If anyone shows up, I can see them from out there. And so far *Onkel* Hezekiah has managed without a business phone, so I don't have to worry about anyone calling."

Nina took the water, her face brightening. "Then I'd love to."

They went outside, and Martha sat down on one side of the picnic table under the tree. As soon as she did, Martha regretted the idea. It had grown hotter throughout the day, and because she'd been inside since morning, she hadn't realized that. Unfortunately, there wasn't much of a breeze either. "Usually it's cooler," she said, frowning. Droplets of condensed water dripped down the side of her bottle, although they hadn't been outside more than five minutes.

"I think it's beautiful." Nina sat down across from her and looked up at the tree. She drew in a deep breath. "So pretty and peaceful."

With sweat dripping down her back, Martha didn't think it was so peaceful. But Nina looked happy and relaxed, in stark contrast to her demeanor inside the shop. "How do you like Birch Creek so far?" Martha asked, wiping her forehead with the back of her hand. She should have brought her handkerchief with her.

Nina's mouth tightened. "It's . . . nice." She lifted her gaze to Martha. "Everyone here is . . . nice."

"*Ya*. It's a great place to live." Martha took a drink of her water. "I thought it would take some time to get settled here, but it didn't take long for this place to feel like home. I'm sure the same will happen for you."

Nina ran a stubby finger down the side of her bottle. Her fingernails were short and ragged, down to the quick, as if she had bitten them off. "I guess."

"I think I heard you're from Wisconsin?"

"*Ya*, a small community hardly anyone's heard of. I lived there all *mei* life. I thought I would live there the rest of *mei* life."

Martha's heart went out to her. This woman was homesick. "Did you leave a lot of friends behind?"

"Not too many. They were special, though. It's mostly the place, not the people, I miss." She lifted her gaze again. "Where did you live before you moved here?"

"Everywhere." She chuckled. "*Mei daed* has a wandering spirit, according to *mei mudder*. We've lived in lots of different districts and three different states. The last one before here was Kentucky. When *Daed* wanted to move from here, *Mamm* put her foot down and said we were staying put. Then *mei onkel* and his *familye* moved here, and he set up this business. Finally, *mei daed* was convinced this was the place to put down roots."

"All that moving had to have been hard on you."

"It was. I didn't know anyone who moved around like we did, and when I was younger it was hard to make friends, knowing that I might move at any minute. *Daed* does carpentry work, and he never had a hard time finding jobs. I eventually got used to it."

"I don't think I can get used to it here," Nina said, her voice barely above a whisper.

Martha decided to change the subject. "*Yer grossmutter* mentioned that *yer familye* is turning *yer English haus* into an inn. Did you run one in Wisconsin?"

She shook her head. "*Mei daed* used to be in construction, but he didn't like the work, at least not anymore. I was surprised when he told us we were moving here and starting a new business."

"It sounds exciting, though. Creating something new from something old. And we really need an inn here. Not that I want the community to get too busy or crowded." Martha paused. "But I think it would be nice if visitors could stay here for a few days and have a restful vacation."

"That's what *mei vatter* thinks." Nina finally opened her water and took a drink. "We'll see how it works out."

A buggy pulled into the driveway, and both women turned to see who it was. "Oh *nee*," Nina said, hunkering down. "What's she doing here?"

"Who?"

Nina looked at Martha and cringed. "*Mei grossmutter.* I snuck out earlier and didn't tell her where I was going. I needed to get away from everything for a little while."

Martha watched as the portly woman got out of the buggy without any effort. She had a pep in her step that was a bit enviable, considering her size and age. Her energy reminded her of Cevilla a little bit, even though Cevilla looked older than Delilah and walked with a cane. She would love to enter her golden years healthy and hardy like these women had.

Delilah turned around and looked at the front door. She headed toward it, stopping when she saw Martha and Nina sitting at the picnic table. "Nina?" She rushed over to them. "What are you doing here?"

Nina turned around. "Making friends." She sat up a little straighter. "Just like you and Levi said I should."

"It would have been nice if you would have told me you'd left," she said with a sniff.

"You didn't realize I was gone?"

"Nina, I've been very busy," she snapped. "In case you haven't noticed, we have plenty of work to do at home."

"Then why are you here?"

Delilah gave her an exasperated look. "I have some business to attend to. We'll discuss your disappearing later." Her grim expression suddenly turned bright as she looked at Martha. "Hello, Martha," she said sweetly.

"Hi, Delilah. Nice to see you." She got up from the table. "I'll walk you into the shop and you can tell me what I can do for you."

"*Nee* need for that," she said, using her hand as a fan and waving it in front of her flushed face. Without asking, she sat down at the table next to Nina, forcing her to scoot over. "You're invited to supper with our *familye*, Martha."

Delilah apparently enjoyed being hospitable, since she had just invited Seth to supper this week. "That's very nice of you."

But Nina didn't look too pleased. Her head dropped into her hands. "Great."

"You met *mei grosssohn* Levi, *ya*?" Delilah asked.

"Um, *ya*. Yesterday." Oh boy. Something was up, something she had a feeling she wouldn't like. Delilah and Cevilla had more in common than being hardy.

"Isn't he a nice *yung mann*? Very successful. Learned how to frame a *haus* at twelve and did one by himself at thirteen. He's an excellent carpenter and handyman. He's also keenly interested in building and running the inn. Maybe more so than his *vatter*."

"That's . . . *gut*?" What was she supposed to say? Levi had seemed perfectly pleasant, but that didn't mean she wanted to have supper with him. Well, it wouldn't be with only him. It would also be with Nina, and her grandmother and father, of course. That might not be too bad. Maybe she was reading something into this that wasn't there.

"Are you busy on Thursday?" Delilah asked, leaning forward.

Martha met her gaze. She had the same brown eyes Nina had, and they were filled with determination. Martha wasn't sure what to do. She wasn't busy Thursday night, unless she managed to convince Seth to let her work in the woodshop again this week, which was unlikely. She didn't want to push the issue, or her luck, with him so early in their woodcarving relationship.

She also didn't want to lie. She'd been doing more fudging and fibbing than she should have lately. "*Nee*," she said. "But—"

"Then it's settled." Delilah pushed herself up from the picnic table bench. "Six o'clock sharp."

"But—"

Nina lifted her head, her expression pained. "Don't bother. It's pointless to argue with her." She took a long swig from her water bottle, then dropped it on the table and wiped the back of her mouth with her hand.

"Nina," Delilah said, "that's unladylike."

Nina rolled her eyes.

But Delilah didn't see that. She was looking at Martha again. "Since you don't have prior plans, we will see you on Thursday. Nina, we're going home."

Martha's mouth dropped open as Delilah flounced back to the buggy.

"I'm so sorry," Nina sighed as she got up from the table. "Once she gets an idea in her head, it's impossible to dislodge it. Trust me, Levi and I have tried." She lifted her lips into a small smile. "It won't be that bad. The food will be *gut*. *Mei grossmammi* is an excellent cook. And *mei vatter* is nice." Her smile grew. "She was right about one thing. So was Levi."

"What's that?"

"I do need a friend. *Danki* for the drink and letting me bend *yer* ear. I feel a little better now."

Martha smiled and stood. "I'm glad." When Nina started to walk away, Martha caught up with her. "There's just one thing I need to make clear."

"*Ya?*"

"I'm not interested in *yer bruder*."

Nina laughed. "You don't have to worry about that. Levi isn't interested in you either." She grimaced. "Sorry, that didn't come out right. I mean he's not interested in anyone. As far as I know, he never has been. That frustrates *Grossmammi* to *nee* end." She paused. "Is it because you're interested in Seth?"

"Of course not. Like we told you and Delilah on Sunday, we're just friends."

"I know. I was just hoping . . ."

"Hoping for what?"

"That you were."

That was an odd answer. "Why?"

"Because then *Grossmammi* would get it out of her head that Seth and I should have a date." Nina balked. "Actually, I'm pretty sure in her imagination she's already moved past the date stage and has planned our wedding."

That was a bit extreme. "Why don't you tell her to mind her own business?"

"Why didn't you tell her you didn't want to come to supper?"

"Oh. You're right."

"Nina, we're leaving *now*!" Delilah hollered.

"Coming!" She turned to Martha. "I'm sorry. I shouldn't have told you all that."

"It's fine. You don't have to worry about Seth either. He's not interested in dating anyone. He's busy with his own . . . stuff."

"Just like we are. I wish she'd get it through her head that she doesn't have to force me or Levi to *geh* out with someone." She paused. "Even if I wanted to date or get married, I'd want to make *mei* own choice."

Martha nodded. "Exactly. You don't want the pressure."

Nina looked at her, brightening. "Right."

Martha wished she could do something to help her. Besides, she wasn't looking forward to a night of Delilah's match-making times two, despite Nina's assurances. "I'm sure Seth and I can set *yer grossmammi* straight Thursday night."

"How? Normal tactics don't work with her."

"We'll come up with something." Great. She was dragging Seth into this now. He wouldn't like that one bit.

"Nina Stoll! Get over here, now."

"I've got to *geh*." Nina grinned at Martha. Her smile made her look like less of a tomboy and more feminine, and a little pretty. "Even if you can't help me on Thursday, I appreciate your trying." She gave Martha a little wave and started toward the buggy, only to turn around. "Do you like to fish?"

"Not really."

"Oh. Well, that's okay." She turned, sprinted to the buggy, and jumped inside. Wow, she was really fast on her feet.

As Delilah pulled out of the driveway, Martha's stomach

twisted into another knot, which seemed to be the norm for her lately. What had she done? She'd given Nina hope, and she didn't want to let her down. She didn't realize how much she missed having a girlfriend here since Selah had moved back to New York, and Martha liked Nina, even though she'd known her for only a short time.

But how could she help her? She picked up Nina's water bottle and her own and headed for the shop. When she got to the door she stopped. An idea had popped into her head. A terrible one, but one that might work. *What if Delilah thought there really was something going on with Seth and me?*

She shook her head and pushed open the door. Yep, that was a bad idea. But the more she tried to forget about it, the more it wouldn't leave her alone. If Nina's grandmother thought Martha and Seth were together, even though they said they weren't, then she would have to drop the matchmaking altogether. That would not only help Nina, it would help Martha. She didn't want to be set up with Levi any more than Nina wanted to be thrown at Seth. "It might do the trick," she whispered as she tossed the plastic bottles into the recycling container behind the counter.

But this was teetering on deceptive territory. First Seth pointed out that she had tried to blackmail him with his secret, even though he had backtracked a little on the severity of it. Now she was considering a plan that meant she would have to fudge the truth . . . again. When had she developed such a criminal mind? *Forgive me, Lord, but desperate times call for desperate measures. This will be the last time. I promise.* All she had to do was hint at Delilah that she and Seth were an item. A very small hint. And she had to convince Seth to go along with it.

Which presented another problem. She was dragging him into another plan, eerily similar to Cevilla's plan B, now that Martha thought about it. A plan both she and Seth had soundly rejected. Now Martha would be asking him to do what he'd already said he wouldn't do. But didn't the end justify the means? Surely Seth would understand that.

Ugh. Her brain started to hurt. Hopefully she would think of another plan, because she wasn't too sure Seth would agree to her crazy idea.

. . .

Tuesday evening, Seth arrived at Martha's house and walked up the front porch steps to the door. But when he lifted his hand to knock, he hesitated. He should have canceled this meal and canceled his session with Martha in the woodshop. This morning his mother had been quiet, her eyes red-rimmed and bleary, and he knew his father had told her about his glaucoma. But she had pretended nothing was wrong as she presented *Daed* with his favorite breakfast—egg and hash brown pie. Right before they bowed their heads for prayer, he and *Mamm* had exchanged a knowing look. They would keep their father's secret as long as he wanted them to. After the silent prayer, when Seth prayed for his father's healing instead of asking God to bless the food, it was breakfast as usual for the family.

But that wasn't the only reason he didn't want to be here. Although he was firmly committed to his father, a tiny niggle of resentment surfaced, and that disturbed him. How could he think about his own plans when his father needed him? The resentment extended to Martha, too, for intruding on his life.

Which was why he was tempted to turn around and forget he'd even been invited to supper. What did he care what Delilah Stoll thought? He didn't even know the woman, and from what he knew, she was too pushy and not all that pleasant. Neither he nor Martha needed to impress her.

Seth started to leave, but then he stopped and hung his head. He was better than this. He'd accepted the invitation, and he wasn't a man who went back on his word. He would muddle through the supper and through his lesson with Martha. He would also set aside his selfishness and focus on the farm. This would be for only the short term, anyway. He firmly believed his father would be healed.

He took in a deep breath. *Here we go.* When he knocked on the door, Martha immediately answered it. "Hi," she said quickly, then stepped out on the front porch and shut the door behind her. She laced her fingers together and glanced over her shoulder before facing him again. "We need to talk."

"About what? And why can't we talk inside?"

Martha took his arm and led him down the porch steps. When they were on the side of the house, she stopped and looked around again, as if she thought they were being watched.

Seth looked around, too, then stopped himself. Why would it matter if someone was around? "Martha, do you mind telling me what's going on?"

She held her head down. "I . . . uh . . . I kind of sort of got us involved in something."

Seth groaned. *Not again.* "What do you mean *something*? And how do you *kind of sort of* do anything?"

She looked up at him, remorse in her eyes. They were such a nice shade of blue, and for the life of him he couldn't understand why he kept noticing that about her. But her pretty eyes didn't change the fact that he wasn't going to like whatever she had to tell him.

"Well, um, it involves Delilah Stoll, and . . ."

He scowled. For a woman he barely knew, she was causing him a lot of trouble. "And?"

"And Nina . . ."

The muscle in his jaw jerked. "And who else?"

"And her *bruder* and her *daed* and supper at their *haus* on Thursday." The words sped out of her mouth like a runaway horse. "And we also kind of sort of like each other, but we only need to let Delilah know that. Now that it's settled, we can *geh* eat." She started to leave, but Seth grabbed her arm. She turned and looked at him.

"I have *nee* idea what you just said." He let go of her arm.

She grimaced, and he listened while she told him about Nina and Delilah's visit to Hezekiah's shop. He could feel his blood pressure spiking as she told him about Delilah's matchmaking plans, not only with him and Nina but with Martha and Levi. He knew that woman had been up to something. "Whose insane idea was this?"

"Mine," she squeaked. She worried her lip. "But I got to know Nina, Seth. She's really sweet, and so homesick."

He couldn't believe this. "So now you're trying to set me up with her too?"

"Not at all. I wouldn't do that to you." She paused and lifted her chin. "But if we don't nip this in the bud now, Delilah will continue to interfere."

"And you think lying to her is the answer."

"Not lying, exactly. We just need to convince her that we like each other." She grinned. "We do, don't we?"

"Martha . . ." He lifted his head toward the sky in frustration,

THE FARMER'S BRIDE   125

then looked at her. "We don't like each other like that. And this is sounding a lot like Cevilla's plan B." Which he didn't like one bit. "I thought we agreed that was a bad idea."

"We did. And it is. But at least Cevilla knows when to back off. I don't think Delilah does."

"Why not just tell her we're not interested in her *grosskinner*?"

She crossed her arms. "You *geh* right on over to the Stolls' and tell her that. I'm sure she'll accept *yer* statement without question."

He hesitated, his gaze darting around the Detweilers' property. He didn't relish the idea of meeting with Delilah by himself. He also had doubts about whether he could convince her. He'd been raised to be respectful, and he wasn't sure how he could respectfully tell Delilah to mind her own business. "Fine." He moved closer to her, and then he leaned down an inch or two, so he was looking directly into those pretty blue eyes of hers. "This is the last time you drag me into something I don't want to do. Got it?"

"Got it," she said, taking a step back from him.

He straightened, continuing to look at her. She'd always come across as a nice, outgoing, levelheaded woman. But lately she was acting more birdbrained than a baby sparrow.

"I promise I won't do this anymore." She started twisting her index finger. "I don't know what's wrong with me lately," she said quietly. "I've been saying and doing things before thinking them through. I'm not normally like that. I just . . ." She looked up at him. "I feel bad for Nina. I never had a problem with homesickness, but I do know what's it's like to leave behind everything familiar. She's having a hard time with it, and I want to help her. The last thing she needs is to be forced into a relationship. Those are hard enough as it is." She averted her gaze and clenched her hands together. "I also don't want to hurt anyone's feelings."

Forced into a relationship? Hurt anyone's feelings? She sounded as though she was speaking from experience, and that experience hadn't been good. As for him, he didn't have any experience to speak of, what with the slim pickings in Birch Creek. He'd always assumed he'd have to find a bride outside the district, and that would be a long time off. But Martha had been hurt, and that hurt still seemed fresh. "It's all right," he said, tempering his tone. "You have a *gut* heart, Martha." Better than his had been lately.

That made her perk up a bit. "I'm glad you aren't mad at me. And I meant it when I said I'm not involving you in anything else. Just supper on Thursday. That's it."

"And woodcarving today. *That's* it."

"What?" Her brow shot up. "You're giving me only one lesson?"

"That's all I agreed to."

"Oh. I guess that's true." She scowled. "I can't learn much in one lesson."

"I can show you a few basics." Her disappointed expression was getting to him. He'd intended to just teach her how to plane the wood, but he might do a little bit extra. "I'm sorry, Martha. I can't commit to anything more."

Her face brightened a little. "It's all right. It's nervy of me to expect more." She rolled her eyes. "Here I am complaining about Delilah being pushy, and I'm doing the same thing."

"*Nee*, you're not. She's taking assertiveness to the extreme."

Her lips curved into a smile. "I appreciate anything you want to show me, Seth. I won't ask for more than that."

He paused. For some strange reason her acquiescence made him want to have another lesson with her, before they started the first one. *What?* That didn't make sense. One lesson only. *No matter how sweet she is, that's it.*

"We should *geh* inside," Martha said. "Supper should be close to ready by now. I told *Mamm* I was going to show you our garden in the backyard."

"She bought that excuse?"

Martha bit her lip. "I don't think so. But lately *Mamm* has been going with the flow when it comes to me."

He nodded and started to follow her into the house. Then an idea came to him. A terrible idea, but that didn't stop him from saying it. He halted. "Maybe we should make tonight a practice run."

She turned around. "Practice run?"

"If we have to convince Delilah, we might as well try it out tonight with *yer* parents." He had to resist slapping his forehead with his palm. What happened to his resolve not to get any deeper into these shenanigans?

She tapped her finger on her chin. "That's not a bad idea."

It's an awful idea.

"But what if *mei* parents believe we like each other?"

Seth hadn't thought that far. Apparently, Martha's short-sightedness was contagious. "We can figure that out later."

"Shouldn't we figure that out now?"

"Martha!" *Daed*'s head poked out the back door. "Supper's ready."

"On our way!" She looked at Seth. "We'll talk about this later, when we're in *yer* shop," she whispered. Then she turned and started for the house.

Seth shook his head. He looked up at the sky again. *Lord, what are we doing? What am* I *doing?* After all this was over, he was getting his head examined.

CHAPTER 8

"We're happy you're able to join us for supper, Seth." *Mamm* passed him a bowl of roasted brussels sprouts.

Martha watched him as he took the bowl. He'd surprised her in several ways during their conversation right before supper, the biggest surprise his suggestion they pretend to like each other in front of her parents. She still wasn't sure why he'd suggested it, since he was upset with her when she told him about supper at Delilah's. Now he had inserted himself even deeper in the charade, and they were bringing her parents into it too. She glanced at her plate, which was full of food, but she didn't have the appetite to eat it. None of this was aboveboard, and she didn't like that, even though she was the one who started the whole thing.

Yet, despite her guilt, she liked the idea of a trial run. If they could fool her parents, they could fool Delilah. Then she would leave them and Nina and Levi alone, and everything could go back to normal—after she confessed the truth to her *mamm* and *daed*, of course.

"*Danki* for having me." Seth placed a spoonful of the sprouts on his plate. "I'll admit I'm surprised that Martha extended the invitation, but I'm glad I took her up on it." He turned to her and smiled.

Her stomach suddenly did a backflip. She didn't know Seth could smile like that. It transformed his entire face, making him look . . . handsome. No, not just handsome. *Gorgeous.* Wait, did she just think Seth Yoder was gorgeous? The same man who was scowling at her a short time ago?

His knee jabbed against hers, yanking her out of her thoughts. Right, they were supposed to be doing a trial run. Of plan B. To help Cevilla . . . uh, Nina. Goodness, her thoughts were a jumbled mess.

She regained her senses and took the bowl from him, making sure her gaze met his eyes. She wasn't all that good at flirting, since she considered it more than a little frivolous, and she'd never engaged in it with Paul. She also didn't want to overdo it, or her mother might wonder if something was wrong with her. "I'm glad you did too." She dropped her voice a bit, and it sounded sultry even to her. She gazed at him from beneath her lashes before plopping a few sprouts on her plate.

When she glanced up, he was still looking at her, surprise on his face. Then he cleared his throat and turned to her father. "How's the cabinet business going?"

"Pretty *gut*. I've partnered up with Atlee, and we're doing some work for Sol Troyer. He's the carpenter the Stolls have hired to help out with their bed-and-breakfast project."

"Inn," Martha corrected, taking the plate of crescent-shaped rolls from the table. She was about to put one on her plate, then stopped. She held the plate out to him. "Would you like one?" Again she looked up at him with her eyes a little lowered, giving him a small smile.

"Uh, *ya*," he said, clearing his throat again. "*Danki*, Martha." Did he just lower his voice too? No, she was just imagining things. Yet the tickle in her stomach was real. Either that, or she was hungry after all.

"Then you've visited with the Stolls?" *Mamm* said, taking a sip of lemonade. "We haven't had a chance to meet them yet."

Martha told her about Nina and Delilah's visit, leaving out the matchmaking details. "We've been invited to supper on Thursday," she said.

"We?" Her father arched a brow.

"Martha and I." Seth glanced at her, meeting her eyes. Good gravy, he had gorgeous eyes too. Why was she just noticing that now? "She told me about the invitation before supper. Of course, I'm happy to *geh* with her." He gave her a wink and picked up his fork.

Martha glanced at her parents, who were swapping baffled glances. Concerned that Seth was laying it on too thick, she knocked her knee against his thigh.

What? he mouthed.

She tilted her head toward her parents, who were now both looking at them with confusion. He smiled, then ducked his head and went back to eating.

"I didn't realize you and Martha were such *gut* friends." *Daed* put down his fork and looked directly at Seth.

Uh-oh. This was something she hadn't planned for—her father's reaction. When she'd thought about it as she and Seth were coming into the house, she was sure he wouldn't pick up on their friendship, no matter how well they faked it. Her mother would be the one to make assumptions. But now her father looked concerned.

Seth froze. "Uh, that's been, uh, a recent development."

"Right." Martha grabbed the plate of canned beets from the middle of the table. "Here you *geh, Daed*. I know how much you like beets." She reached over Seth to pass the plate, brushing against his shoulder. A shiver went down her spine.

"Allow me." Seth took the plate from her, his hand covering hers for a split second before she released the plate. Again, another shiver. What was happening to her?

Daed nodded his thanks and took the beets, then put a few on his plate, as if the pickled vegetable had made him forget about interrogating Seth.

Eager to change the subject, Martha turned to *Mamm*. "Were you able to finish *yer* puzzle yesterday?" Then she looked at Seth. "*Mamm* is making wall art out of old puzzles."

"Really?" Seth said as though Martha had stated the most interesting thing he'd ever heard.

Mamm smiled. "I've found some pretty ones at a few yard sales and thrift shops. Naomi and I like to visit those, and *yer mudder* joins us when she can."

"She always loves a *gut* sale."

"I found I enjoy doing puzzles. It's relaxing, and they do make pretty pictures."

Seth nodded. "I'd like to see one, if it's finished."

He was being utterly charming, so much so that Martha kept staring at him. This wasn't the Seth Yoder she'd always known, the one who'd been standoffish in the past year, although she knew the reason now. He seemed genuinely interested in her mother's new hobby, and from the growing smile on *Mamm*'s face, she was pleased he was showing such interest. Her father had looked at the half-finished puzzle last night and said, "Nice," before heading upstairs to bed.

"I can show you after supper," she said. "I'm hoping Martha might take an interest in it too."

Surprised, Martha said, "You are?"

"You need a hobby. Something to keep you busy when you're not working. I think that will help you with . . ." She stopped. "Never mind." Then she glanced at Seth before looking back at her with a knowing grin. "Although . . . maybe you don't have time for a hobby after all."

Bingo. She and Seth turned to each other at the same time and beamed. They'd achieved their objective, at least with *Mamm*. Later she'd explain to her the real reason they did this, but right now she was relieved that they'd managed to pull it off. Then she looked at her father. He was eating the beets, giving Seth a few glances, but not saying anything, which Martha took as a good sign. She hoped he wouldn't be mad when he found out what they were doing.

After he finished the last beet, *Daed* asked Seth, "How's *yer familye*? *Yer daed*'s got a nice spread there. I never was much into farming, but *mei onkel* was, and they did rather well for themselves." He pointed his fork at Seth. "I like *yer vatter*. He's a *gut* bishop, and a *gut mann*."

"*Danki*," Seth said. He pushed a bite of rice casserole around on his plate.

"Seems like things are going well for all of you."

Seth didn't look up. "They are."

"Glad to hear it." *Daed* pushed away his plate. "Excellent meal, Regina. As always. Any dessert?"

Mamm chuckled. "As always." She turned to Martha. "Why don't you show Seth the puzzle on the coffee table in the living room. It's almost finished."

"I can help you with dessert," she said.

Mamm waved her off. "*Nee* need. *Yer vatter* and I can handle it." She looked at *Daed*. "Right?"

Daed gave Martha and Seth a long look, as if he was trying to decide if letting them be alone with a puzzle was a good idea. Finally, he nodded. "*Geh* on into the living room. We'll bring dessert and *kaffee* to you."

"How do you take *yer kaffee*, Seth?" *Mamm* asked.

"Black, please."

"That's how Martha likes hers." She gave Martha another knowing smile as they left the kitchen and went into the living room.

Martha blew out a long breath as Seth plopped onto the couch. He looked up at her, any flirty or endearing expression gone. "I think we did it," he said, glancing over his shoulder as he kept his voice low.

"We definitely did it." Without thinking, she sat down next to him. Then she frowned. "I feel terrible about it. "

He ran his palms over his pants legs. "Me too."

"I'm going to talk to *Mamm* after we're finished with wood-carving," she whispered. "I don't think she'll be happy about our misleading them, but I don't want to deceive *mei* parents anymore."

"I agree. Nice acting, by the way. You almost had me convinced in there."

"Speak for *yerself*." She laughed. "I was . . ." She'd almost admitted to the butterflies in her stomach. She didn't dare do that. She would look like a fool for letting his fake flirting get to her. "I was pleased with our performances."

"Is that the puzzle?" Seth leaned forward and looked at the incomplete project. About a dozen pieces were left.

"*Ya. Danki* for pretending to be interested in it. You made *Mamm* happy."

"I'm glad she's happy, but I'm also interested. I used to love doing puzzles when I was *yung*, and I've seen the picture puzzles you two were talking about." He picked up a piece and examined it. "I think this is pretty old."

"Vintage. That's what *Mamm* said, anyway." She picked up the box from the floor next to the table. "It's supposed to look like this." A peaceful scene of an old thatched house and a row-boat on the shore of a lake was on the cover.

"Very nice." He carefully set the piece back down. "I haven't done a puzzle in a long time. I'm the only one who really liked to do them, and the more complicated the better. *Mei schwesters* would do the simple ones with me, but they refused to do the harder ones. Which was fine by me, since I was happy doing them by myself." He leaned against the back of the couch and looked at Martha. "There's something gratifying about completing a challenge."

She nodded and had to agree. That's how she felt about learning something new. While it might be hard at first, she was satisfied when she was able to do what she'd set out to do. Like tonight. Convincing her parents that they were interested in each other had been a challenge, and she and Seth had conquered it. Now she was ready to conquer woodcarving. Or at least learn more about it than she knew now.

Daed came into the room carrying two slices of pecan pie, and *Mamm* followed with two cups of coffee. Seth stood and took the coffees from her. *Daed* handed the dessert plates to Martha.

"*Danki*," Seth said as he sat back down. He gestured to the table. "Nice puzzle. A *gut* choice for a wall picture, in *mei* opinion."

Mamm smiled. "I thought so too." She nudged her husband toward the kitchen. "You two enjoy visiting," she said. "We'll take care of the cleanup."

"We think we'll *geh* for a walk a little later," Martha said, giving them an excuse for when they'd disappear to the woodshop.

"Take *yer* time." *Mamm*'s smile widened. "It was nice having you over, Seth. Don't be a stranger."

"I won't." He grinned and waited until they left the room. His grin slid from his face as he turned to Martha. "It's over." He set Martha's cup on the coffee table, well out of the way of the puzzle. "*Yer* parents are nice people, by the way."

"They are." Which compounded her guilt. But what was done was done, and she would rectify it as soon as possible. She handed Seth one of the pie slices, then sat back down next to him, even though two other empty chairs were in the room. "When do you think we should leave?"

"Ira told me he and some of the Bontragers are heading to Chupps' pond to fish tonight. I don't want to run into them on our way to the woodshop. We should wait until they're already there. That should be in half an hour or so." At Martha's nod, he asked, "What should we do until then?"

She looked at the puzzle. "I don't think *Mamm* would mind if we finished this."

"Sounds *gut* to me."

They both reached for the same puzzle piece, their hands brushing against each other. "Sorry," he said, snatching his hand back. He took a sip of coffee. "You *geh* ahead."

Martha nodded, but her mind wasn't on the puzzle piece, and that was clear when she couldn't remember where the piece fit, even though a moment ago she knew exactly where it went. Her fingers tingled where they had brushed his, more than they ever had when she and Paul held hands.

She glanced at him. He was already tearing into the pie, eating the slice with gusto. If he was affected by that light touch, he didn't act like it. *Get it together, girl.* She focused back on the puzzle and moved the piece around, trying different configurations.

"It goes here." He put his empty pie plate on the floor next to the couch and took the piece from her. "See?"

"Oh." She let out an awkward chuckle. "Silly me. I should have figured that out."

He looked at her. "Are you sure you're *gut* at puzzles?"

Ya, when I'm not behaving like an idiot. Determined to prove herself, she picked up another piece and quickly found where the edges matched up. Satisfied, she said, "See?"

"Guess that will teach me to doubt you."

Her breath caught. There it was again. That gorgeous smile accompanied by a hearty laugh. *Very attractive.*

She froze. Her parents were nowhere in sight. He didn't have to keep up the ruse. She watched him as he fit another piece in the puzzle. Now she was more concerned than just deceiving her parents and trying to help Nina. Something was going on here—something inside her. She didn't want to like that feeling, but she couldn't deny it.

· · ·

Nina glanced at her grandmother, then focused on the road ahead. She held on to Happy's reins as he pranced down the road. He was living up to his name, and she was growing to love the gentle black gelding. Back home she loved going on evening rides in her father's open buggy, usually by herself as she headed for the fishing hole. Fishing. When she first moved here, she hadn't cared about her favorite pastime, but now she was itching to fish. She hadn't expected Martha to be interested, but it never hurt to ask. She liked Martha, and although she'd heard an earful from her grandmother about taking off without telling her, it was worth spending some time with a new friend. A girlfriend, which she hadn't had since her school days.

But now they were headed to Seth Yoder's house, at her grandmother's insistence, of course. "I'm sure this could wait until tomorrow," she grumbled.

"We have a full day tomorrow. The flooring people are coming in, plus I want you to help me choose the linens and quilts for the inn bedrooms. I have a stack of catalogs for us to peruse." She settled into the seat. "I want to get Seth's confirmation for supper on Thursday. We don't want this to be a last-minute affair."

Nina cringed at the word *affair*. Her grandmother could be so pretentious sometimes. Nina knew it was because she'd had a stern upbringing when she was little, more stern than normal since her mother had been a stickler for manners. Yet sometimes *Grossmammi*'s attitude could be quite snobby. "I'm sure Seth's not home from Martha's yet."

"Then we can wait for him and have a nice visit with the Yoders." *Grossmammi* sat up and moved the tray of sweet rolls from her lap to the seat. They'd purchased them from Yoder's Bakery on the way home from the optics shop yesterday.

It dawned on Nina that the Yoders could have the bakery's sweet rolls anytime, since the bishop's sister, Carolyn, owned and ran the bakery. But she didn't dare say that to her grandmother. "What if they're busy?"

"Then we'll leave the sweet rolls and *geh* back home." She huffed. "Why do you have to be so contrary, Nina?"

"I'm being realistic," she mumbled.

"What did you say?"

"*Nix.*" She focused on the road, glancing at the directions to the Yoders' house on the piece of paper in her lap. Yes, *Grossmammi* wanted to nail down her plans, but Nina knew she also wanted to see the bishop's home. To measure how he lived. She was nosy, and she always had been. The comparison trap had been a problem in their community. Even Nina had been aware of that. The women were also competitive, fighting to be the first one to get the wash out on the line or making sure their pie had the highest peaks of meringue. It was a contradiction of their faith, but in their tiny community, everyone knew everyone else's business and foibles. Nina thought they were all being stupid. That was another reason she liked hanging out with the guys. They didn't care about comparison, except when it came to fishing. She usually caught the biggest fish anyway.

As they approached the Yoders', Nina wished she would have put her foot down about coming here, but her grandmother would have gone anyway. It was already dusk, and she didn't like the idea of *Grossmammi* driving home in this still-unfamiliar area after dark. Besides, she could at least try to keep her grandmother from being too nosy or embarrassing. She'd probably fail, but she'd rather have firsthand knowledge of *Grossmammi*'s well-intentioned mischief.

She pulled into the Yoders' driveway, parked the buggy, and met her grandmother on the other side. *Grossmammi* didn't need any help, so she stood there while she got out, glancing around at the large house and pristine farmland. Cows lowed in the background, and she heard a few sheep bleating. Several other nice houses were on this street, along with expansive farmland.

Grossmammi looked at her. "For goodness' sake." She pulled a handkerchief out of the pocket of her apron. "Didn't you look in the mirror before we left? You have a smudge of chocolate on *yer* chin."

Nina took the handkerchief and scrubbed at the spot. She rarely looked in the mirror, and when she did it was on Sundays. "Did I get it?"

"*Ya.*" She sighed, then took the handkerchief and stuffed it back in her pocket as she looked around. "These people have money, obviously." She sniffed.

Nina looked at her. "Does that matter?"

She shrugged. "It all depends on how you use it."

"That's not our place to judge."

Grossmammi smirked. "Who's judging? I'm simply making an observation. Now, let's see if Seth has returned from Martha's."

Nina followed as her grandmother confidently made her way to the Yoders' porch, then rapped on the door without hesitation. After a few moments, a young man opened it. Nina knew from her grandmother that Seth had two brothers, but she hadn't met either one of them. Her gaze met his. He was taller than Seth—and bulkier, maybe stronger. His shoulders were wide, and the hems of his short sleeves were a little tight around his biceps. He had dark-brown hair, blue eyes, and a startled expression on his face.

"Hello," he said.

"Hello, *yung mann.* I'm Delilah Stoll, and this is mei *grossdochder*, Nina. We stopped by for a visit." *Grossmammi* tried peeking around him to look inside, but his large body filled up the doorway. Nina vigorously rubbed her nose. Her grandmother was in fine form.

"Come on in." He held the door open for her, and the two

women went inside. "I'm Ira. I don't think we've met." He shut the door and turned to them. "*Mei* parents are out back. I'll let them know you're here."

"Is Seth home, by any chance?" *Grossmammi* asked.

Ira paused, his welcoming expression dimming. "*Nee.* He's . . . out."

"I see. Then we'll wait right here for *yer* parents."

"Okay." He looked at Nina, a little confused.

All Nina could do was shrug and try to smile. If it was this awkward to pay a visit to the bishop, she could only imagine what it would be like at supper Thursday night.

After Ira left to get his parents, Nina resisted the urge to bite her nails while *Grossmammi* inspected the room. She'd never been a nail-biter, but lately she couldn't leave her hands alone. Her grandmother didn't say anything, yet Nina knew she was taking in every detail. One graying eyebrow raised, she scanned the room. Nina wasn't as thorough, but she did notice this was a nice, lived-in living room. She felt immediately at home here, which was surprising since this was her first visit. Yet something about the place was welcoming, and she got the feeling the Yoders never turned anyone away.

Soon Freemont and Mary walked into the room, and *Grossmammi*'s attention swept to them, as if she hadn't been nosily scrutinizing their living room. "Hello," she said, walking toward them.

"Hi, Delilah," Mary said. "Lovely to have you drop by for a visit." She turned to Nina. "It's nice to meet you too. I'm Mary."

"Freemont." The bishop extended his hand to Nina and gave her a firm handshake. His palms were calloused from farmwork.

"It won't take me but a second to put on a teakettle or the

percolator." Mary turned to *Grossmammi*. "Do you prefer tea or *kaffee*?"

"Tea, please. And we brought some—" She let out a small gasp and turned to Nina. "I can't believe I left the sweet rolls in the buggy. Do you mind getting them, Nina?"

"Glad to," she said, and then hurried outside, grateful for the escape. Maybe it had been a bad idea for her to come. She felt like she was on pins and needles every time her grandmother opened her mouth.

Nina stood on the Yoders' front porch and let out a long breath. The air was thick and muggy, as it had been ever since she'd moved here. But at least she had a moment to herself. After breathing in the comforting smells of the farm—sweet timothy grass, the perfume of the slightly wilting flowers in the pots on the porch, and even the scents of the pastured animals nearby— she started toward the buggy. On the way she swatted at a stray horsefly. Then another. Then two more. What was it with the insects in Birch Creek? They seemed to like her far too much.

"The horseflies have been pretty active lately." Ira walked up to her, fishing pole in one hand, a wicker creel in the other. "Surprising since it's so hot."

"I had the same problem with wasps," she said, swiping at another fly. For some reason they were leaving Ira alone. She turned to him. "I'm sorry about coming over without an invitation."

"Why? We have an open-door policy here." He smiled, and whatever had bothered him earlier when her grandmother mentioned Seth didn't seem to be bothering him now. "Although *yer grossmammi* seems to have her own visiting policy."

"That she does." Nina took in his fishing pole, and the sweet rolls were forgotten. "You're going fishing?"

He nodded. "With Zeb and Zeke Bontrager. It's been too hot to fish during the day, so we decided to give it a try tonight."

"What are you fishing for?"

"Mostly sunfish. The pond doesn't have a big variety. It's in the woods over there." He pointed to the large house next door. "The Chupps let us fish whenever we want. They ought to, since we're *familye. Mei schwester* is married to a Chupp and . . ." He shook his head. "I won't bore you with all that. Do you like to fish?"

She nodded, facing him, barely holding in her excitement. "I do. I fished all the time back home. We had several ponds, but like *yers*, they didn't have a wide variety of fish. A couple of times a year I would *geh* with *mei bruder* and *vatter* to Lake Michigan. The walleye and perch are plentiful there."

"Sounds like Lake Erie. I went fishing there for the first time last year, with Zeb. We booked a charter."

"That's what we would do." She took a step toward him. "What kind of bait do you use?"

"Worms, mostly." He opened the creel and took out a Styrofoam container.

"Mind if I take a look inside?"

His brow lifted. "You're joking, right?"

"Not at all."

Ira handed her the container and she pulled off the lid. "Oh, these are nice ones." She burrowed her fingers into the moist dirt and pulled out a fat worm. "Did you dig these up *yerself*?" She held up the worm and inspected it. What an excellent specimen. When he didn't answer, she looked at him.

His mouth was agape. "Um, *ya*. Yesterday morning, before 4:00 a.m. That was the coolest time of the day, believe it or not." He looked at the worm dangling from her hand, then back at her. "I gotta say, I've never seen a *maedel* so excited about worms and fishing."

Feeling self-conscious, she put the worm back in the container and closed the lid. Her grandmother would be appalled at her reaction. "I like to fish," she said quietly, handing the worms back to him.

"Do you dig *yer* own worms?"

She nodded, not looking at him. Now he probably thought she was weird. Well, he wouldn't be the first one to see her that way. Normally she didn't care, but she'd been more than a little sensitive lately.

"Do you like to use minnows?" Ira asked.

Nina lifted her eyes to him, surprised he was still asking her questions about fishing. She figured he would have been gone by now. "I prefer live bait, *ya*."

"Me too. Zeb and Zeke like using lures, but there's *nix* better than live bait. Say, you want to *geh* fishing with us? We'll probably be gone an hour or so. Think *yer grossmammi* can do without you for a little while?"

Nina had never been more tempted in her life, but she shook her head. Her grandmother didn't approve of her fishing, despite cooking up anything edible Nina brought home. "I can't," she said, remembering she was supposed to be getting the sweet rolls. *Grossmammi* was probably wondering what was taking her so long. "*Danki* for asking me."

"Okay. Guess I'll see you later, then."

She paused. Was that a flash of disappointment in his eyes? How could she assume that, when they'd just met? He turned and headed for the backyard. She watched him go, wishing she could go with him.

Her shoulders slumping, she walked to the buggy, got the

sweet rolls, and returned to the house. She knocked quietly on the front door since she didn't feel comfortable just walking inside.

Mary opened the door and smiled. "Oh, Carolyn's sweet rolls," she said as she let Nina in. "Those are delicious."

"What took you so long?" *Grossmammi* was seated on a hickory rocker in the corner. Freemont was sitting on the couch opposite her.

"Sorry. I was dawdling." She didn't want to bring up her conversation with Ira to her grandmother. She wasn't in the mood for a lecture about how unfeminine fishing was, especially not in front of Mary and Freemont.

"Normally Nina is very polite," *Grossmammi* said. "She must have been taken by *yer* beautiful property."

She was, but Nina didn't say anything as she offered the rolls to Mary.

"I'll bring these out with the tea," Mary said when she took them. "*Danki*, Nina."

"Have a seat." *Grossmammi* pointed at a comfortable-looking, cloth-covered chair near the couch.

"*Ya*," Freemont said with a slight smile. "Have a seat, Nina."

She cringed as she sat down. The Yoders were seeing all sides of Delilah Stoll—confident, pushy, in command of all situations. Nina had none of those traits, and she wished she had the ability to disappear, preferably to Ira's fishing pond. But she sat down as ordered.

Soon Mary came back to the living room carrying a tray laden with a teapot, mugs, napkins, and a plate of the sweet rolls. The three of them were chatting, but Nina tuned them out. She should have taken Ira up on his offer. She would love to be sitting on the bank of a pond, line in the water, the sounds of nature around her, forgetting about her homesickness, the inn, and her grandmother controlling her life.

She didn't know what the topic of conversation was until she heard her grandmother ask about Seth.

"Do you know what time he'll be back?" *Grossmammi* asked.

"I thought he'd be home by now. He said he was having a quick bite of supper at the Detweilers'." Mary looked at Freemont. "Did he say anything else to you about his plans for tonight?"

"*Nee.* I'm sure he'll be home anytime. Must be having a great time with Martha and her parents."

Nina caught the pinched look on her grandmother's face. Seth and Martha having fun together was not in Delilah Stoll's plans.

After a little bit more small talk, it became clear Seth wasn't coming home anytime soon. Nina was relieved by that. Martha had said she would come up with something to help all of them escape *Grossmammi*'s plans, but Nina didn't expect her to. That wasn't Martha's responsibility; it was Nina's. But Nina couldn't get up the courage to put a stop to her.

It was still dusk when they left, not dark as Nina had thought it would be by the time they'd be going home. "I like those two," *Grossmammi* said.

"They're nice."

Nina expected her grandmother to say something else, but she could see she was deep in thought. Maybe she had reconsidered supper Thursday night. Before they'd left Freemont's, she'd told Mary that Seth was invited over, but surely her grandmother had the idea that Seth and Martha were closer than she'd thought. Nina knew the truth, but maybe tonight would be the only convincing her grandmother needed to get the notion of matchmaking her and Levi with Seth and Martha out of her mind.

. . .

Delilah stared out into the scenery while Nina drove the buggy. Her plans were being thwarted left and right, and she didn't appreciate it one bit. She knew in her mind that Birch Creek was the place for her family, but it had taken a lot of convincing to get Loren to move, although she let her grandchildren think it was his idea. Her son could be so passive sometimes, a trait he'd inherited from his father. He'd also inherited Wayne's loyalty and love for his family, two qualities she had loved most about him. While her son had been a widower for a long time, Delilah knew better than to push him to find someone else to love. Instead she focused on Nina and Levi. They required more than enough of her attention.

She didn't understand either of them. Any young man and woman would be chomping at the bit for the privilege to court them if her grandchildren weren't standing in their own way. Levi was outgoing and friendly with everyone, and he had surprised Delilah with his eagerness to move to Birch Creek and open an inn. Yet he wasn't focused on marriage or a family of his own at all. As far as she knew, he'd never had a date, and she made it her business to know her grandchildren's business. He was twenty-one years old. High time he'd started planning for his personal future.

Nina was a more difficult case. Beneath her rough exterior was a lovely woman, but Nina did everything she could to keep that buried from the world. Delilah couldn't relate. Back in her day, she'd been one of the prettiest girls in her community, and she'd enjoyed attention from the boys until she'd fallen in love with Wayne. But all Nina had wanted to do ever since she was a child was roughhouse with boys. Oh, and fish. Delilah scrunched her nose. More than once she'd found a hook or a dead worm in Nina's laundry. She wouldn't get a husband by acting like a boy. The fact that she hadn't been approached by any young men for a date proved that.

It was up to Delilah to take charge, just as she had ever since she'd been in her teens and her mother had passed away. She had raised her younger siblings, then raised Loren, and now she was coming to the end of raising Levi and Nina. Truth be told, she was a bit weary of being so responsible. But God had seen fit to give her this purpose in life, and she wouldn't fail him, or her family. Unfortunately, her family members needed a kick in the pants to get moving. And she was just the one to do the kicking.

She shifted in her seat. Too bad Seth hadn't been home tonight. He was a handsome man, from a good family. God wouldn't have chosen Freemont to be bishop if he didn't deserve it. She'd always believed bishops and their families were particularly blessed by God, even if she didn't know any Scripture to back that up. And from the looks of the Yoders' farm and house, they were well off. It was easy to say money wasn't important, but not having to scrape out an existence alleviated a lot of worry, in her experience. Which was why she wanted Nina and Seth together. She wanted to see Nina happy, not struggle the way Delilah had when she was her age, before she'd married Wayne.

Then there was Martha. Delilah wasn't all that sure about her, other than she was pretty, in a fresh and lively way. But it wasn't as though her grandson had any other choices to pursue in this district. She'd already learned Martha was the only single woman close to his age, which was the only downside Delilah had seen about Birch Creek so far. Levi was so charming that she was sure Martha would be smitten after they'd spent some time together. And because Levi would be part owner and a manager of the inn, he would also be set financially. *He's such a catch.*

She smiled to herself. All she had to do was make sure Thursday evening went off without a hitch. As long as Seth and Martha were there, she would guide the rest, especially Nina. She relaxed a bit. Her plans might not be going perfectly, but they were heading in the right direction.

CHAPTER 9

"Do we really have to sneak around like this?" Martha asked.

Seth stopped a few feet from the copse of trees by Jalon Chupp's house. More than once he'd wished he'd built his shed farther away from the pond. But if he had, he'd be spending precious time traveling, taking away from the time he could be woodcarving. "Shh." He put his finger to his lips and cocked his head. "Do you hear anything?" he whispered.

"Birds. Crickets. Then there was that goat screech back there—"

Seth put his finger over her lips. "Don't you know how to whisper?"

"*Ya,*" she said against his finger, then moved his hand away.

He took a step back. What had gotten into him tonight? From the moment he'd agreed to Martha's scheme and then come up with his own—he was oh so very tired of schemes— he'd given 100 percent to making her parents think they fancied each other. Surprisingly, it hadn't been that difficult. It also hadn't been that unpleasant. During their meal, he'd felt comfortable with her parents, and the food was delicious. He'd also noticed how pretty Martha's eyes were again, since they had sat so close to each other purposely. Not just her eyes, but her whole face. And when they were putting the puzzle pieces together, he also realized how elegant her hands were.

Normally he didn't care about such things, but for some reason he couldn't take his eyes off her—when she wasn't looking, of course.

And now he had touched her lips. Granted, she was being a bit loud. Well, loud might be an exaggeration, but she certainly wasn't quiet. He knew Ira and the Bontragers had to be at the pond by now, and he didn't want to draw their attention. But he didn't have to put his finger over Martha's lips to accomplish that. He could have just shushed her verbally.

But then he wouldn't have felt her soft lips. Her very *soft* lips.

"Sorry." He whirled around and headed for the shed. He needed to get tonight over with. Then things could go back to normal. Except they wouldn't. Not with his father's glaucoma and the responsibility he'd handed Seth. Responsibility he honestly didn't want but would make sure he fulfilled.

To Martha's credit she didn't say another word as they made their way to the shed. It was dusk, but he had plenty of lights in the woodshop. He unlocked the door, turned on the lamp on the table near the door, and walked to the back while Martha closed the door behind them. He plugged his two fans into battery power and then flipped them on. The muggy, still air stirred. The fans didn't do much to cool off the shed, but they provided a bit of relief. He didn't anticipate they would be here that long anyway.

He went to the pegboard against the wall where he hung all his tools. At least he'd hung all his tools at first. Now almost all of them were scattered all over his workbench and the shelving unit. He wasn't exactly a neatnik. The two still hung were there only because he hadn't used them since the last time he cleaned up his shop, weeks ago. He pulled his planer off its peg. "We'll start with this." He held up the tool.

"A planer?" Martha put her hands on her hips. "*Mei daed*'s a carpenter, Seth. I learned how to use a planer when I was six years old."

"*Yer vatter* let you use a tool when you were six?"

"Actually, when I was five. That's when I first used a hammer." She went to the pegboard and looked at the one tool left hanging. "I want to learn carving, not building." She took it off the hook and turned to him. "Teach me how to use this."

Her words sounded bossy, but her tone was sweet. Feminine. A little cajoling. Not in a bad way, but in a way that made his mouth go dry, for some strange reason. He went to the corner of the shed where he kept his bottled water, cans of pop, and snacks. Usually he brought a cooler of ice with him when it was this hot, but he didn't have the chance this time. He took a can of Coke from the plastic rings, popped the top, and took a sip. It was hot and tasted terrible, but it took away the dryness.

Seth set the can on one of the shelves and took the tool from her. "This is for advanced work." He wouldn't admit that he needed more practice with the fish tail too, but she didn't need to know that. He hung the tool back up and lifted another basic one off the shelf. "How about trying the chisel again?"

She smiled. "*Ya*. That's *gut*."

Even her smile was pretty. He grabbed the pop and took another swig. *Blech*. "Let's get this over with," he muttered.

"I heard that."

He turned around and saw the annoyed look on her face.

"Look, Seth, if this is such a chore for you, forget it. I don't want to force you to show me anything." She headed for the door. "I'll get *mei* own tools and book and figure it out from there."

A vision of her slicing her finger open, like he had when he first started using the tools, came to his mind. "Come back," he said. "It's not a chore. I'm just tired, that's all." Which he was. He hadn't slept well last night, thinking about *Daed*. And he'd worked all day on the farm. "I said I would teach you, and I always keep *mei* word."

She peered at him. "Are you sure?"

"Positive." He held up the chisel. "Let's get started."

. . .

It wasn't long before Martha was wiping sweat from her face. Her shoulders ached a little from using the mallet to hit the handle of the chisel, and her hands were cramping from her unfamiliar grip on the tools.

She'd never had so much fun in her life.

Seth stood right beside her, helping her adjust her grip, showing her different ways to sink the blade of the tool into the aspen wood, and gently correcting her when she made a mistake. Which wasn't too often, she was surprised to find out. She was also surprised to discover how much she liked working with wood. A lot. Even if it felt like one hundred degrees in the woodshop. She'd anticipated the joy and challenge of learning something knew, but this was different from tying knots and training horses. The feel of the wood, the way the chisel chipped at it, exposing new grain . . . This feeling reached into her soul.

"Here." Seth handed her a rag from a stack on the shelf above the workbench. "Don't worry. It's clean. I've been keeping a stock of them this summer."

She looked at it and smirked. "You don't have any more of those attractive headbands?"

He did, but he wasn't about to pull them out, because he was sure she would want him to wear one. "Do you want this or not?"

She grinned and took it from him, then wiped her face, which was no doubt red. She handed it back to him and resumed her work.

He looked at the damp rag. "What am I, *yer* assistant?" He set the rag on an empty space on the shelf, then studied her progress. She'd caught on quickly, much more quickly than he had. "I think you're ready to move on." He went to the pegboard and took down a tool that resembled the chisel but had a U-shaped curve at the end. "This is a gouge," he said, flipping the tool over in his hand and giving it to her handle first. "You saw me using it when you were here before. Use the curved edge down, on the side of the wood."

She took the tool and looked at the wood in the vise. She had chiseled the end of the small piece until it was smooth. She did as Seth instructed, and it gouged a nice edge into the side of the wood.

"Now turn it over and use the other side in the middle."

She did as he instructed. This time the gouge created a shallow trench in the wood. She looked at Seth and grinned. "What a useful tool."

"It's one of *mei* favorites. That's a wide gouge. I have some smaller ones for more detailed work." He went to the shelving unit on the opposite side of the room and pulled down a block of wood, then brought it over to Martha. "I used the smallest one to carve around the bird's wings."

She took the wood from him and examined it. He was a good carver, in a rustic sort of way. The bird wasn't very detailed; it was simple, like the seashell she'd seen the first time she was here. But she liked its charm. "How long did it take you to make this?"

"A while." He frowned. "Hard to be exact since I can get only snatches of time to work out here." He took the wood and put it back on the shelf.

She watched him, more beads of perspiration slipping down the side of her face. "Why do you keep this place a secret?" she asked.

He turned around, giving her the first scowl since before suppertime. "That's not any of *yer* business."

She felt the tips of her ears heat, which they always did when she was embarrassed. "You're right. I'm sorry I asked." She turned and focused on the wood in front of her. Her mind started to visualize what she could make with the scrap wood and the two tools. It would make a nice base frame for one of the smaller puzzles her mother had purchased, one she hadn't started on yet. But once *Mamm* finished, Martha could glue the completed puzzle to the frame, then put some clear varnish on it to seal it and make it shiny. Her father had shown her how to use stain and varnish a few years ago, but she'd never had the opportunity to apply what she learned.

She quickly used the gouge to hone the side of the wood, then took it out of the vise and turned it to the other side. She decided to use the palm of her hand instead of the mallet to push the gouge along the edge. The wood was soft enough for that. Then she did the same to the other two sides. Once finished she turned to see Seth organizing his tools. He'd already cleared off one of the shelves on the unit, and she saw that a large plastic tub was full of trash. She'd been so engrossed in her work she hadn't heard him moving around behind her. "Do you have any sandpaper?"

"*Ya.*" He pulled open a drawer in the small cabinet near the worktable, then took out two sheets of sandpaper. "Rough and fine," he said, handing them to her.

"Perfect." She went to work sanding the board, fine wood dust gathering on the backs of her hands.

"What are you making?" Seth said, as he leaned over her shoulder.

She jerked, the sandpaper skidding across the wood, but she kept her grip on the paper. He shouldn't startle her like that. He also shouldn't be standing so close to her. It was hot in here, and she was already a sopping mess, and she was sure she didn't smell that great either. But that wasn't what bothered her. It was that annoying tickle in her stomach that kicked up again. He hadn't moved, and if she turned her head just right, the top of her *kapp* would brush against his cheek. She did *not* want that to happen. "A frame."

"Doesn't look like a frame." He moved to her side.

She blew out a relieved breath, then explained what she planned to do with the wood. "I'm sure frame isn't the right word, but I don't know what to call it."

"A plaque. And it's a great idea. They have several of those in that gift shop in Barton."

The pause in sanding made her realize how much her hand hurt. She wasn't used to using her hands like this, and she looked down at the dust on them. She set down the sandpaper and rubbed her fingers. "How long have we been here?"

"Let me check." He glanced at the same small clock on the worktable he'd looked at the other day, then grabbed it. "This says seven, but that can't be right." He went and opened the door. "It's dark outside. Must be past nine." He shook the clock, then looked at it again. "This thing must be broken."

They'd been out here for almost two hours? She quickly brushed off her hands. "I've got to get back home. *Mamm* and *Daed* are probably worried about us."

"I'm not so sure they are." He gave her smirk. "They told us to take our time, right?"

Right. Now she was remembering the sly look on her mother's face when they left. Oh boy. It was going to be hard to admit the truth about her and Seth. "Still," she said, "I don't want to give them any ideas."

"Too late—"

"Any *more* ideas." She turned to him and smiled. "*Danki*, Seth. This was so much fun. May I take the plaque and finish it at home? *Daed*'s got more than enough sandpaper around. I'll pay you for the wood."

He walked over to the bench and picked up the plaque. He looked at it before handing it to her. "You don't have to pay me." Then he looked her up and down. "By the way, you're covered in sawdust."

She glanced at her dress. She could brush that off easily enough, but when she touched her face, it felt grimy. A dry rag wasn't going to help. How was she going to explain that to her parents? "I'll stop by the pond and wash up before I *geh* home."

"What if Ira and the Bontragers are still fishing there?"

"Then I'll say I came by to cool off. I'm just going to rinse *mei* face and neck and arms. Besides, they won't think anything of it if I'm by myself."

His expression grew stern. "You're not going there by *yerself*."

"Seth, the pond isn't that far away."

"It's dark."

"It's also a full moon."

He crossed his arms. A bead of sweat ran down the side of

his face. His dark hair curled at the ends from the heat and humidity in the woodshop. "I'll *geh* with you."

"And what will you tell *yer bruder* if he's there? We don't want him to get the wrong idea about us, right?" She didn't want to tell Seth she was already worried Ira was mad at her.

"I'll figure something out." He opened the door and motioned for her to leave.

She walked out of the shed and waited while Seth turned out the lights and locked up. It was still warm and sticky outside, but she felt a slight, welcome breeze. Only then did she realize how stifling it had been in the shed. She had so much fun carving she hadn't really noticed.

"You don't have to come with me," she said. "I am a grownup, you know."

He gave her a long look. The moon was bright tonight, so much so that she could see his expression. He didn't look upset or put out or irritated. He looked . . . Okay, she had no idea what that look meant, only that she shivered, which made no sense because she was the furthest thing from cold.

Then his expression changed again, becoming inscrutable. "Come on."

With a sigh she followed him, clutching the plaque, and put shivering in front of Seth from her mind. She was pleased with her idea and decided to hit some garage sales herself and find her own puzzles. She'd get a nice one to put together and attach to the plaque, then give it to her mother for her birthday next month.

When they reached the pond, no one was in sight. "Thank you, Lord," Seth said, looking at the sky. He seemed to be doing that a lot tonight.

"Could you hold this?" Martha handed him the plaque. He

nodded and took it, and she leaned down at the edge of the bank and dipped her hands into the cool water. She'd been to this pond several times. It was a well-kept place, always mowed, with a bench on one side. That was good, since she didn't have to worry about any critters jumping out at her. She splashed the water on her face, then her neck, then finally her arms. She got up and went back to Seth. "That felt great," she said, grinning, not caring that her face was wet. She wiped her hands on her dress and reached for the plaque. "*Yer* turn."

. . .

Seth had never been more annoyed with a full moon in his life. Which was ridiculous, since the moonlight would keep them from having to use a flashlight to get home, which would decrease the chances of them being detected. He also realized he'd forgotten his pocket flashlight in the shed. Then again, his mind hadn't been firing on all cylinders tonight. Especially right now.

He'd noticed how pretty Martha was at her house, but she was downright beautiful in the moonlight. He also realized that some of that attraction was because of the confidence she'd displayed back in the woodshop. She used the tools as though she'd been woodcarving all her life, and even if her father had given her some rudimentary instruction on woodworking, the plaque looked almost professionally done. Far better than his first attempt had been. And while he'd had to find ideas from books he checked out from the library, she had come up with a pretty clever one of her own on the spot. That was creativity, something he suddenly realized he didn't have very much of. At least not as much as Martha had.

But all that was in the far recesses of his mind. All he could do was gaze at her lovely, fresh face illuminated in the silver light. Droplets balanced on the tops of her cheeks, and when she blinked he noticed a few of them falling from her eyelashes, which didn't seem to bother her. A bead of water slid down the side of her face, and he almost reached up and wiped it off. If he hadn't been clutching her plaque in two hands, he might have done it.

"Seth?" she said, bringing him out of his stupor.

"Oh. *Ya*." He handed her the plaque and hurried to the pond. The water here was never stagnant because of a mega battery–powered pump Jalon had installed a couple of years ago. The pump didn't interfere with the ecosystem, but it kept algae at bay. He crouched down and scooped up as much of the water as he could. He needed to splash his hot face, and not because it was warm and muggy out. This whole evening had turned out to be more than he bargained or prepared for.

He cooled off his face and neck, then stood and turned to see Martha looking up at the sky. He gulped. That didn't help matters much. The moon cast her profile in a silvery glow, and his mouth went dry again. Oh, this wasn't good. It wasn't good at all. He knelt and dunked his entire head into the pond, then jumped to his feet and swiped his hand over his face before shaking the water out of his hair.

"Seth," Martha said, giggling. "You're getting me all wet."

"We need to get back," he said, rushing past her toward the opening in the woods. He didn't slow his steps, not even when they had reached Jalon's backyard. The house was dark except for one light in a window on the top floor. When it went out, he realized it was probably later than he'd thought. "I'll walk you home," he said, turning to her.

"You don't have to—"

"I'm walking you home, Martha."

"All right," she replied quietly, holding the plaque to her chest and looking a bit wounded.

Great, now he was snapping at her. He was starting to rue the day Ruby had planned that hunt. That was the start of all his troubles where Martha Detweiler was concerned, and he had more troubles to deal with other than her. He didn't have time for . . . for whatever this was he was feeling.

"Seth, can you slow down? *Yer* legs are longer than mine."

He slowed his steps and turned to look at her, walking backward. "Sorry," he mumbled. "I just don't want *yer* parents to worry."

"You weren't concerned with that a little while ago."

Because I'm not thinking clearly. If he had been, he wouldn't be here, walking in the moonlight with Martha and fighting his feelings. He glanced at her. She was still holding the plaque against her chest, and he remembered her intense focus as she worked with the chisel. He wondered if she realized she'd stuck out her tongue a little bit when she concentrated. He thought about how she hadn't seemed to notice the sandpaper dust all over her clothes, and about the sweet sparkle in her eyes when she talked about her idea.

It was all so . . . attractive. And he didn't need to be attracted to anything right now.

They reached Martha's house, and just like Jalon's house, the lights were out. He stopped at the end of the driveway. "You're home," he said, not taking a step farther.

She glowered at him. "Don't sound so disappointed." Then she lifted her chin. "*Danki*, Seth. I know I've already said this, but I really enjoyed tonight."

He had, too, unfortunately. All he did was nod.

Martha's shoulders drooped slightly, and she started to head for the house. "Oh," she said, turning around. "Don't forget about Thursday. Do you want to meet me at the Stolls'? Or pick me up here?"

He squeezed his eyes shut. He had forgotten about the Stolls. That was the whole reason he was pretending to like Martha tonight. But somewhere the line between reality and fiction had blurred. "Right. The Stolls. I'll meet you there." He didn't think it was a good idea to be alone with her in the buggy. At least not when they were pretending to be a couple. *Or until I can get* mei *scrambled egg of a brain figured out.*

She nodded, turning around too fast for him to see her reaction. When she was inside, he spun on his heel and headed home. Tomorrow he would have to tell his parents he had another supper invitation for Thursday. He was rarely invited anywhere lately, and now he had two social events in one week. *Nee, that doesn't look suspicious at all.*

When he arrived home, a small lamp was glowing in front of the living room window. He appreciated his parents keeping it on for him. He turned it off, about to head upstairs, but then decided to go into the kitchen. Maybe a snack and some water would still his thoughts enough that he could get some sleep tonight.

He turned on the lantern on the kitchen table, and when he saw a note lying next to it, he picked it up.

Nina and Delilah Stoll stopped by. Said you were invited to supper on Thursday. I'll make a dessert for you to take over there.

He set his *mamm*'s note back on the table. As long as she didn't make donuts. Normally the thought of his mother's hockey puck–like donuts brought a smile to his face. She could make anything else, but decent donuts eluded her. Right now, though, he couldn't even smile. He sat down and ran his hands through his hair, still damp from the pond. How was he going to get through another night of pretending with Martha? Especially when he wasn't sure if he *was* pretending?

Then there was Delilah. She was a woman on a mission, one he didn't want to deal with. He thought Cevilla was forthright, but she had nothing on Delilah Stoll.

He pushed up from the table and got a drink of water. His dad came to mind, and he immediately felt ashamed. His father was facing blindness, and Seth was worried about a stupid supper. He needed to get his priorities straight. His father and the farm were the most important things right now. And after he finished his obligation to the Stolls, he would focus his attention on him.

Yet despite his vow, he thought about Martha.

. . .

Nina settled on the bank of the pond and set her creel beside her. She opened it and pulled out a fat, slimy worm. Perfect. She baited her hook and cast it into the middle of the pond. Then she waited, digging her toes into the warm grass, peace settling over her.

It was midday, another hot one, and she had snuck away from her grandmother, this time with Levi's help. He knew how important it was that she get in some fishing time, and he said he would give *Grossmammi* some excuse for Nina's absence this afternoon. Nina had hurried and fetched her fishing pole from the barn, then walked over to the Chupps' house. She would have arrived sooner in the buggy, but she'd made good time on foot.

After seeing Ira with his fishing pole, she couldn't get fishing off her mind. She also needed to fortify herself for tomorrow night, and nothing was more fortifying for her than fishing. She had stopped to ask Jalon permission to fish, mentioning Ira's name. Hopefully Ira wouldn't mind. Jalon had happily given it to her. He seemed nice. So had Ira and his parents. And of course, Martha. Everyone she'd met in Birch Creek had been. That, coupled with some quality fishing time, eased her homesickness a tiny bit.

She closed her eyes, holding the pole with a loose grip, but not too loose, in case she got a bite. Then she heard something moving in the trees. She looked over her shoulder and saw Ira approaching. She was so surprised that the pole slipped out of her grip and fell onto the ground. It suddenly zipped off into the pond. A fish was taking off with her pole.

"Oh *nee*," she said, bounding to her feet. "That's *mei* favorite rod."

"I'll get it." Ira shoved off his boots and socks and waded into the water without hesitation. He ducked under for a moment, then came back up with her pole.

She clasped her hands together. "Oh, *danki!*"

He sloshed to the bank and handed her the pole. "I'm afraid you lost *yer* fish," he said.

"I'm not worried about that." She took her rod and ran her palm over it. "I was afraid of losing this. *Danki* for getting it for me."

"The fish in here aren't big enough or strong enough to drag that very far." He moved to the side of her and shook the water out of his hair, then looked at her. "Did I get you wet?"

She couldn't help but giggle. "A bit. Were you trying to?"

He shook his head. "*Nee.* Sorry about that."

"Don't be. The water feels *gut.*" She grew serious as she took in his wet clothes. "You're soaked. I'm sorry about that."

"Trust me, I'm glad for the chance to cool off." He wrung out the hem of his shirt, which now clung to him like a second skin.

That didn't escape Nina's notice. He was a very, *very* well-built man. She turned, her face heating for some weird reason. "I-I'm g-glad." She was stuttering? She never stuttered.

"I realized I forgot *mei* tackle box," he said. "I came by to get it. I didn't know you were back here."

"I thought you used live bait." She turned slightly, now more curious about the tackle than his wet shirt.

"I do. But I keep a few lures around." He scanned the bank of the pond. "There it is." He went to a small, neatly trimmed bush a few feet away. "I set it down last night, and then Zeb distracted me." He turned to her. "Are you enjoying *yerself*?"

"*Ya,*" she said, her self-consciousness leaving her. "This is the most well-kept pond I've ever seen."

His damp bangs hung above his eyes. "It used to be wilder than this. But Jalon decided to clean it up since so many of us use it." He glanced around. "It's a bit fancy for me, though."

"I agree." She faced him fully now, sitting with her legs crossed. "I always loved the wildness of ponds and lakes. Some things should be kept pristine."

"Does that mean you don't want to fish here again?"

She smiled and shook her head. "Not when the fish are biting this *gut.*"

"Speaking of, I'll let you get back to it. I've got a ton of work to do this afternoon."

She watched as he took his tackle box and walked away. "Bye," she called after him. She'd sat back down on the bank when she heard his voice.

"Nina."

He stood at the edge of the copse of trees surrounding the pond. "*Ya?*" she said.

"Maybe you'd like to *geh* fishing sometime." He glanced down at the ground before looking back at her. "We could, uh, meet here."

Usually she liked to fish by herself, but she was pleased by his invitation. "I'd like that, Ira."

He gave her a small smile. "I'll let you know when." Then he disappeared.

Nina cast her line back into the pond. Fishing with Ira sounded nice, and hopefully they would catch a lot of fish. She liked to cook and eat them almost as much as she liked catching them. She pulled her legs up to her chest and smiled, holding on to her pole more tightly this time. She was happier than she'd been in a long time. Thanks to fishing.

But a little voice in the back of her mind spoke to her. *Thanks to Ira.*

CHAPTER 10

"Your turn, Cevilla."

Cevilla looked at Richard, her friend's face coming into focus. Today he was dressed nearly Amish, with the exception of his short haircut and the fact that his shirt was tailor-made instead of Amish-sewn. He insisted on visiting the barber every two weeks. Cevilla couldn't imagine him with an Amish haircut. She wasn't sure she could imagine him Amish, despite seeing him in a plain shirt, black suspenders, and blue jeans. This was the most casual she'd seen him dress since they'd reunited.

However, she wasn't thinking about Richard's clothes, or the chance he might never join the Amish, which would put their relationship on even more uncertain ground. She was still distracted by her meeting with Delilah last Sunday. They had parted on the wrong note, and that hadn't set well with her. She needed to make some kind of friendly overture to the woman. At the time she'd decided to invite the family to supper, but now she wasn't so sure that was the best thing to do.

"Cevilla?" Richard waved his hand of cards in front of her face. "Are you in there?"

She set down her cards, even though she was one card away from gin, and pushed away from the table. "I need to bake something," she mused out loud as she stood and then walked to her pantry. She opened the door. "Now, what would Delilah and her family like?"

"Um, Cevilla. The card game?"

"We're finished, and you won," she said with a wave of her hand. She looked over her supplies. "I don't have much time to make anything complicated."

Richard's chair scraped on the hardwood floor as he stood. "Mind cluing me in on what's going on in that pretty mind of yours?"

She smiled and peeked around the door. Leave it to Richard to give her an excellent compliment. "I'm going to pay the Stolls a visit tonight. Are you free to drive me over?"

"Usually I'd have my stamp club meeting in Barton, since it's Thursday, but it was canceled this month. So yes, I'm free to take you. Do you want me to drop you off?"

She shook her head and pulled out a bag of flour. Peanut butter cookies sounded good. Besides, those were Richard's favorite, and she would make some extra for him to snack on this week. He was good about not eating too much sugar because of his diabetes, but he couldn't resist peanut butter cookies. She'd make sure his cookies were on the small side.

"Do you want me to stay with you at the Stolls'?" he said. "I need a little clarification here."

"Yes." She shut the pantry and carried the flour and jar of peanut butter to the counter, balancing it in her arm while she leaned against the cane as she walked to the counter. "Please stay with me at the Stolls'."

Richard rose and took the small bag from her. "Mind telling me what tonight's visit is about?"

She set down the peanut butter. "I want a fresh start with Delilah Stoll. We didn't part on friendly terms last Sunday. I want to make that right ASAP, and I've decided this makes the most sense."

"I see." He went to a cabinet and pulled down a bowl. He owned his own house next door, but he'd been here so many times that he felt comfortable in her small home—as though it were his home. She pressed her lips together. *It could be.* But they weren't ready for that. She sighed. They were acting as though they had all the time in the world, which wasn't true for either of them. Yet she wasn't going to marry a man who wasn't Amish. No matter how much she loved him. And she did indeed love Richard.

Cevilla looked up at him, a lump forming in her throat. "Thank you."

He glanced at her. "For what?"

She swallowed. She wasn't used to being this open with her emotions with a man. She'd never had the experience. "For being you."

Richard smiled, the creases around his mouth deepening, making him even more handsome. "You're most welcome. You know I'd do anything for you, Cevilla."

Except join the church. But she didn't want him to do that for her. She wanted him to do it for the Lord—as long as it was God's will.

After she made the cookies with a little bit of Richard's help—mostly taste testing the batter—and had a quick bite to eat, they made their way over to the Stolls'. Again, she thought how nice it was to have another woman in their district closer to her age. She could imagine them spending time together drinking peppermint tea, talking about issues only women of their age would fully understand. She hadn't realized how much she missed peer camaraderie until it was possible to experience it again. She had always been the wise old woman of their community, even when she first moved here. It would be a relief to be plain ole Cevilla to someone other than Richard.

Richard pulled into the driveway and turned off his car's engine. "Is it all right to stop by unannounced? I'm still unsure about the rules of etiquette here."

"I can't exactly call her up, so yes, it is acceptable." She opened the door, but he didn't get out of the car. "Are you coming?" she said, frowning. Had he changed his mind?

He hesitated, then nodded. "Guess I'm still not used to the Amish way. It seems a little presumptuous to be here without an invitation."

She chuckled as she got out of the car. "This isn't California, Richard. We don't stand on ceremony."

She took in the Stoll residence. They had done a lot to this old house in only a short time, and even from the driveway she could see a framed-in addition on the back. She could also see that they'd kept the thin, light-green boards that ran vertically across the front of the house, giving it a nice, if a bit fancy, look. That surprised her. Part of the grass in the yard had been dug up, and she assumed they were expanding the driveway and parking for future guests. The house itself needed fresh paint on the outside. Maybe they were waiting to paint everything one color at the same time. However, the front porch had been cleaned and freshly stained.

Since meeting Delilah and Nina, she'd learned why the Stolls had come to Birch Creek. Cevilla had decided this bed-and-breakfast or inn or whatever they were calling it would be a good addition to the community. A place for visitors to stay was long overdue.

Richard put his hand on her elbow, and they both slowly

walked up the porch steps, taking their time and making good use of their canes. When they reached the front door, she knocked on it, then a moment later gave it another knock, harder this time.

"Give them time to open the door, Cevilla," Richard said, although his tone was gentle.

He was teaching her patience, which had always been in short supply for her. She did as he said and waited a few moments, but there was still no answer. She was about to knock again when it opened. Delilah stood there, her eyes widened with surprise. Then her expression became impassive. "Hello, Cevilla."

"Hello, Delilah."

Delilah looked at the plastic-covered plate of cookies, then at Richard, then back at Cevilla. "Is there something I can do for you?"

"I've been a bit remiss about my hospitality." Cevilla held up the plate and smiled. "These are for you. I thought we could visit for a while. Get to know each other better."

Delilah peered down at the cookies. "I'm allergic to peanut butter."

Cevilla's jaw tightened. "Oh. I'm sorry about that. Perhaps your family members could enjoy them."

"Perhaps."

Cevilla glanced at Richard, who gave her a confused look. Normally it wasn't a problem to drop in uninvited, but Delilah seemed on the verge of proving her wrong.

"Who is it, *Mudder*?" Loren Stoll came up behind Delilah.

"Cevilla Schlabach." Cevilla held out her hand to him and he shook it. "This is my friend, Richard Johnson."

"Loren Stoll." Loren shook Richard's hand, then opened the

door a bit wider. "Come on in. We were just about to start supper. Would you like to join us? Nina and *Mamm* made plenty. We always have room for more."

Loren radiated hospitality, and Cevilla could see that he would make an excellent innkeeper. They'd already eaten, but her curiosity got the best of her. How far along was the construction inside? She glanced at Delilah, who looked like she had downed a bottle of vinegar. Why were her petticoats in such a twist? "We'd love to." Cevilla handed the peanut butter cookies to Delilah and stepped inside.

"Cevilla," Richard looked perplexed. "We've already—"

"Come along." Of course he was going to try to keep her from accepting Loren's invitation, since neither of them were hungry. But unfortunately for Cevilla Schlabach, there were times when nosiness overcame common sense.

"The kitchen's this way," Loren said. "Don't mind the dust." Loren laughed as he gestured around the living room. "We're under construction, as you can see."

Cevilla hobbled through a living area that was neat but had seen better days. This house had been abandoned for a long time, so it was to be expected that it needed repair. She followed him to the kitchen, where the doorway wasn't framed in.

When she walked inside, she froze. *What have we here?* She looked at the stunned faces of four young people and smiled. Martha and Seth were sitting next to each other, across from Nina and a young man she assumed was her brother, Levi. She hadn't met Levi yet, but he had the same cheery face his father had. Nina didn't look as sour as she had on Sunday, but she wasn't as bright as her sibling.

Wait. Cevilla's smile slid from her face. Martha, Seth, Nina, Levi . . . She looked at Delilah, who was putting the plate of cookies on the counter, shoving them far into the corner as if they were contaminated. Well, well, well. Cevilla recognized matchmaking machinations when she saw them. This supper was obviously a setup, and Delilah had to be behind it. This put a kink in plan B, which, as far as Cevilla was concerned, was still in play no matter what she'd led Martha to believe when she'd visited her at Hezekiah's shop. At least Cevilla's version of plan B.

This wouldn't do. Cevilla wasn't going to let this woman get in the way of Martha's and Seth's happiness—even though Martha and Seth had yet to discover said happiness. They never would if Delilah continued to interfere.

Levi stood. Even though he wasn't smiling, he still looked welcoming and good-natured. "I'll grab two more chairs." Then he did smile at Cevilla and Richard. "Welcome to our home."

"*Danki*, Levi," she said, forgetting that she made a special effort to speak only English in Richard's presence. She looked at Martha and Seth, their expressions resembling a deer staring down three sets of headlights. *Don't worry, dears. I'll handle this.* Then she turned to Delilah. "It appears I came just in time."

. . .

Martha watched as the newcomers sat down in the chairs Levi provided, at the additional place settings Nina had made. Good gravy, what was Cevilla doing here? It was bad enough that Delilah had given them all assigned seats, with her sitting next to Levi. But Nina had skillfully bypassed that, taking her seat next to Levi when Delilah had her back turned as she stirred noodles on the stove. Martha had quickly sat down, practically yanking Seth down next to her. Delilah had looked shocked at the change in seating, and then she frowned. Martha was sure she was going to insist they go back to the original seating arrangements, but then they heard the knock at the front door.

"I'll get it," Levi had said, getting up from his chair.

"*I'll* get it." Delilah gave Levi a pointed look, and he sank back into his seat. Loren had followed her a minute later.

Then they both returned, with Cevilla and Richard in tow. Martha saw the sly look on Cevilla's face when she saw her and Seth sitting next to each other. Then she saw it disappear when she glanced at Delilah. Now they were all sitting at a table too small for eight people, with Cevilla and Delilah exchanging narrow glances. Martha had known tonight was going to be difficult, even with Seth's cooperation and then Nina's, once she'd managed to get her alone earlier, just long enough to explain the plan. With the two older women glaring at each other, it felt like a powder keg was about to go off.

"Let's pray." Loren, who seemed oblivious to the tense undercurrent, bowed his head.

Martha followed suit. *Lord, please don't let this become a disaster. I promise I will tell* Mamm *and* Daed *everything tonight when I get home.* She should have done that yesterday, but she'd avoided it. *Mamm* hadn't said anything to her about Seth, which relieved her, but she couldn't bring herself to admit that she and Seth had only pretended to like each other. Yet that was the least of their worries. With Cevilla here, how could she and Seth pretend to like each other? Cevilla would either know they were faking, or worse, she would believe them. Either way, she would take credit for thinking of the idea in the first place.

She felt a nudge against her leg and opened her eyes. Turning to Seth, she saw the tight smile on his face. Then she looked at the rest of the people around the table and saw they were all looking at her. "Needed a bit of extra prayer," she mumbled, trying to smile. But she couldn't pull it off, not with her stomach churning, her guilt growing, and, great, now she was sweating. It was hot in the kitchen, and that didn't help. She tried to inconspicuously wipe the perspiration from underneath her eyes as Loren picked up the platter of fried chicken.

He turned to Cevilla. "White or dark meat?"

"Dark, if you please."

He nodded, took the tongs, and then placed a chicken leg on her plate. He handed the plate to Nina, who was sitting next to her. Nina peered over the plate at Martha, looking as strained as Martha felt. *Just get us through this, Lord.*

"If I had known we would be having *extra* company," Delilah said, picking up a basket of sliced bread, "I would have fried a few more pieces of chicken."

"We don't eat much." Cevilla took the napkin near her plate and placed it in her lap.

"I appreciate your hospitality," Richard said. He sounded polite and looked calm, but Martha thought she detected a glint of annoyance in his eyes. When he glanced at Cevilla, she could see it for sure.

"The more the merrier." Loren eyed his mother. "We need to get used to this, *Mudder.* Lots of extra people will be here once we open the inn, the Lord willing. That's the whole point of starting this business."

Delilah sniffed and put two pieces of bread on her plate. "Not during our personal meals, *sohn.*"

Seth nudged Martha again with his leg. She turned to him, expecting to see that irritated scowl he so often wore. Instead, she saw amusement in his eyes. He leaned closer and said in a low voice that sent a shiver down her spine, "Would you like a slice, Martha?"

"Uh, *ya*." She nodded, and he handed her the basket. She knocked her knee against his thigh. Didn't he realize they had to abandon their plan now? She took the breadbasket and glanced at Cevilla, who was looking mighty pleased with herself. *Oh nee.* Now Martha would have to make explanations to her too.

"Martha, I didn't realize you and Seth knew the Stolls so well," Cevilla said.

"We don't," they said at the same time, making Cevilla's smile grow wider. She looked so smug, they both chuckled, and for a moment Martha forgot this was the worst supper party she'd ever attended.

"I'm glad you came." Nina gave the coleslaw to her father. "Martha and I have become friends."

"Yes," Martha said, smiling at her. "We have." She was glad everyone was speaking English for Richard's sake—even Delilah.

"It's always nice to have *friends* over for supper." Cevilla looked at Delilah. "Don't you think?"

Delilah picked up a plump chicken breast. "*Ya.* Much better than wrangling for a free meal."

Cevilla's expression turned cold.

"The chicken is excellent," Richard said, although he hadn't taken a single bite of the wing he'd selected earlier. "I'm always impressed with Amish cooking."

"I don't normally cook for"—Delilah looked him up and down—"*English* people. But I suppose that's another thing I need to get used to."

"The inn was your idea, Grandmother." Levi poured gravy over his mashed potatoes. "Remember?"

"I didn't realize you knew that," Delilah said tightly.

Martha and Seth exchanged glances again. While this was certainly an uncomfortable conversation, at least everyone seemed to have forgotten the matchmaking goal of the evening. *Thank you, Lord.*

"And it was an excellent idea." Loren smiled at his mother. "I haven't been this happy in a long time."

Nina looked at her dad with a pensive expression. "You haven't?"

"Your grandmother was right. It was time for me to make a change."

Nina nodded and looked down at her plate, but she made no move to eat.

The table grew quiet, except for the sound of people eating. Martha saw Cevilla and Delilah glancing at each other, their expressions strained. Richard kept his head down as he nibbled on his chicken wing, while Levi and Loren, who both still seemed oblivious to the tension, ate their meal with gusto.

Martha looked at Seth. He was using his bread to sop up the leftover gravy on his plate, obviously enjoying the food. Maybe he didn't notice the tension either.

"That was delicious, *Mamm*. You outdid yourself with this meal," Loren said. He turned to Levi. "I think we can get the last of those boards up on the house before the sun goes down. Sol made a good dent in them today."

Levi nodded.

"Wait." Delilah set down her fork. "You haven't had dessert."

Loren pushed away from the table and stood. "No room for dessert."

"I'll have mine later," Levi said, following his father toward the back door.

"But we have company!"

"Can I give you both a hand?" Loren and Levi halted, and Seth set his napkin on the table and looked at Martha. "You don't mind, do you?"

She couldn't figure out if he was serious or playacting. Either way, he didn't need her permission to help Loren and Levi. "Not at all," she said, giving it anyway.

"Thanks, Seth. We can use all the help we can get." Loren looked at Richard. "Interested in supervising?"

"You bet." He didn't look at Cevilla as he took his cane and stood up. "I used to be in construction myself."

"Richard—"

He turned to her. "Come get me when you're ready to go."

Cevilla clamped her mouth shut as the men left the room.

An eerie silence descended on the room as the women stayed in their chairs. Martha wasn't sure what to do. Should she offer to clear the table? Make an excuse for leaving early? Crack a joke to break the tension? She looked at Delilah and Cevilla. No, a joke would be the wrong thing right now.

"*Grossmutter* made a chocolate cake," Nina said, her voice barely above a whisper. "She was famous in our community for her cakes."

"Oh really." Cevilla sat back in her chair. "I make a pretty *gut* blueberry pie myself."

"Pies," Delilah scoffed. "Everyone can make a pie."

"I can't."

They all looked at Martha. She shrugged. "I've tried, but the crust is always soggy. Cooking isn't one of the *mei* strengths."

Delilah frowned. "What about sewing?"

"I can make *mei* own clothes. That's about it."

"Cleaning?"

"Passable." Why was she suddenly being quizzed like this?

"Martha has many admirable qualities. Homemaking isn't the measure of a woman, anyway." Cevilla's gaze softened as she looked at Martha.

"It's the measure of a wife," Delilah said. "Then again, how would you know? I heard you've never been married."

Martha jerked her head toward Delilah, who picked up her napkin and dabbed at the corner of her mouth. Martha didn't appreciate her tone. "A woman doesn't have to be married to be fulfilled."

"Perhaps. But one also wonders what failings a lifelong single woman might have that would drive away a *mann*."

"Cevilla has Richard." Martha lifted her chin.

"Oh, right. An *English mann*."

Cevilla spoke up. "An honorable *English mann*. One of the finest I've ever known."

"Be that as it may, I didn't realize this community was liberal when it came to couples cohabitating."

"We are not cohabitating, as if that's any of *yer* business." Cevilla's voice took on an ominous tone. She stood from the table and took her cane. "Now, if you'll excuse me, *mei friend* and I will depart now." She looked at Nina. "It was a pleasure to meet you, Nina. You have a lovely personality. Clearly you don't take after *yer grossmutter*."

"Cevilla." Martha shot up from the chair, but she didn't say anything else. Cevilla was being rude, but Delilah had asked for it with her distasteful comment.

Cevilla was already opening the back door. Martha had never seen her like this. She was really upset. Martha hurried and followed her outside. "Cevilla," she said. It didn't take long for her to catch up with the woman.

Cevilla turned around. They weren't that far from the house, and there was a possibility their conversation would be heard, but that didn't stop her from speaking her mind. "I have never met a more *insufferable* woman in *mei* life."

Martha thought Cevilla had been insufferable, too, especially a minute ago. "That doesn't mean you can be rude to her. We turn the other cheek, right?"

"Can't you see what she's doing? She wants to match you and Seth with her grandchildren." She tapped her cane on the concrete patio. "How impudent."

"You're trying to do the same thing with Seth and me. We've figured that out, by the way."

"That's different."

Martha put her hands on her hips. "How? You're both trying to force something that isn't there."

"That's not what I saw." Her expression turned crafty. "Seems you and Seth are getting along quite well."

"That's because . . . Oh, forget it." She was tired of this. Tired of everything that had to do with romance and relationships. "You need to apologize to Delilah."

Cevilla paused, her heated expression dissolving into contriteness. "I do. But not now. I need to cool off before I say something I really regret." She turned and yelled, "Richard! We're leaving."

Richard, who was talking to Loren near the front of the addition while Levi and Seth nailed plywood to the floor beams, turned to her. "One minute," he said.

"Now!"

Richard's bushy eyebrows went up, but he didn't move. He

continued to talk to Loren while Cevilla tapped her foot impatiently. Finally, he shook Loren's hand and made his way slowly, walking more slowly than normal, in her direction. When he reached her, he looked at Martha. "Have a pleasant evening," he said, a sweet smile on his face. But that changed when he turned to Cevilla. "Now I'm ready to go."

Martha watched this interaction in shock. She'd never seen Richard lose his temper, or even raise his voice. But his eyes were steely cold as he faced down Cevilla. He wasn't a man who would be bossed around.

Cevilla nodded, her lips in a thin line. Then she followed Richard to the driveway. When they disappeared around the corner of the house, Martha heard the back door open. She turned to see Nina walking toward her.

"That went well." Nina sighed and stood next to Martha.

"I guess it could have been worse. And it spared Seth and me from having to pretend in front of *yer grossmutter.*"

Nina frowned. "Weren't you pretending in there?"

Martha shook her head. "What do you mean?"

"The way you two looked at each other." Her frown turned to confusion. "You even giggled at the same time."

"We didn't giggle." She lifted her chin. "More like a small chuckle."

"It was a giggle." A smile lifted at the corner of Nina's mouth.

"*Anyway,*" Martha said, setting aside what Nina was insinuating, "I'm sorry about Cevilla."

"And I'm sorry about Delilah."

"Do you think they realize how alike they are?" Martha asked, finally able to crack a smile. Bossy, nosy, and both 100 percent sure they were right.

Nina laughed. "They have *nee* idea."

CHAPTER 11

Seth nailed the last board into the floor of the Stolls' addition, then stood up. His back was dripping with sweat, but he wasn't as tired as he thought he'd be after another night of tossing and turning, then a full day's work on the farm before coming here for supper. A supper that turned out to be more entertaining than expected. Cevilla and Delilah were two peas in a pod, all right. Hopefully they would get over their differences and become friends, but so far they were acting like sworn enemies.

Even better, he'd been spared from faking any romantic feelings for Martha. He also enjoyed the food. The fried chicken was perfect, and the gravy didn't have a single lump. He was willing to lend a hand when it came to construction projects, so he felt good about helping Loren and Levi. Other than the questionable behavior of two women who should have known better, he had a decent time.

Still, he was ready to go home. He'd met Martha here, so he didn't have to take her home. But he needed to talk to her before he left—alone.

"*Danki* for helping us," Levi said, handing Seth a bottle of water.

He opened it immediately and drained it. "*Nee* problem," he said, gasping a little. He'd put that away a little fast. "Glad to help."

"Don't worry. Next time you come over, you won't have to pitch in."

Next time? Did Levi have the same agenda his grandmother did?

Levi flipped his empty bottle in his hand. "I was glad *Daed* suggested working on the *haus* tonight. It's bad enough that *mei grossmutter* is doing her matchmaking thing again, but her and Cevilla . . ." He shook his head and laughed. "I think Delilah has met her match. I didn't think I'd ever see the day."

Seth nodded, glad Levi and his grandmother weren't on the same side when it came to her matchmaking attempts. Relief washed over him. Not only was he finished pretending tonight, but because Martha had set things straight with her parents, he didn't have anything to worry about. Finally, he was free of this mess.

His relief was short-lived, though. Cevilla was tenacious when it came to matchmaking, and he imagined Delilah would be too. *Don't borrow trouble.* His father's stance, straight from the Bible, applied to this situation. He didn't need to guess at the future.

He turned and saw Martha and Nina standing on the patio, talking. This was his chance to speak to Martha, if he could get her away from Nina. "If you don't mind, I'll skip dessert," he said as Loren joined them. "I need to head home."

"Not at all. I'm bushed too." Levi pushed back his damp hair.

"We all are. It's been a long day." Loren turned to Seth. "It was nice having company tonight." He chuckled. "Our unexpected visitors, especially."

Seth was glad to see Loren and Levi were both good-natured

about the whole thing. "Cevilla and Richard are great people, once you get to know them."

"I can tell they are," Loren said. "And *mei mamm* means well. She can be prickly sometimes—"

"Sometimes?" Levi said, raising his eyebrow.

Loren gave him a warning look, but then turned back to Seth. "She cares a lot about *mei kinner*. She took the place of their *mamm* after she died."

"I'm sorry for *yer* loss," Seth said.

Both Levi and Loren looked somber. "Don't hold tonight against her," Levi said.

"She has *gut* intentions," Loren added.

The three men walked to the house, stopping when they reached Martha and Nina. "Can I talk to you for a minute?" he said to Martha. "After I *geh* inside and thank Delilah for the meal."

"She went to bed," Nina said. "Said she had a headache."

Seth wasn't surprised to hear that. "Will you thank her for me, then?"

"Of course."

He gave Martha a questioning look, then tilted his head in the direction of the driveway.

Confusion passed over her face, but she nodded. "I'll be right back," she said, then walked with Seth to the front of the house. "Is everything all right?"

"*Ya.*" He dug into his pocket, then pulled out a key. "Here."

She looked at it as it lay in the palm of his hand. "I don't understand."

"This is a key to the shop." Although his father said he needed some time to get things together to teach Seth about the farm, *Daed* had already started his lessons. Today's lesson had been about cultivation techniques, and tomorrow bright and early he was going to the livestock auction with his father to bid on a bull and a few dairy cows. "You'll do this on *yer* own," *Daed* had said. "I'll be there if you have any questions."

"Seth?"

"Right. The key." He put it in her hand. When she didn't fold her fingers over it, he folded them for her. "I'm going to be busy in the near future." He frowned. "Really busy. I won't have much time to work in the shop."

"I still don't understand why you're giving me a key."

He didn't completely understand it himself. When he woke up this morning, he knew he couldn't continue giving Martha lessons, and this time it wasn't because he didn't want to. A part of him did. He had enjoyed seeing her enthusiasm, and he had to admit it was nice to have somebody with him in the shop. She was also talented; anyone could see that. But he'd shifted his priorities to his father, and he didn't think Martha should pay the price for that. "If you want to use *mei* tools and the spare wood to practice, you can. I also have some books I purchased with *gut* instructions. Feel free to look at those if you need to."

"Seth?" She looked up at him, her eyes wide with surprise. "Are you serious about this?"

He nodded. "The only thing I ask is that you continue to keep the shop a secret." He leaned down and looked into her eyes. "I need you to promise me that you will."

She put her fist to her chest. "I promise." She grinned. "I can't believe you're letting me do this."

"I can't either," he muttered. Maybe he was making a huge mistake. Maybe he might as well be putting an ad in *The Budget* announcing the existence of his secret woodshop. Maybe he—

She threw her arms around his neck and hugged him hard. "*Danki*," she said in his ear. "*Danki* so much."

His hands went around her waist, as automatically as if they belonged there. He inhaled the scent of her shampoo, the freshness of her dress, and possibly the lingering scent of fried chicken. He'd never smelled anything so wonderful in his whole life.

She pulled away from him. "I promise, promise, *promise* I won't tell anyone about the shop."

"Or take anyone there."

"That too." She opened her hand and peeked at the key, grinning the whole time. "I'm so excited. I can't wait to *geh* to the shop tomorrow after work."

He shoved his hands into his pockets and smiled. His heart swelled, seeing her so happy. He paused. When did it matter to him that Martha was happy? Sure, he didn't want anything bad to happen to her, but until she'd discovered his woodshop, he hadn't thought about her too much. Seeing her beam with joy, he was grateful he'd listened to that small voice in his heart telling him to trust her with a key.

"I've got to get going," he said, still grinning and unable to stop. "I'm so glad tonight's over, by the way."

"Me too." She clasped her hands together. "*Nee* more pretending."

"Right," he said softly. "*Nee* more pretending."

"I'm heading home too. I just want to say good-bye to Nina."

"All right." He didn't move. It seemed weird that they didn't have another plan to see each other. But wasn't that the way he wanted it?

Martha headed for the house. "Bye," she said, waving. "And thank you again!"

He watched her go before he turned and headed home. Tonight had turned out better than he'd imagined it would. That wasn't much of a stretch, since he'd expected disaster. But he'd had a good meal, had been entertained by the Cevilla and Delilah standoff, and then had lent some elbow grease to a good cause. To top it off, he'd made Martha happy. That was better than any dessert, no matter how good a cook Delilah was.

He didn't realize he hadn't told Martha when he wanted the key back until he was almost home. Now that he thought about it, though, he wasn't sure when he'd be back to the shop. He only knew he was leaving it in good hands.

· · ·

"Pouting doesn't become you, Cevilla," Richard said as he pulled his Mercedes into Cevilla's driveway. "Neither does nosiness, bossiness, or rudeness."

Cevilla crossed her arms over her chest. She was aware that she looked like a spoiled child, and she had to admit she felt like one. She also knew better than to behave like this. What was it about that woman that pushed her buttons? "We were invited," she said. "What was I supposed to do, decline?"

"Yes, especially after we saw that Seth and Martha were there." He shut off the engine and turned to her. "We crashed their dinner party."

"It wasn't a party." She looked out the window, unable to face Richard. She was embarrassed. She shouldn't have bossed him the way she had. He had deservedly put her in her place. And he did not deserve her derision for it. "I'm sorry," she said.

"I know you are."

She turned at his gentle tone and saw the forgiveness in his eyes. "I behaved badly, didn't I?"

"A tad." He took her hand and held it. "More than a tad."

"She was trying to set up Seth and Martha with Nina and Levi."

"They're lovely young people, so I don't blame her."

"But Seth and Martha are meant to be together." At Richard's stern look, she added, "I believe they are."

He rubbed his thumb over her hand. The skin was wrinkled, and the veins poked out from her thin skin, but that didn't stop him from kissing the back of her hand. "Cevilla, your heart is in a good place. But you need to let these young folks find their way to each other without your interference."

"And what about Delilah? She's interfering too."

"So that makes it okay for you to do the same thing?"

Cevilla was about to say that she was the one who started the matchmaking ball rolling, but she knew Richard wouldn't like that answer. "No," she said, looking at their clasped hands. "It doesn't."

"Why don't we go on a trip together? Any place you'd like to visit, we can. Just name it."

"Are you trying to get me out of Birch Creek?"

"I'm trying to keep you occupied enough so you won't meddle in other people's business."

"I can't go on a trip with you." She pulled her hand from his. "You know why." She opened the door. "It's getting hot in here. I'm going inside."

"Can I come in?"

She turned. She wanted him to come inside. But it was getting late, and she had some praying—and asking for forgiveness—to do. "Not tonight."

He nodded. "All right. But I want you to know . . . I've been thinking about the future."

Her heart leapt a tiny bit. "I don't want you to rush into anything. This has to be God's timing."

"I know, Cevilla. I won't make a decision unless I'm sure God is leading me to it." He touched her cheek. "I know this isn't easy on you. It's not easy for me either."

"We aren't promised easy," Cevilla said. "We're promised that the Lord will be with us during the hard times." She smiled. "God brought us together after all these years. We can wait as long as he wants us to."

"That's what I believe too." He leaned over and kissed her cheek. "I'll see you tomorrow, then?"

Butterflies multiplied in her stomach. Richard had a way of making her feel decades younger. "Tomorrow."

As he always did, he waited for her to get inside the house before he left. She shook her head. Who would have thought that at eighty-something years old she would be dropped off at her house like a teenager after a date?

She'd meant what she said about God's timing. She was willing to wait for Richard to make his decision. She wanted God's will above all else.

Cevilla hobbled to her bedroom, exhausted. Tonight had been draining. She had good intentions about visiting Delilah. But the way she had sneered at Cevilla's peanut butter cookies had really burned her butter. Then she started insulting Richard, and that had been the end of that.

In her younger days she wouldn't have put up with Delilah's insults, but she didn't have it in her to verbally hit back the way she used to. That was probably a good thing, since she'd been known to impart harsh words when she should have kept her mouth shut.

Cevilla sank onto the edge of her bed. Richard was right. She needed to leave the kids alone. It wasn't the first time she'd realized her meddling wasn't needed—or wanted. But what if Seth and Martha didn't see how good they were for each other? What if they let their lack of awareness get in the way of love? *That's not for me to worry about.*

"Lord," she whispered, "I need some straightening out—and only you can do it."

· · ·

Delilah took off her *kapp* and placed it on the empty spot on her dresser. She unbound her hair, brushed it out, braided it, and tried not to throw the hairbrush across the room. She had spent years trying to keep her spitfire temper in check. Cevilla Schlabach had almost undone all her training.

She placed the hairbrush on the dresser next to the *kapp* and sank onto the edge of her bed. "Lord, I was not at *mei* best today." She looked up at the ceiling, then down at her hands in her lap. Tonight had been a disaster, and she knew she was partly to blame. But she had recognized that look in Cevilla's eyes when she showed up on her doorstep. She was being nosy, plain and simple. *Just like you were when you went to the Yoders'.* Delilah really didn't like it when God pointed out her hypocrisy.

Well, none of it mattered anymore. Seth and Martha may have told her they weren't interested in each other, but anyone with eyeballs could see they were. At least Birch Creek had other prospects for Nina. But what about Levi? Martha was his only hope, at least when it came to a local girl. She knew her grandson well enough to know he would be completely entrenched in their innkeeping business, possibly for years. When would he have time to find a wife?

A knock sounded on the door, and she lifted her head. "Who is it?"

"Me, *Mamm.*"

"Come in, Loren."

Her son entered, still wearing dusty clothes from working on the addition. He looked tired, but not bone weary, the way he had for years after his wife died. She hadn't realized there would be so much work to be done getting this inn started. She also hadn't anticipated that Loren would want to do a lot of the work himself, even though he'd hired Sol Troyer too. *He really could use a wife.* But she wasn't sure she had the strength to find him one after tonight's debacle. "Do you need something, *sohn*?"

"We need to talk." He came inside and shut the door. "I'm too dirty to sit on the bed," he said, gesturing to his clothes. "I'll take only a moment of *yer* time." His chest heaved as he took a big breath, then blew it out. "I want you to stay out of Levi and Nina's business."

Shocked, she pressed her hand against her chest. "I'm not in their business," she said, fibbing.

"*Ya*, you are. I know you think I'm oblivious, and sometimes I'm too passive when it comes to *mei kinner*. But this time I'm putting *mei* foot down. Let them be, *Mamm*." He swallowed. "You've done an excellent job raising them. Miriam would be pleased."

Tears sprang to Delilah's eyes. "I never wanted to take her place as a mother."

"I know. But you did, and we needed it. They're grown now, though. And whether they get married or stay here in Birch Creek or *geh* back to Wisconsin isn't our business anymore. Let them live their own lives." He smirked. "I let you keep on railroading mine."

"I don't railroad anyone—"

"I'm kidding, *Mamm*." He chuckled.

She regarded her son for a moment. He did look happy, despite being tired. Even now, when he was exhausted from work and annoyed with her meddling, she saw a joy in his eyes she hadn't seen in a long time. "You're glad we're here, then?"

"I am. I know I was uneasy about making this move and investing so much money, but I really believe we can make this a success. And I don't know how to explain it, but I feel like Birch Creek is home. You were right, as usual. I needed a kick start." He backed toward the door. "Do we have a deal, *Mamm*? Will you let the *kinner* live their lives their own way?"

"*Ya*," she said, her throat thick. His words had hit home. She needed to step back and give her grandchildren space. She'd always trusted God with everything, but she now saw she hadn't trusted him when it came to Nina and Levi. Nor had she trusted them. That was going to change—right now. "I'll mind *mei* own business when it comes to Levi and Nina's love lives."

"All aspects of their lives."

"All right. But don't expect me to not offer *mei* two cents from time to time."

"Oh, I wouldn't dare." He grinned. "What would we do without *yer* two cents? It usually ends up being a nickel's worth anyway."

After Loren left, Delilah pondered his words—and her

behavior tonight. Wayne had always been the one to keep her in check. But he died when Loren was a teen. It had been just her and her son's family ever since. Now Loren was stepping into the role of her conscience, just like her husband had. Her chest squeezed. She missed that man every day.

She'd been terrible to Cevilla, and she had seen the look in the woman's eyes when she made the dig about her being single. She blew out a breath. *You're right, Lord. I have to make amends.* Not just to Cevilla but to Nina and Levi too.

. . .

On Friday evening, Nina tossed her baited hook into the water, crossed her legs, and looked up at the trees. It was near dusk and after suppertime, and as she'd expected, no one was here at the Chupps' pond. What she didn't expect was for her grandmother to suggest she go fishing tonight.

"I've seen a couple of ponds around here," *Grossmammi* said as they washed the supper dishes. "You haven't been fishing in a long while, have you?"

She'd bitten the inside of her cheek. She didn't want to lie to her grandmother, but she also didn't want to tell her about her fishing expedition the other day. Levi would get caught in a fib too.

Fortunately, *Grossmammi* didn't stop talking long enough for Nina to answer. "Why don't you *geh* fishing this evening?"

Stunned, she turned to her grandmother, her hands covered in soapy water. "What?"

"*Geh* fishing. There's plenty of daylight left. I'll take care of the rest of the dishes."

"Are you sure?"

Grossmammi looked at her. "I'm sure. You love fishing. You should get to do what you love. I'm sorry I held you back from that."

Nina smiled as she remembered the conversation. Her grandmother had shooed her away after that, and she had sped to the barn to get her pole and fishing tackle. She watched the ripples on the pond as a light breeze fluttered over the water. She didn't know what had gotten into her grandmother, but she wasn't going to question it.

She pulled her knees to her chest, rested her chin on them, and closed her eyes. She wasn't sure how long she'd sat there with her eyes closed, holding the pole and listening to the sounds of the birds and cicadas and a hoot owl she hadn't noticed the last time she was here, but when she opened them, she saw Ira standing beside her. Instead of being surprised like she had the last time, she was pleased. Deep down she had been hoping she would see him.

"I didn't want to disturb you," he said, looking down at her. "Mind if I join you?"

She didn't mind at all. She patted the grassy spot next to her. When he sat down, she noticed he didn't have a pole or bait. "You're not fishing?"

He shook his head. "Nah. Sometimes I come out here just to enjoy the peace and quiet."

"But it's Friday night. Don't you have plans?"

"Like a date?" He raised a dark eyebrow, then looked away.

"I was thinking more of a social event. Don't you have singings and frolics here?"

"Yeah, but I've decided to quit going to those." He tugged on a blade of grass. "I used to think I might have a chance with someone . . ." He shook his head. "She's made it clear she's not interested." He looked at Nina. "I'm not gonna beg someone to like me."

Nina couldn't imagine him having to beg anyone to like him. He was very attractive, not to mention friendly and nice. She didn't know him that well, but what she did know she found appealing. It also dawned on her who he was interested in. "You're talking about Martha."

"Obviously. She's the only *maedel* in Birch Creek."

"I see." She looked at her bare feet. Martha wasn't the only girl in the community now. Then again, why would Ira notice that? Nina was used to being treated like one of the boys and ignored as a girl. Why would Ira see her any differently? The bigger question was why did being ignored as a girl matter to her? It never had before.

"Sorry," he said, touching her shoulder. "I shouldn't be dumping *mei* problems on you."

"That's all right." She lightly tugged on the line, so the bait and hook would move in the water and hopefully catch a fish's attention. "I've been told I'm a *gut* listener."

"You are." He kept his gaze on hers for a moment, then spoke. "Anyway, there's not much to do tonight. Judah's next door with the Chupps, and Seth and *Daed* have been thick as thieves lately. They've got the farm ledgers spread out on the table at home, and they're looking them over for some reason." He shrugged. "Can't think of anything more boring than that, so I decided to come here and talk to the fish. They're *gut* listeners too." He grinned.

She smiled back. "Where's *yer mamm*?"

"At *mei schwester* Karen's. She and Ivy and *Mamm* are doing some kind of craft thing. They usually do when they get together." He laid back on the grassy bank and clasped his hands behind his head. "I wonder when we're going to get some rain. We sure do need it."

She looked at her pole, then glanced at him over her shoulder. "Do you want to use *mei* fishing rod? I don't mind sharing."

He shook his head. "I'm fine here."

Nina faced the pond and tugged on the rod again. Maybe the fish weren't biting tonight. That would be okay. She didn't always have to catch something to enjoy fishing.

A few seconds later she felt a pull on her line. She jumped to her feet and started to reel it in.

"You get a bite?" Ira scrambled up from the ground and stood next to her.

"*Ya.*" She pulled on the pole, then turned the reel again. A sunfish dangled from the hook as she pulled it out of the water.

"That's a *gut*-sized one," Ira said.

Nina nodded. It was a nice-looking fish. She brought it closer, released it from the hook, and then let it go back into the pond.

Ira looked at her. "Catch and release tonight?"

"*Ya.* I forgot to bring *mei* creel. I don't feel like taking fish home and cleaning them tonight anyway." She turned and looked for her container of bait.

Ira spotted it before she did and handed it to her. She opened it and pulled out a ball of bread. She hadn't had time to find any live worms.

"Do you want some live bait? I can run to the *haus* and get some."

"*Nee.* This seems to be working fine." She cast the line back into the pond, then sat down.

Ira paused. Then he said, "I'll be right back."

After a few minutes Ira returned with a pole and some bait.

"I changed *mei* mind," he said, plopping down next to her. "Couldn't sit here and just watch you fish." He baited his hook, then cast his line.

They didn't say anything, just sat in the dusky evening and waited for the fish to bite again. To the west the sun had disappeared behind the trees, and fireflies began to appear. Nina couldn't think of a better way to spend a Friday night. Her grandmother had encouraged her to fish, which was a miracle. She'd made a friend in Martha, and now possibly with Ira. Birch Creek wasn't as horrible as she'd initially thought it would be.

"This is nice," she said, turning to him.

Ira looked at her and smiled. "*Ya.* It definitely is."

CHAPTER 12

As the rest of July and half of August passed, Martha couldn't have been happier. She spent two, sometimes three nights a week in Seth's woodshop. She pored over the dusty woodworking books on his shelves and familiarized herself with each tool. By the end of the second week she was already carving some fancy designs in the wooden plaques she enjoyed making. She'd even bought stencils and had started to carve some simple signs with short verses or inspirational words on them. She often lost track of time while she was working.

Except at church, she hadn't seen Seth since their supper at the Stolls'. Other than at the shop and church, she hadn't seen anyone, really, as she had become consumed with her new hobby. She now understood why Seth wanted to keep this a secret. No one was here to bother her or question what she was doing. She was free to create.

The only exception to her happiness was the fact that she still hadn't told her parents she and Seth weren't together. When she arrived home from the Stolls' that night when Cevilla and Richard had unexpectedly showed up, her parents had been in bed. She had decided to tell them the next morning. But when she woke up, they'd left on an impromptu trip to Holmes County, and when they returned, she was in the woodshop. When she got home and her *mamm* asked if she'd been with Seth, she'd said yes.

"Have you decided to keep *yer* dating a secret for now?" her mother asked.

Martha knew some couples preferred that, unwilling to face scrutiny from the community. "*Ya*," she'd quickly answered, glad for a plausible excuse. "We have. If you and *Daed* could keep this to *yerselves*, and not even talk to Seth's parents about it—"

"Of course. We understand."

Those were outright lies, but she didn't want to break her word to Seth, and she realized it was better if her parents thought she was spending time with him. That way she could keep his secret, and they wouldn't ask any more questions. They seemed pleased about her and Seth being together.

But now as she unlocked the door to the woodshop, guilt plagued her, and it was growing stronger each day. She would have to tell them the truth soon, or the guilt would swallow her up. Nothing was going on between her and Seth, and it never would.

For now, she was going to focus on her woodworking. She chose a stencil and took the sanded plaque she'd made the other day to the worktable. Carefully, she started to carve the word *love* on the plaque in large letters.

The door to the shop opened.

Martha whirled around, her heart thumping in her chest. Then she saw it was Seth. "Goodness, you scared me," she said, leaning limply against the worktable. "I thought I locked the door."

"You did. I have a key too." He walked into the woodshop and looked around, then let out a low whistle. "Wow, is this *mei* shop?"

Hearing him talk about the shop so possessively was a stark reminder that she was the interloper here, even though he'd given her free rein. How long would he allow her access? Surely he wanted to get back to the hobby he loved—a hobby he preferred to do alone. The thought of not being able to come here and work made her heart wrench. She shoved the feeling aside. "I did a little cleaning," she said, giving him a smile not 100 percent genuine.

"I'd say you did more than a little." He walked around the shop. She had cleaned all the shelves, organized his tools, brought bins for the different sized wood and categorized them, wiped off his books and put them all in the same place, and always left the shop clean and swept before she left. Since she had barely started on today's project, it looked pristine.

"I can't think in chaos." She bit her lip. "Not that I'm saying *yer* shop was chaotic."

He laughed. "Oh, it was. I don't have a problem with it, though."

Her teeth sank into her lip further. "Do you have a problem with it now?"

Seth looked at her, his expression sincere. "*Nee.* I absolutely don't."

Relieved, she picked up her plaque and prepared to put it away. "I can work on this later."

But he didn't answer her. He was looking at two of the shelves she'd cleared off to put her finished projects. They were full of the lacquered plaques. He pulled one down. "God is love," he said, reading the words aloud.

She set down the plaque and hurried to him. "That was *mei* first one," she said, taking it from him, feeling self-conscious. "It's not that *gut.*"

He touched the plaque. "May I?"

After a pause, she nodded and let him take it. He studied it for a few minutes, then set it back on the shelf. "You're doing *gut* work."

"*Danki*," she said softly. His compliment meant a lot to her.

He took down another plaque, looked at it, and then replaced it and looked at another. She put her hands behind her back, the self-consciousness coming back. The plaques had a variety of small designs on them, from flowers to ladybugs to curlicues that weren't perfect, but gave the end product homemade charm.

"You learned all this in a month?" Seth turned and faced her.

She nodded. "You have some great instructional books."

"I guess I do," he mumbled, glancing around the shop again.

Martha went back to the worktable and picked up the plaque she'd been working on. "Like I said, I can work on this later." She looked at him. "If it's all right with you, that is."

His expression was impassive. Then he spoke. "You can work on it now. I can't stay long. I just came because . . ."

"You missed being here?"

"*Ya.*"

"Then why don't you come back?"

He sighed. He looked hot and tired, his forearms tanned and muscular. "I don't have the time. I've got plenty to keep me busy." He gave her a half smile. "I'm glad *mei* things are going to *gut* use."

She saw a forlorn look in his eyes, as if he'd given up on his hobby completely. But there was no way he'd do that. He couldn't give this up. She understood that now more than ever. To cheer him up, she gestured to the shelving unit. "Did you see where I put *yer* projects?" She'd set them up in a nice display.

"*Ya*," he muttered, looking away. "I saw them."

For some reason he seemed disappointed, and she didn't want that. She searched her mind for something to bring a smile to his face. *A smile I've missed.* "I need some help with sweep cuts," she said.

"*Yer* sweep cuts look *gut* to me."

"They could be better. Would you show me?"

He hesitated, then finally nodded and walked over to the worktable.

They practiced sweep cuts on scrap wood for a little while. "I can see where you're having the problem." He put his hand over hers on the handle of the tool. "Keep *yer* wrist relaxed. Like this."

The shiver down her spine was back. It intensified when he moved to stand behind her. Because he was several inches taller, he could guide her hand with the tool and still see what he was doing.

"Right," he said, his voice low. "You're getting the hang of it."

In truth she had lost her concentration the moment he put his hand on hers. She had no idea if she was getting the hang of anything. All she knew was that the shiver was gone, replaced with a wildly thumping heart. But instead of warning bells going off in her brain, she began to relax.

Seth took a step closer until her back was against his chest. Thinking he would move after he realized he was so close, she was surprised when he remained in place. His hand stilled in the middle of the cut, and she could feel him breathing near her ear.

Then he cleared his throat and moved away. "Uh, yeah. You've got it now."

She turned to see him backing up. "Yeah," she said, feeling a little breathless. "I think I do."

He stopped when his back hit the door. "I, uh, I've got to get home. Lots of, uh, work to do there."

"Right." She couldn't keep her gaze from his. Her heart still hammered in her chest, and she realized she didn't want him to leave. "You don't have to—"

"Bye." He threw open the door and ran out.

She leaned against the worktable, willing her heart to slow. As it regained its normal rhythm, she began to think clearly. Oh bother. Why had she reacted to him like that? As though she liked him? As though she were attracted to him? *Very attracted*.

Martha sighed, confused, her woodworking completely forgotten. All she could think about was how she'd felt when Seth was close to her. It felt right being that close to him in the woodshop he loved so much. Very right, even though she knew it was wrong.

· · ·

Seth slowed down in the middle of the woods before he reached the field that backed up to his father's land. He bent over, put his hands on his knees, and drew in a deep breath. He'd run the entire way from his woodshop—in the heat, no less. What had happened back there? All he'd wanted to do was show Martha a different way to hold the tool. That had turned into moving closer to her . . . and then wanting to turn her around and hold her in his arms.

He stood up and blew out a breath. How stupid was he to think Martha would want him to embrace her? He'd expected her to elbow him in the stomach when he moved near her. Instead she stood there, and he thought he heard a small sigh.

That had nearly undone him, and he knew he had to get out of there. Because if he hadn't, he would have gone with his impulse. And from the crazy way he'd been acting this summer, he would have done something completely wrong . . . like kiss her.

He started to walk, although slowly. He hadn't expected her to be in the shop, much less see everything she'd done to it. The transformation was impressive. He hadn't realized how messy his shop had been until it was cleaned up, and he did like it. He also liked her carvings. She had innate talent, that was plain. With a little more practice and some polish on those plaques, she could easily sell her creations.

She was ahead of him already, and he'd been doing woodworking for more than a year. His creations paled in comparison, and a stab of jealousy hit him. This was his dream, not hers. She didn't have the right to be better at it than him. Then he realized the ridiculousness of his own thoughts. She had a gift. He didn't.

Not that it mattered anyway. His father had started to show some more signs of poor eyesight over the past month, and tomorrow he had an appointment in Cleveland to see a specialist. That made their time together more urgent, and Seth had been consumed with the ins and outs of farmwork, both the technical side and the nuances of it. He had to admit that he was starting to reevaluate his feelings about farming. No doubt it was demanding work, but it was also challenging and satisfying. He had a new appreciation for the food on the table now that he knew exactly what it took to get it there. Before he'd seen the work as chores; now he was seeing it as more.

But he still missed being at the shop and had planned to do some simple whittling this evening. Then he'd found Martha there. He'd genuinely thought she might do a bit of fiddling around with the wood and tools a few times, get bored, and then give up. Now he could see that wasn't going to happen. It shouldn't happen.

He'd used the farm as an excuse to get away from Martha, but he had a little time before he had to get back. He started to walk down the road, away from his house. The temperatures in August had been as hot as they were in July, but today they were a bit cooler. They'd had a few pop-up showers over the past couple of weeks, but the ground was still parched, and some of the leaves were already brown. They'd skipped their normal autumn color.

A buggy approached. He recognized the couple inside as it neared. Martha's parents. He waved at them, expecting them to pass him by. Instead, they pulled to a stop beside him.

"Hi, Seth," her mother said, a surprised look on her face. "Where's Martha?"

"Martha?"

"We know you two want to keep *yer* relationship a secret. You haven't even been to our *haus* for weeks. But we already know how you feel about each other." She tapped her husband's knee. "Don't we, John?"

He nodded and looked at him. "We thought Martha was with you tonight."

"She told you that?"

"She didn't have to," her mother said. "She's usually with you when she goes out during the week. Right?"

Realization dawned. Martha had never told her parents they'd been pretending to like each other that night at their house, all for the sake of implementing plan B at the Stolls'. "I was with her earlier," he said, anger rising inside him as he tried to think of an excuse to tell them. He wasn't about to ruin his secret because Martha couldn't stop lying. "I needed to run home for something."

"Isn't *yer haus* in the opposite direction?"

"Um, *ya*. But I'm heading to . . . Ruby's *haus*. Martha's meeting me there."

Her mother tilted her head, a puzzled expression on her face.

"Regina, we need to get to the Beilers'. We're late as it is." Martha's father tapped the reins on the horse's back.

"Nice to see you," her mother said, the confusion still there as Martha's father chirruped to the horse. "Don't be a stranger, now."

Seth waved and grinned, the grin falling from his face as they disappeared down the road. He continued to walk a little farther as if he were really going to Ruby's. When the Detweilers had turned at the end of the road, he took off in the direction of the woodshop.

He was out of breath when he got there. He'd run more in the span of a half hour than he had all summer. He tried to open the door, but Martha had locked it after he left, something he would have appreciated if he wasn't so upset. Maybe she'd left too. He hoped not. If she had, he'd have to go to her house and find her. The thought of running back there made him even angrier.

His key clicked in the lock and he opened the door. She was placing her plaque on the shelf with the rest of them, a satisfied look on her face right before she turned her head toward him. Her eyes widened with surprise. "Seth, what are you doing back—"

"You didn't tell *yer* parents, did you?" He stormed over to her until he was almost standing on her toes. "You didn't tell them the truth."

. . .

Martha's stomach turned with dread. "How did you find out?"

"I just saw them. They thought I was with you, or you were with me. Whatever, they thought we were together. Apparently, they think we've been together all this time." He leaned over her, furious. "Don't they?"

"*Ya*," she squeaked.

He groaned. "You said you were going to tell them it was all a ruse."

"I know. And I intended to. I promise I did." She threaded her fingers together. He was really angry, and she didn't blame him.

"Who else thinks we're an *item*?" He made quotes in the air.

"*Nee* one else. I haven't said a word about us to anyone."

"Us?" He ground out. "There's *nee* us, Martha."

She was painfully aware of that, now that she truly wished there was. She'd thought she'd given up on men, only to find herself with intense feelings for Seth. Feelings he clearly didn't return. "I know. But it was a *gut* excuse. They didn't question where I went as long as they thought I was with you. So I didn't have to lie to them to be here." She tried to smile. "See, I was keeping *yer* secret."

He glared at her, looked away, then rubbed his eyes with his thumb and finger. "So you're saying this is *mei* fault."

She held two fingers close together. "A little."

Seth blew out a breath, looked up at the ceiling, then looked at her. "I guess I can see that." He sounded calmer, and the redness in his face had subsided. "This is both our faults."

"But mostly mine." Martha shook her head. "I'm sorry, Seth." Her voice started to wobble. "I didn't mean to cause you trouble."

"Hey." He put his hand on her shoulder. "It's all right. We'll figure this out."

She looked up at him, and their gazes locked for a moment. Then Seth moved away from her. He shoved his hands into the pockets of his grass-stained work pants. "We need to tell them. Together. *Tonight*."

Martha's mouth dropped open. "Tonight? Why don't we wait until tomorrow—"

"Because it's time to end this. All of it, once and for all."

She tilted her head, stunned. It really was her fault they were in this mess, all because she'd been a coward. She was hiding behind lies and running away so she wouldn't have to do something hard—be truthful. Seth had only wanted to keep his secret safe, which he had a right to. She wouldn't even know about this place if she hadn't barged into it when she was running away from the other single men at Ruby's. He didn't need to face her parents. She did. "*Nee.* I'll tell them. It's *mei* responsibility."

He shook his head, looking at her intently. "*Nee.* It's both of ours."

Something pulled inside her chest. She had given him an easy out—one she probably would have taken, considering her track record lately—but he was standing his ground. How could she not like this man? How could she not—

No, this couldn't be happening. She hadn't fallen in love with him, had she? That was nonsense. They hadn't even officially dated. Yes, there was a spark of attraction. She had to admit that. But love? That was something different. Something far deeper. Something she had never felt before. Not with Paul.

Only with Seth.

Now what was she supposed to do?

"*Yer* parents were on their way to the Beilers'," he said.

"Huh?" She looked at him, and that same warm sensation filled her, like a jar of honey that had spent the day in the sunshine. She ignored it. She wasn't in love with Seth Yoder. That wasn't possible. Besides, they had just agreed to tell her parents they felt nothing for each other. Yet Martha knew that would be another lie, at least for her.

"Hello?" Seth leaned down and looked her in the eye, annoyed. "Are you listening, Martha?"

"I'm listening," she said, her voice quiet, her mind trying to focus on what he was saying. "*Mamm* and *Daed* said they were visiting the Beilers for a little while tonight. They won't be gone that long, since they don't live too far away."

"Then we'll *geh* to *yer haus* and wait for them."

Did she have a choice? Just because she'd realized her feelings for Seth didn't mean she didn't have to fix things with her parents. She nodded, dread reaching to her toes. Seth deserved to have the record set straight. "*Ya*," she said, unable to fake a shred of enthusiasm. At least she was being honest for once. "Let's *geh*."

• • •

Delilah knocked on Cevilla's front door. She'd been invited to her house for supper, via Richard dropping by yesterday and hand delivering an invitation. Delilah had been surprised to read what the card said, written in neat script.

Please do us the honor of having supper with us tomorrow night.

Cevilla

P.S.—I hope you like pork chops.

She did like pork chops, but that's not why she accepted the invitation. She had yet to make amends with Cevilla. They had nodded to each other at church, and God was urging her to apologize for her past behavior. The excuse of having lots of work to do and decisions to make with the inn wasn't enough. She'd been avoiding Cevilla. It had never been easy for Delilah Stoll to apologize, but as she held the still-warm peach cobbler in her hands, she knew she couldn't avoid Cevilla forever. The woman had extended an olive branch, Delilah assumed. It would be poor form not to accept it.

The door opened, and Richard stood there. He smiled, his eyes pleasant and warm. "Hello, Delilah. We're glad you could make it."

She nodded. "Thank you for inviting me."

"Cevilla's in the kitchen finishing up the potato salad. I'm just about to put the pork chops on the grill. Please make yourself at home."

Delilah nodded, and more than once she wondered what type of relationship Cevilla and Richard had. She'd never seen the man at church, and he was wearing typical *English* clothes—light-brown trousers and a short-sleeved checked shirt—and his hair was cut short. It was clear he and Cevilla were close . . . but how close? And why did no one in the community seem concerned about it?

She stopped her thoughts. She wasn't here to snoop. She was

here to apologize, get through supper, and go back home, her duty done. She walked into the kitchen just as Cevilla put a small bowl of potato salad on the table.

"Hello," she said, looking up. She smiled, as if she and Delilah had been friends for a long time.

"Hello." Delilah was thrown a little off guard. She held up the cobbler. "I brought dessert."

"Wonderful. I have some pudding setting in the fridge, but we'll have *yer* dessert instead. You can set it on the counter near the sink."

Delilah followed Cevilla's instructions, then turned around. She looked around the kitchen. It was small, but neat and adequate. In addition to the potato salad, the table held a plate of pickles, a loaf of sliced bread, butter and jam, and a small plate of raw carrots, cucumbers, celery, and cherry tomatoes. It all looked delicious.

"Richard's been eager to use his new grill," Cevilla said, gesturing to the back patio. "I've never grilled in *mei* life, but he says it's the one aspect of cooking he's confident in."

"How long have you two known each other?" Delilah couldn't help asking.

"Sixty plus years, I guess." Cevilla looked at her. "I suppose you have some other questions too."

She sniffed. "I don't want to be nosy."

Cevilla laughed. "I'd be disappointed if you weren't." Then she sobered. "We got off on the wrong foot, Delilah, and I'm sorry about that. I behaved badly at *yer haus*." She frowned. "I'm embarrassed by *mei* behavior."

Her sincere apology helped spur on Delilah's. "*Nee* need. I was just as much in the wrong. It's just that when it comes to *mei grosskinner*, I want what's best for them."

"I understand." Cevilla looked at her. "I don't have children of *mei* own, but I've lived in Birch Creek for more than twenty years. The *familyes* here have become *mei familye*, their *kinner mei grosskinner*. You were wise to choose Seth and Martha. They're fine *yung* adults."

"I didn't have much of a choice when it came to Martha," she said, then grimaced. "That didn't sound right."

"You're being honest. I appreciate that."

Delilah nodded, understanding. Now that she was admitting things, she said, "I've been told I meddle too much."

"Funny, I've been told the same thing." Cevilla chuckled. "It's true, unfortunately." She turned and shuffled back to the stove. "I'm trying to stop, though. It's not easy."

"*Nee*, it isn't."

"What do you want to drink?" Cevilla asked as she put a teakettle on the stove.

"I've always been partial to peppermint tea."

Cevilla turned and smiled. "So am I. I think we might become friends after all."

Delilah lifted her chin. She wasn't ready for friendship, but a nice supper would be a start. "Perhaps we will . . . someday."

CHAPTER 13

Martha tapped her foot as she sat in the living room with Seth and waited for her parents to return from the Beilers'. It was eight o'clock, and she'd thought they'd be back by now. She stared at her untouched glass of iced tea on the table with droplets of condensation running down the side. In contrast, Seth had downed his tea as soon as she handed it to him. "Do you want something else to drink?"

"I'm fine." He was seated next to her on the couch, which she thought was confusing since they had plenty of other places for him to sit. It did present them as a united front, though. Perhaps that was what he was thinking. Not her. Her thoughts were all about being so close to him. Her foot tapped faster.

"Do you mind?" He sounded agitated.

She stilled. "Sorry." So much for him enjoying their proximity. "Do you want to do a puzzle?" They both needed something to distract them while they waited.

He shook his head. "I thought you said *yer* folks were gone for a short visit."

"Maybe they decided to stay longer." She started to get up. "It's getting late. We can do this another—"

Seth pulled her back down. "We'll do it tonight. I don't care how long we have to wait."

Martha folded her hands in her lap. From this moment on

she was going to be honest. Fudging the truth, deception, lying by omission—none of that was worth the guilt and anxiety she was experiencing. If one of the boys wanted to ask her out, she would politely and gently tell him no, not run away. If Cevilla came up with any more matchmaking plans, she would politely and gently tell her no too. Then she would tell her again, because Cevilla could be stubborn. Last, she was never, ever going to drag someone else into her problems. "I really am sorry, Seth."

"You've said that already. Several times." He looked at her, his expression softening. "It's okay, Martha. We both wove this tangled web, and we'll unravel it together."

"That was poetic," she said, managing a small smile.

He grinned. "You want to put that on one of *yer* plaques?"

"It would take a big plaque." She paused. "And a lot of skill."

"You have the skill." He sobered. "And the talent."

"You think so?"

"I know so. *Yer* work is far ahead of mine."

"*Nee* it isn't." But she blushed at the compliment.

"You should think of selling your work."

Her eyes widened. "*Nee*, I couldn't do that."

"You could." Seth looked at her intensely. "I'm sure *mei schwester* Ivy would love to have some of *yer* pieces in her shop."

"Doesn't she run an antique store?"

"*Ya*, but they also sell some locally created things. She's been working with Noelle O'Brien, the woman who owns the yarn and craft store next to her. They've been cross-selling and promoting. I didn't realize Ivy had such savvy business sense."

"Still," she said, shaking her head, "those plaques aren't *gut* enough to sell."

"Try it and find out."

Martha ran her hand over her knee. "What if they don't sell?"

"Then you haven't lost anything, have you?"

"Have you sold some of *yer* pieces?"

He shook his head. "Mine aren't for sale."

"They're *gut* enough, though."

"They're not for sale."

Martha wondered why Seth didn't want to sell his wood-carvings, but she wasn't going to pry. He didn't owe her an answer. He didn't owe her anything.

He stood, went to the front window, and looked outside. It was nearly dark, but he would be able see the lights on her parents' buggy when they arrived home. They must not have been in sight, because he turned around and looked at her. Then he shook his head and chuckled.

"What's so funny?"

"It's not exactly funny," he said. "More like ironic. Everything that's happened recently was because you ran into *mei* woodshop." Then he frowned a little. "The guys you were running away from are *mei* friends, and one is *mei bruder*. They really are *gut* people, Martha. You don't have to be afraid of them."

"I wasn't afraid of them." She glanced up at him. "It was . . ."

"It was what?"

The way he phrased the question with a soft, encouraging tone spurred her to continue. "Three years ago, I had a boyfriend. His name was Paul." She smoothed imaginary wrinkles from her dress. "We didn't date very long before I broke up with him. I knew we weren't right for each other even before that, but I didn't want to hurt his feelings." She wouldn't go into the details of how possessive and mean he could be, or how he wanted to know what she was doing every minute of the day. Her life hadn't been her own, and she had the same drowning feeling when the men of Birch Creek were pursuing her.

"When I ended the relationship, he didn't take it well. He said some terrible things to me." She averted her gaze, her throat growing tight. "He said I was selfish and heartless. That I didn't care about anyone else's feelings but *mei* own, and he felt sorry for anyone who would get mixed up with me, because I would ruin their life the way I ruined his."

Seth's mouth turned into a grim line, and he sat down next to her. "He's wrong. You know that, don't you?"

"I do, but sometimes I can still hear him saying those words."

He shook his head. "He sounds like a loser to me."

Martha looked at him. "I don't want to speak badly of him, any more than I already have."

"See, that right there shows you aren't heartless. This guy treated you horribly, and you're not lashing out at him behind his back." Seth paused. "Do you still have feelings for him?"

"Absolutely not. But I never want to hurt anyone like that again. I'd rather avoid a relationship than be the source of someone else's pain."

He stared at her for a long moment, then got up and looked out the window again.

The tightness in her throat vanished, and a sense of calm came over her. He didn't judge or blame her for what happened with Paul. Telling him about her past had been difficult, but he had supported her. Her heart warmed. Seth Yoder was special.

"They're coming," he said, rushing back to sit next to her on the couch. He was in such a hurry that when he sat down, he almost sat on top of her. "Sorry," he mumbled, then scooted over.

I don't mind. She pressed the heel of her hand against her forehead. She had to get her thoughts straight before her parents walked in. *I don't like Seth. I don't have feelings for Seth. I don't love—*

Her mother came into the living room, having entered the house from the back door, the closest entry to the barn. She still had her black purse slung over her shoulder when she halted. "Hello," she said, her grin wide. "I wasn't expecting you two to be here."

Martha swallowed. "Hi, *Mamm*. Is *Daed* putting up the horse?"

"*Ya*." She started to head for the stairs. "But don't mind us. We stayed a little longer at the Beilers' than we expected, and we're going straight to bed. You two can *visit* for as long as you want."

Seth let out a sound between a choke and a cough, and Martha knew she had to put him out of his misery. "Actually, we need to talk to you and *Daed* about something important."

Excitement leaped into *Mamm*'s eyes. "You do? Let me *geh* get him. The chores can wait for a few minutes." She tossed her purse on the rocking chair and hurried out of the living room. Martha hadn't seen her mother move so fast in ages.

"What did you do that for?" Seth said, glaring at her.

"Do what?"

"Now she thinks we're announcing our engagement."

"*Nee* she doesn't." Then she realized that her mother never hurried, and she never took *Daed* away from his chores. "Oh *nee*."

"It doesn't matter." But now his foot was tapping in time with hers. "We'll clear that right up too."

She felt terrible. Couldn't she do anything right when it came to Seth? As soon as they told her parents the truth, she was staying far, far away from dating. There was less chance for trouble if she did.

Her mother and father hurried back into the room, *Mamm* more quickly than *Daed*. Dread pooled inside her again. She was too old to be grounded for lying, but she would experience something even worse—their disappointment.

Mamm started to sit down, then straightened. "Should I get some *kaffee*? Tea? Lemonade? Water?"

"*Nee*," Seth said, his voice sounding a little strained. "We're fine."

Mamm smiled at him and sat down in the easy chair next to *Daed*. "Whatever you have to say, we're all ears." *Daed* nodded.

Martha opened her mouth, but no sound came out. Oh, this wasn't good. How could her voice betray her like this?

"Um . . ." Seth cleared his throat and shifted in his seat. "You see, Martha and I, well . . ." He cleared his throat again.

She tried to speak again, but she only squeaked. What was wrong with her? Why couldn't she tell her parents she didn't have feelings for Seth? Why was she letting him do the hard and awkward thing?

"Don't be nervous, Seth." *Mamm* gave him a reassuring smile.

"He can be a little nervous." *Daed* smirked. "It's not every day you make a life-changing decision."

"I . . ." Seth suddenly turned pale. "Oh *nee*, I've got to *geh*." He jumped up from the chair, grabbed his hat, went to the front door, stopped, and faced Martha. "I . . ." His face turned whiter than *Mamm*'s sheets after she bleached them, and he ran out the door.

"What in the world?" *Mamm* looked at Martha, bewildered. "Is he all right?"

Finally, Martha found her voice. "I have *nee* idea."

. . .

For the third time that day Seth found himself running. He sprinted down the road and made a left turn until he was completely out of sight from Martha's house. He stopped, winded, sick to his stomach, and full of regret. More importantly, he had no idea what he was supposed to do next.

He moved to a nearby field and leaned against a large tree, sweat dripping down his face. That was nothing compared to the cold sweat he felt when he started talking to Martha's parents. *Tried* talking, to be exact. And it wasn't because her parents were looking at him with expectant expressions, or that they had an even more wrong idea about his and Martha's relationship than before.

It was because he couldn't lie to them.

He closed his eyes. He couldn't tell Martha's parents he didn't have feelings for their daughter, because he did. That realization had hit him like a punch in the gut when her parents came into the room. No, it was before that, when he and Martha were sitting next to each other on the couch. He could have sat in one of the other chairs, but he didn't want to. He wanted to be near her, especially after she had told him about Paul. What a jerk. That guy had no idea what a special woman he'd lost, and it angered him that someone would treat her that way.

He yanked off his hat and pushed his fingers through his damp hair. Now what was he supposed to do? He couldn't tell Martha he liked her. Not when he'd made such a huge point of needing to end their fake relationship, and especially not when she didn't return his feelings. But he also couldn't leave things the way they were. He let out a bitter laugh at the irony. He was going to have to go back to Martha's and tell a lie to erase another lie. A partial verse came to mind from the book of Colossians. *Lie not to one another* . . . Lying was all he'd been doing lately. Lying by omission about his woodshop. Lying about his feelings for Martha to trick people. And now he was considering lying about the most important thing of all—his true feelings for Martha.

Seth picked up his hat and rammed it back on his head. He didn't need this. He was worried about his father and feeling more and more responsible for the farm with each passing day. He didn't need to fall for Martha. He didn't need her in his life.

But he wanted her in his life. He wanted to tell her about his father, about the pressure of running the farm, about the reason he wouldn't try to sell his woodcarvings—they weren't good enough. He wanted to pour out everything to her because he knew she would understand. She would comfort him with her sweet voice, and he would believe that everything would be all right. He trusted that God would work things out for good for his father. Yet having Martha on his side would make that conviction more . . . tangible.

It was well past dark, and he couldn't go back to the Detweilers' tonight. Early in the morning he and his father were planning the crops for next year, which Seth hadn't realized his father did *every* year. Then *Daed* and *Mamm* were going to Cleveland for his appointment. He would have time to see Martha's parents in the afternoon, while Martha was at work, making it easier to get the words out. He would say what he should have said tonight. Surely Martha told them the truth after he'd run out. Now it was his turn, both to confess and apologize.

"I don't have feelings for Martha," he sent into the night. The words pained his heart, but at least he did get them out. If he could speak them now, he could make himself speak them tomorrow.

. . .

Early the next morning Martha poured herself a cup of black coffee and sat down at the kitchen table. *Daed* must already be outside, and *Mamm* was probably with him. Sometimes she joined him after she put on the coffee, before making breakfast.

She stared at the cup, unable to take a sip. She still couldn't make sense of what happened last night. One minute Seth was fine, and the next minute his face was as white as the milk in the pitcher on the table, and he was running away like his pants were on fire. She'd gone after him but then lost him as he turned the corner at the end of her street. Did he suddenly become sick and not want her to see him that way? That shouldn't have mattered to him. She would have taken care of him no matter how sick he was.

She gripped her spoon. She wanted to take care of him, and that was a huge problem, along with the fact that her parents still didn't know the truth about her and Seth. Although she was sure they'd wanted to, they'd refrained from asking any questions when she'd returned and said she just wanted to go to bed.

What happened had eaten her up inside last night, and she hadn't slept much at all. That didn't bode well for her, because she had to go to work today. Friday was often busy, because, next to Saturday, they had more *English* customers at the optics shop than on any other day of the week.

"Martha?"

She turned and looked at *Mamm*, who was setting a jar of raspberry jelly on the table. She'd never heard her come into the room. "*Ya?*"

"Are you all right?" *Mamm* sat down next to her. "I'm surprised to see you up this early, but from the shadows under *yer* eyes, you should probably *geh* sleep a little longer. I'll take care of breakfast."

Martha stared at her coffee cup again. "I can't sleep."

"Because you're worried about Seth?"

She started to nod. Her mother was speaking the truth. She was worried about Seth. But that wasn't the only reason behind her mother's comment, and she couldn't stand to lie to her anymore. "Seth and I aren't . . . together."

"Oh? But last night . . ." *Mamm* paused. "Is that why he ran off? Because you broke up with him?"

"*Nee.*" She pushed the coffee cup away. "I didn't break up with him. He didn't break up with me."

Mamm frowned. "I don't understand."

Martha took a deep breath, then explained everything to her mother, including Cevilla's plan B and Delilah's plan to set her and Seth up with her grandchildren. "I'm so sorry," she whispered, unable to meet her mother's eyes. "Forgive me for lying to you all this time." She waited for her mother to say something. When she didn't, Martha lifted her gaze.

Her mother's expression was firm, but there was sympathy

in her eyes. "I'm definitely not happy that you lied to *yer vatter* and me, although we were guilty of jumping to conclusions."

"I knew you had. And we should have never led you to believe we were together."

"*Nee*. You shouldn't have." *Mamm* shook her head. "You've always had a kind heart, Martha. But sometimes it's kinder to be honest and straightforward." She touched Martha's hand. "Although after what Paul put you through, I know it's hard for you. Still, this was a convoluted way to avoid telling everyone how you truly feel. The truth would be only fair to them, and to *yourself*."

Martha nodded. "You're right."

"I'm disappointed in Cevilla, too, although I'm not surprised." *Mamm* half-smiled. "From what I've heard, she has a history of meddling in other people's romantic affairs."

"She has *gut* intentions."

"That's not an excuse." She moved the coffee cup back in front of Martha. "I'll tell *yer daed* what happened."

"*Nee*, I'll tell him. This is *mei* problem. Not anyone else's."

"That's true." She paused. "If you and Seth were supposed to tell us the truth last night, then why didn't you? And why did he run off like that?"

Her cheeks heated at the thought of how she couldn't get the words out last night. She still hadn't told her mother about her feelings for Seth, only about their ruse. This morning she'd realized that her lack of words was because she couldn't bring herself to lie anymore. But that didn't explain Seth's actions. "I don't know. I hope he's okay."

"So do I." *Mamm* glanced at the clock. "*Geh* lie down for a few minutes. Like I said, I'll take care of breakfast." She got up and went to the stove.

"That's it?"

"What do you mean?"

"You're not disappointed in me?"

Mamm turned to her. "I'm disappointed in the lying, *ya*. And next time you're struggling, I want you to come to me. We can work through it together. But I think you're in the process of reaping what you've sown. Those are consequences enough."

Martha breathed out a sigh of relief, even though she thought her mother was letting her off the hook a little too easily. But Martha still had to talk to Cevilla—and yes, even Delilah—and set things straight. She wasn't looking forward to that.

"By the way," *Mamm* said, pouring a cup of flour into a bowl, "if you haven't been with Seth all this time, where have you been?"

She sucked in a breath. She hadn't anticipated this question, and she couldn't spill Seth's secret. *Lord, what am I supposed to say?*

"Never mind." *Mamm* poured some milk into the bowl and started to stir. "You're an adult, and what you do with *yer* private time isn't *mei* business. I'm sorry I pried."

"It's all right." She took a gulp of coffee, which was now lukewarm. "I think I will lie down," she said.

"I'll call you when breakfast is ready."

Martha left the kitchen, went to the living room, and laid on the couch. She closed her eyes. *Thank you, Lord.* Yet she still wasn't settled in her soul, and she wouldn't be until she set everyone straight about her and Seth's deception . . . and until she was able to forget about her feelings for him once and for all.

. . .

Seth stood on the porch as his mother and father waited for the taxi to take them to Cleveland. "We should be back this evening," *Daed* said.

Seth looked at his parents, seeing the firm set of his father's jaw beneath his beard and the worry in his mother's eyes. "I'm sure the doctor will have *gut* news," he said, hoping he sounded more confident than he felt.

"God willing." *Daed* turned to him. "Whatever happens, *sohn*, it will be God's will."

Seth was familiar with that line of reasoning—it was at the core of his faith. But sometimes God's will was hard to swallow, especially when it was possible his father would become blind. Seth nodded. If his father believed, Seth would believe too.

"There's not too much to do today, other than the regular chores," *Daed* said. "You and *yer bruders* will probably have them done this morning, and when you finish you can have some free time this afternoon. Judah plans to spend the rest of the day with the Bontragers, and Ira told me he could use some free time too."

"You two have been working especially hard," *Mamm* added. She gave her husband a sharp look. "Too hard, I think."

A blue sedan pulled into the driveway. *Daed* and *Mamm* made their way to the car, and Seth stayed on the porch until they drove away. He closed his eyes and prayed. As he finished his prayer, Ira came outside and stood beside him.

"I'm surprised they're going to Cleveland," he said. "They rarely travel past Barton."

Seth turned to him. "How did you know where they were going?"

"I overheard them talking this morning," Ira said quietly.

Seth paused. Had his brother heard anything else? From the blank expression on Ira's face, he couldn't tell.

They didn't say anything for a moment as a hot breeze fluttered through the trees in the front yard. Finally, Ira spoke. "I told *Daed* I'd be gone this afternoon," Ira said. "I have some, uh, business to attend to."

Seth nodded, barely hearing him. He wasn't just thinking about his parents. Martha and her folks were also on his mind. He hadn't slept a wink thinking about what happened. All he'd done was delay the inevitable.

"Seth?" Ira said.

"Fine," he said with a wave. "Do whatever you need to do."

"Who put vinegar in *yer* milk this morning?" Ira muttered, then walked back inside.

After they finished the chores and ate the lunch *Mamm* had made for them, Ira and Judah both left. Although he could always find things to do around the farm, he decided to go ahead to the Detweilers'. He had to get this over with. He started in the direction of their home, but his gut started churning. He turned in the opposite direction and headed for the woodshop. He was surprised he hadn't thought to come here in the first place. With Martha at work, he knew she wouldn't be there. He needed to alleviate some stress, and woodcarving would help.

A few hours later, he looked at his halfway-finished project and grimaced. He'd tried to make a plaque similar to Martha's, but it didn't have her charm. He didn't have her skill. He threw it into the bin of scrap wood. His mind hadn't been fully on carving anyway. Between his father, Martha, and now realizing that he might never be good enough at woodcarving to make it a career, he was angry. His world was upside down, and he had Martha Detweiler to blame.

Seth hung his head. He couldn't blame her, not completely. It wasn't her fault he'd fallen for a woman who didn't feel the same about him. The blame for that was squarely at his feet.

He looked around the woodshop, seeing Martha's touch everywhere. The place was filled with her presence. This had been his sanctuary. It didn't feel like that anymore. He flung open the door, then pulled it shut, not bothering to lock it behind him. What did it matter if someone else found this place? It would never be the same for him again.

He trudged into the woods, his feet feeling heavy. It was cooler today than it had been in a long time, and a strong wind had kicked up. He should be grateful for it, but he felt only bitterness—about everything.

A strange scent filled the air. He sniffed. Smoke? Who would be burning on a day like this? A burn ban had been in place in their county all summer. But as the wind kicked up, the scent of smoke grew stronger. He saw a plume of smoke rising in the direction of Jalon's property. *Fire!*

He burst through the woods only to see that Jalon's farm wasn't on fire. His was.

CHAPTER 14

Martha held Seth's old clock in her hands. She'd asked her uncle to repair it, and now it kept perfect time. She put it back on the shelf, impatient. The shop wouldn't close for another hour.

Onkel Hezekiah had been happily working in the back most of the day, like he always did. She finally understood the passion he had for his job. He could make a living doing something he loved. Not everyone had that good fortune. For her the day had been slow, and her mind had bounced from woodworking, to Seth, to Cevilla and Delilah, then back to Seth. It was as if she had a ping-pong game going on in her head, and she couldn't let it continue.

She had decided she was going to give Seth back his key. Staying away from him was the only way she could get rid of her feelings for him, and even though he was too busy to work in his shop, his presence permeated the space. She wouldn't be able to keep her mind off him when she was there, remembering how good it felt to be so close to him. But that didn't mean her decision was an easy one. She couldn't stand the idea of not being able to work in his woodshop, yet she couldn't keep going there either. How was she supposed to give up these two things she loved?

She tamped down her worry, which was making her head

ache, and went back to the workroom, needing a distraction. Her uncle was hunched over a pair of glasses, replacing the nose pads. Ever since he'd repaired Levi's frames, more people had brought their glasses to him instead of going to the optical shop in Barton. As usual, word got around quickly in Birch Creek.

"I'll be outside cleaning off the front walk," she said. He nodded in response, not looking at her. She went outside and grabbed the broom she used specifically for outdoor use.

As she swept the dust and bits of gravel off the short concrete walkway, she heard a siren wailing in the distance. She paused, a strong breeze making her *kapp* strings flutter against her shoulders. The sound sent a cold shiver down her spine. She hadn't heard a siren that close since she'd moved here. She closed her eyes and said a quick prayer that wherever the emergency vehicle was heading, there would be a good outcome.

She finished sweeping the walk and leaned the broom under the awning. She looked at the store's front. An empty space next to the door would be perfect for a small sign. Her uncle already had a large one near the road, but a simple, yet decorative wood sign would add a nice touch to the building. Maybe she could make one for him. But then she remembered she was giving Seth back his key, which sent her emotions into another tailspin.

"Martha!"

She turned to see her mother running toward her. Panic crashed through her. Her mother didn't run. Martha hurried to meet her.

"There's a fire at the Yoders'," she exclaimed, trying to catch her breath. "All available hands are needed. *Yer daed* is already there."

Onkel Hezekiah came outside, pushing his magnifying

glasses to the top of his head. "I heard a siren." He looked at Martha's mother.

"Fire at the Yoders'," *Mamm* said, still breathing hard.

He yanked off the glasses and handed them to Martha. "Lock up the shop," he said, then took off toward the barn to hitch up his buggy.

Martha barely nodded, gripping the glasses in her hands. *Seth*. Was he home? Was he injured . . . or worse? Her hands started to shake. "I'm going to Seth's." She spun around to put her uncle's glasses away and lock up the shop, but her mother stopped her.

"*Nee*, you're not." *Mamm* went to her.

"They need help."

"They'll need our help after they put out the fire." *Mamm* looked worried. "We'll let the men handle the blaze."

"But what if Seth's hurt?" Martha blinked back sudden tears. "What if he's burned or . . ."

Mamm put her arm around her and led her back inside the shop. She took Martha's hand. "We'll pray that none of the Yoders are injured."

She closed her eyes and listened to her mother praying for the family, the animals, the farm, and the men and firefighters putting out the blaze. But when Martha opened her eyes, she didn't feel a sense of calm. "I'm scared," she whispered.

"God's in control," *Mamm* said gently. "Believe that."

She squeezed her eyes shut, trying to have her mother's depth of faith. But she couldn't stop imagining something horrible happening to Seth. *Please, Lord, don't let anything happen to him.*

. . .

The firefighters and several men from the community had helped put out the fire, and both Seth's body and mind were numb as he stood looking at the cloud of smoke that still hung in the air. No one had been hurt, except Aden. He'd burned his hand when he arrived and tried to help Seth and Judah save their animals. He was with the firefighters by the fire engine now as one of them taped it up. The burn wasn't serious, Aden had insisted. That didn't make Seth feel any better.

He turned and looked at Judah, huddled on the back-porch steps. The house had been almost untouched, the fire stopping at the patio's edge after scorching the rest of the yard. But they had lost the barn. They lost livestock. They lost the crops. They had lost almost everything on the farm.

Seth went to Judah and sat down. His brother didn't look at him. He stared straight ahead, his face covered with soot. They had managed to save some of their livestock, which were now finding refuge at Jalon's, where the rest of the men in the community had gone to help with the relocating process. He put his hand on Judah's shoulder. Judah shrugged it off.

"Don't," his youngest brother said. "Don't try to make me feel better."

"It was an accident."

"It was *mei* fault." Judah looked at him, his eyes red-rimmed. "You've been helping *Daed* a lot more lately, and I came back this afternoon because I started thinking I should help him too. That pile of splintered pallets has been rotting by the barn for months. It's not as hot today, so I thought I could burn them." He gulped. "I forgot all about the burn ban."

Seth nodded but didn't say anything. What could he say? Judah thought he was to blame, but Seth blamed himself more. His father had put him in charge. Instead of keeping an eye on the farm, he'd been preoccupied with his problems. He'd been irresponsible and selfish. If he had been here, he would have stopped Judah, told him it was too windy and too dry to set the pile on fire. Judah was fourteen, and he lacked Seth's experience and knowledge.

Judah hung his head. "How am I gonna tell *Daed*?"

"We'll both tell him."

Judah's head jerked up. "You didn't do anything wrong."

Ya, I did.

One of the firefighters came over to them. He'd taken off his helmet but was still wearing his full gear. Sweat poured down his face. "You two okay?"

They both nodded, and they were both lying. "We're fine," Seth said, trying to act like he had everything in control, that losing the farm in a span of an hour hadn't broken him into pieces inside.

"Your friend with the burned hand said he was going to go help with the animals that survived," the man said. His expression grew more somber. "I'm sorry we couldn't save more of them."

"We appreciate everything you did." Seth's voice was flat, and Judah's head was down again. He heard his brother sniff, and his heart tore in two.

"If there's anything we can do to help . . ." The firefighter shifted on his feet. "A couple of us have a day off tomorrow. We can help with the cleanup."

"Thanks, but we'll take care of it."

"All right. Just know the offer stands." He went back to the fire engine and spoke with the rest of the firefighters. They all looked at Seth and Judah, then packed up their gear and prepared to leave.

Just as the fire truck pulled away, a familiar blue sedan turned into the driveway. The car had barely come to a complete stop when *Daed* scrambled out of it and rushed toward the house. "What happened? Are you two okay? Where's Ira?"

Seth stood. "We're fine. Ira isn't here, and he wasn't around when the fire happened."

His stoic father's entire body started to shake as their mother appeared beside him. "Tell me what happened," he said, his voice trembling.

Judah started to speak, but Seth interrupted him. "It's both our faults, *Daed*. Not just Judah's." He explained about the fire, about the livestock, about the farm.

When Seth finished, his father sank to his knees. "It's all . . . gone?"

"Almost."

"The *haus* is all right." His mother put her hand on *Daed*'s shoulder. "Our *kinner* are safe."

His father nodded but remained on his knees. Judah started to cry, and Seth was close to it.

"Come inside," *Mamm* said, putting her arm around Judah. Unlike her sons and husband, she was calm. "You too, Seth."

Although his mother's demeanor was serene, Seth caught the flash of pain in her eyes. She was holding it together for the rest of them. "I'm staying here," he said, and his mother and Judah went inside.

He went to his father and knelt in front of him. "I'm so sorry," he said, the tears flowing now. "I . . . I failed you."

His father looked at him, a blank expression in his eyes. "God's will," he whispered.

"How can this be God's will?" Seth almost shouted the

question. "This was a human mistake. *Mei* mistake." He hung his head. "*Mei* fault," he said, sobbing.

His *daed* stood, then helped Seth to his feet. "Something *gut* will come of this," *Daed* said in an unsteady voice. "God will see to it. Now, mind *yer mudder* and *geh* inside. I'll be there in a minute."

Seth rubbed the tears from his face with the back of his sooty hand and went inside. He didn't want his brother or mother to see he had lost control, and he was grateful they weren't in the kitchen. He went upstairs to wash and change his clothes, but the bathroom door was closed. As he passed by, he heard his brother sobbing from inside. His chest tightened.

He went to his bedroom and stood in the middle of it, unable to move. He wanted to believe his father. He wanted to have his faith and confidence. But all he could think about was his failure. The farm was everything to his *daed*, and it had started to be important to him too. Their loss was worse than anything they had experienced in the past, even during the hardest of times. It would take a long time to come back from this. They'd had everything, and in a flash, it had all turned to ashes.

· · ·

Nina sat in the front seat of the taxi while Ira sat in the back. He had asked her earlier in the week to go fishing with him at the Grand River this afternoon, and she had agreed. She hadn't told her grandmother where she was going today, other than fishing. Surprisingly, *Grossmammi* hadn't asked. She'd been less controlling since the supper last month with Seth and Martha. Nina hadn't seen much of Martha other than at church, but between working on the house and the inn and fishing with Ira, she'd had little time to do anything else.

She glanced over her shoulder at Ira, who gave her a smile. He was becoming a good friend, and his companionship, along with their fishing trips, had eased her homesickness until she barely felt it. Her grandmother had kept in touch with two of her friends back in Wisconsin, but they didn't seem to have much news to share, and Nina had noticed that no one asked about her in the correspondence *Grossmammi* received.

It was as if the cord between her and her old community had been severed, and she was surprised that she wasn't all that upset about it. If anyone had told her almost two months ago that she would be content in Birch Creek, she wouldn't have believed them. But that's exactly what had happened, and she was grateful. She slept well at night now, and the longing in her heart had faded. Like the rest of her family, she was starting to believe Birch Creek was home.

"I'm sorry the fish weren't biting," Ira said, leaning forward in the backseat.

"That's not your fault." She looked at him over her shoulder. "I had a great time anyway."

He grinned, and she smiled back. He had told her about Martha, and that he was taking a break from romantic relationships. She was falling into a familiar habit with Ira—platonic friendship. Which was fine with her. Even *Grossmammi* hadn't dropped any hints or nagged her about being more attractive to the opposite sex. Her grandmother had changed, for the better.

Ira had told the driver to drop off Nina first. The taxi pulled into her driveway, but before she could fully get out of the car, *Grossmammi* burst out of the inn and hurried toward them, faster than Nina had seen her move since she and Levi were little kids. "Nina, is Ira with you?"

Ira rolled down the window as Nina got out of the car. "Hi, Delilah."

Her grandmother's face paled. Nina put her hand on her shoulder. "*Grossmammi*, what's wrong?"

"There's a fire at *yer* farm, Ira." Her voice broke.

"What?"

"Loren and Levi are there to help put it out. You need to get over there right away."

Ira yelled out his address to the taxi driver as he rolled up the window. Nina put the fishing pole and tackle in her grand-mother's hands. "I'm going with him."

"You will not." *Grossmammi* held her arm. "I won't have you put in a dangerous situation. We don't know how much dam-age that fire has done."

"I don't care." She stared her down. She wasn't going to be intimidated this time. "He's *mei* friend, and I'm going whether you like it or not."

Grossmammi let go of Nina's arm. "All right. But don't do anything foolish."

Nina scrambled into the car and turned around to check on Ira. His face had turned snow white. "Small fire," he whispered. "Must be a small fire."

The taxi driver had to have broken the speed limit with how fast he drove to the Yoders'. There wasn't a fire truck there, which Nina took as a sign that the fire was out. Yet as soon as she got out of the car, she smelled the smoke, and she saw gray, wispy tendrils of it rising from the pile of black wood and ash that used to be the barn. Waves of smoke blew across the black-ened pasture behind it. Her stomach dropped.

"*Nee*," Ira said, dashing past her toward the house.

The front door opened, and Seth came outside. He looked freshly showered, but his expression was tortured as he went to Ira.

"*Mamm* and *Daed*? Judah?" Ira asked, panic on his face.

"We're all fine."

"Is everything . . . ?"

"*Ya*. All but the *haus*. Almost everything else is gone."

Ira froze. His expression became emotionless, the opposite of how he'd been behaving before they arrived. That worried Nina. She went over to him and lifted her hand to his shoulder. "Ira?" When he turned to her, she reached for his hand, not thinking about how it would look to Seth or whether Ira even wanted her there. "It's okay," she said softly, moving closer to him. "Everything will be okay."

"You should *geh* home," Seth said quietly. "*Yer bruder* and *daed* should be there soon. They helped get the few animals we saved over to the Chupps'."

Ira squeezed her hand, but his expression didn't change. She lifted her chin. "I'm not leaving," she said. "Not unless Ira wants me to."

"Do you want her to stay?" Seth said.

Ira looked at her and nodded. "*Ya*. I do."

"Okay. But please talk to me before you ask Judah or *Mamm* and *Daed* any questions. Judah . . ." But then Seth turned around without finishing and went back into the house.

Ira let go of Nina's hand and walked over to where the barn had stood. He crouched and stared at the ashes, the residual smoke blowing in the breeze.

She crouched beside him, a lump in her throat. "I'm so sorry, Ira. What can I do to help?"

He turned to her, his expression bewildered. "I don't know what happened, but worse, I don't know what we're going to do." He stared at the ashes again. "It's not just the fire. *Mei daed* . . ." He swallowed. "There's something wrong with his eyesight."

Nina sucked in a breath. "There is?"

He nodded. "I don't think I'm supposed to know. I overheard him and *Mamm* talking about his appointment in Cleveland this morning. I have *nee* idea if Seth and Judah know . . . Although now that I think about it, Seth must know. That explains why he and *Daed* have been working so closely together recently." His shoulders slumped. "I'm sure *Daed* has his reasons for not telling me, and I don't care that he didn't. But if his eyes are bad enough that he has to see a specialist . . . and now this . . ."

"Ira." Nina took his hand in hers. "If there's one thing I've learned about the people in Birch Creek is that they take care of each other. You and *yer familye* won't *geh* through this alone. And I'll help you any way I can. I know *mei familye* will too."

He looked at her, his eyes glassy. "*Danki* for being here, Nina."

"I wouldn't want to be anywhere else."

. . .

The next day the community of Birch Creek shut down for the day as everyone gathered at Seth's house to help clean up and assess the damage. Women brought food and set up tables for lunch while the men went through charred wood, looking for anything salvageable from the barn. Asa Bontrager, who was an accountant and in charge of the community fund, had a private discussion with Seth's father inside the house. Everyone else stayed outside, continuing to work and clean up. Zeb and Zeke, along with Owen, Jalon, and Adam, were at Jalon and Adam's farm, building temporary shelter for the animals. "We'll keep them as long as you need," Jalon had said. "They'll be well taken care of."

Deep down Seth was grateful for everyone's help. This was what their community did in times of crisis—it came together. That wasn't the case before his father had become bishop, but *Daed* had unified a fractured community with his strong, yet quiet leadership.

Judah was with Malachi and a few of his friends, who were doing their best to cheer him up while they picked up discarded charred wood and put it in a pile. Unlike yesterday, the air was still, without a trace of breeze. *Daed* and *Mamm* had forgiven both him and Seth, but they couldn't hide the disappointment and sorrow in their eyes. Seth was exhausted after another night of not sleeping, but he threw himself into cleaning up the cornfield the best he could before it would be plowed over, probably on Monday. Despite the challenge of such a dry summer, the ears would have been ready for harvest in a little over two weeks, but only scorched and shortened stalks were left. He cut them out of the ground and tossed them into a wheelbarrow, then rolled it over to the growing pile on the other end of the field.

He was on his third wheelbarrow trip when he saw Martha coming toward him. Despite everything, his heart did a little flip at seeing her. The feeling subdued when she neared. She was the last person he wanted to see . . . and yet she was still the only person he wanted to see.

"Seth," she said, stopping a few feet away from him.

He used his hatchet to cut a stalk, refusing to look at her. The sun beat down on him, and he was flush with heat and sweat. The day was blistering hot again, adding insult to injury.

"I brought you something to drink."

"I'm not thirsty." He hacked at another plant, then tossed it into the wheelbarrow.

"Maybe not, but you're going to dehydrate out here if you don't drink something." She put her hand lightly, hesitantly, on his shoulder.

He stilled. How was he supposed to refuse her when she touched him like that? Although the gesture could have meant anything, and probably was meant only to get his attention, it meant so much more to him than that. He tossed down the hatchet and took the cold bottle of water from her. After he drained it, she handed him another. She had come prepared.

"Be careful," she said. "You don't want to get sick."

Her nurturing made him feel good. But he didn't deserve to feel good. He stopped drinking and wiped his mouth with the back of his hand. He screwed the lid back down, dropped the bottle, picked up the hatchet, and started cutting again.

After a few moments Martha asked in a quiet voice, "Are you okay?"

He stopped, holding the hatchet high. Was she seriously asking him that question after everything that had happened? After he'd left the farm unattended while his father was away? "*Nee*," he said, angry, not looking at her. "I'm not okay. I don't think I ever will be. This is *mei* fault."

"*Yer* fault? You blame *yerself*? You can't do that, Seth—"

"*Ya*, I can." He started hacking again, hoping she'd get the hint that he wasn't in the mood to talk to her or anyone else.

She didn't move, and she waited until he'd tossed the stalk in the wheelbarrow before she said, "I brought back *yer* key."

He looked at the key in her outstretched hand, the sun glinting off the metal and making it shine. "Keep it," he said, moving to the next stalk.

"I don't need it. I won't be going to *yer* shop anymore. You'll be able to work alone."

He sneered. "Do you think I'll have any time for a stupid hobby after this? It's going to take months to rebuild this place, and years to get it back to what it was." He shook his head, defeat filling him. "Keep the key. Keep the tools. You're better at using them than I am."

"Seth, that's not true."

"Leave me be, Martha. I've got work to do." He grabbed another cornstalk, this time hacking harder than he had before. Only when he finished cutting the stalk to ribbons did he stop to look at her.

She was gone.

CHAPTER 15

Two weeks later, Martha carried two heavy tote bags into Ivy Schlabach's antique shop. The little bell above the door rang as it opened, and she felt the cool air of the fans in the shop that stirred the air. She looked around for Ivy or her husband, Noah, who helped Ivy run the shop, but she didn't see either one of them.

The little store was filled with antiques, some of them with that musty old smell she didn't really care for. But she saw some new items too. Books on antiquing and refinishing old furniture were displayed near an antique cash register. She set her tote bags on the floor and rang the bell on the counter.

Since the Yoder fire, she hadn't sought out Seth. The pain in his eyes when she tried to give him back the key had shaken her heart. She wanted to do something to help, but she hadn't been sure what. Seth didn't want her around, and she didn't blame him. He and his family were consumed with trying to get back on their feet. The community had gathered for a barn raising last weekend, and her father had gone over there this week to help with repairs to the back of the house. It had sustained some smoke damage, but nothing structurally. When he returned later that night, *Daed* said the Yoders were in good spirits. But Martha couldn't imagine that applied to Seth.

She knew Seth had pushed her away for a reason besides

rebuilding the farm. He didn't trust her, and she had given him plenty of reason not to. She still didn't know why he'd run from her house that night, but what did it matter now?

Noah, a tall, lanky man who wore hearing aids, came from the back of the store. "Hi, Martha," he said, moving behind the counter. "I almost didn't hear the bell. We might have to get a louder one." He smiled. "What can I help you with today?"

"I thought maybe I could help *you*." And Seth, too, although she was fairly sure he wouldn't want her help. "Sometimes you sell new items, right?"

"Depends on what it is."

She lifted one of the bags and put it on the counter. "Wood-carvings." She pulled one out, and Noah examined it.

"Nice," he said. "Do you know who made it?"

"I do. But this person prefers to remain anonymous."

"I see. Well, anonymity won't stop me from selling an item. May I look at the rest?"

She showed him all the woodcarvings, and he studied them. When he put the last one on the counter, he said, "I think we can make a deal of some sort. What are *yer* terms?"

Martha smiled. Seth might not like what she was about to do, but she would deal with the fallout later. She was determined to help him, whether or not he liked it.

· · ·

Cevilla picked up the old iron she'd heated on the stove. She touched the flat side of it with her finger. It was hot enough, and she applied it to the simple pale-blue fabric on her ironing board and smoothed down a seam. She couldn't sew worth a hoot, but Delilah sure could. They were in the freshly painted living room at the Stolls' new house, which had been finished earlier in the week. Levi and Loren had done an excellent job building the two-story house, and now they were focusing all their time and energy on the inn. Delilah manned the sewing machine while Cevilla ironed the seams. They were making curtains for the Yoders' master bedroom, which was at the back of the house. where the fire had caused some smoke damage.

"I appreciate you helping me," Delilah said. "Work always goes faster with two extra hands."

Cevilla took the curtain panel to Delilah, relying on her cane to keep her balance. "That it does." She went back to the ironing board to press another one.

"So what's going on with you and Richard?" Delilah said over the whirr of the sewing machine.

"That's a rather personal question." Cevilla set down the iron on its flat end. "And quite out of the blue."

"We've been friends for a month now." Delilah gave her that sharp look of hers. "You expect me to keep *mei* nose out of it for longer than that?"

Cevilla chuckled. "I suppose not, especially when I would have asked you the same question long before now." She picked up the iron again. "Richard and I are *gut* friends."

"Only friends?"

"A little more than that," she said, admitting the truth. "But as you can see, he's still attached to his *English* ways."

"Is he going to join the church?" Delilah asked.

"I don't know."

"What if he doesn't?" Delilah turned in her chair.

Cevilla had thought about nothing else, of course, especially since he continued to muse on his decision without her input. That was his right, and it was a good thing he hadn't talked about it for a long while, because she wasn't sure she wouldn't say something to sway him either way. Thus, she refused to worry about it. Worry wouldn't change anything anyway. She needed patience in this situation, usually in short supply. She was sure this was God's way of teaching her some, and she had been leaning on him more than ever. Although she could have done with an easier lesson. "I will have to accept whatever decision he makes."

"Do you love him?" Delilah asked softly.

"*Ya*," she said. "I do. I know he loves me too."

Delilah sighed. "You're blessed to have that, Cevilla. Especially at this time of life." She gave her a sad smile before starting to sew again.

Cevilla knew how blessed she was, which made her feel guilty for wanting more. Having Richard in her life, in any way, should be more than enough. But sometimes, more times than not lately, it wasn't.

Nina entered the house, carrying a basket of laundry fresh off the line. It was September now, and Cevilla prayed every night that the rain would come with the cooler temperatures. The weather had thrown everyone for a loop this summer, not to mention what had happened to the poor Yoders. Now everyone was extra careful with anything that could start a fire.

"I'll put this away," Nina said, "and then I'm going to the Yoders'. I promised Ira I'd help him with the horses. Now that the barn is finished, they're ready to bring them back from Jalon's."

"How is the *familye*?" Delilah asked. "I thought about stopping over there earlier this week, but I didn't want to intrude."

Nina gave her a surprised look, then replied, "They're making *gut* progress on restoring the land. I worry about Ira and his *bruders*, though." She set the basket on the coffee table and started to fold dish towels. "They're working day and night to recover what they've lost."

Cevilla wondered about Nina and Ira's relationship. Delilah did, too, and they had discussed it several times, but both had vowed never to meddle again. Cevilla was still smarting from being wrong about Martha and Seth. The two of them actively avoided each other now. Fortunately, Richard hadn't said a word about the situation, although a good dose of *I told you so* would have been warranted.

"We should be finished with these curtains today." Delilah stopped sewing and examined the panel. "Would you mind taking them over early next week?"

"Of course not." Nina set the last folded towel on the stack on the table, then picked up and started folding a white pillowcase.

Cevilla watched her, noticing how different Nina was from when she first came to Birch Creek. She was still tomboyish, but there was a softness to her rough edges now. *Did Ira have anything to do with that?* Cevilla shut down that thought. She was finished interfering, and that included thinking about interfering.

She and Delilah finished the curtains, and Richard came by later that afternoon to pick her up. When they got to her house, he held the car door open for her. "What's for supper?" he asked.

She turned and looked at him. "Meat loaf sandwiches. Ready for a gourmet meal?"

"*Ya.*" Richard stilled. "In a minute."

"Is something wrong?"

He shook his head, and a line of tension formed around his mouth. "No, but I have a favor to ask."

"Anything."

"I'm not saying that I've made a decision," he said, "but will you teach me about the Amish faith? I want to know everything—the history, the rules, the doctrine. I want to learn about the faith you've dedicated your life to."

Cevilla's heart soared, but she tempered her response. "Of course. I'm glad you asked me."

"I was just thinking it would be good to have all the facts," he said, grabbing his cane out of the backseat. "Knowledge is important."

"Yes, it is." The knowledge she would give him could drive him away from or draw him closer to the Amish. Whichever way he chose, she would love him.

He shut the car door and grinned. "Now, how about that meat loaf sandwich?"

. . .

In mid-September, Martha picked up an envelope of money from Noah and Ivy. It was a good-sized sum and had surpassed her expectations. All the woodcarvings had sold. "Everyone is wondering who the artist is," Noah had said after handing her the envelope. "I'm curious myself."

Martha simply smiled and thanked him. Then she took a taxi back to Birch Creek.

Instead of going home, she went straight to Seth's. They still weren't talking to each other, and Martha's heart ached every time she looked at him. Freemont and Mary seemed to have recovered from the tragedy faster than their sons, although Judah was starting to show signs of his outgoing personality again. Ira was still serious, and she knew he had been working hard on the farm and spending time with Nina. Martha had hoped she and Nina would be close friends, but she spent her free time with Ira, and she seemed to have overcome her homesickness.

The single men in the community also seemed to have given up on her as any thoughts of dating and socializing had gone to the wayside after the fire. They'd been spending their free time helping the Yoders. That was exactly what she wanted, though—for her life to get back to normal, simple again, the way she'd hoped it would be.

Yet she was more unhappy than she'd been before. And more lonely. She was glad Nina and Ira were friends and that she had stuck by his side through the whole ordeal, but that left her alone. She was being selfish, but she couldn't help it.

She'd thought about writing to Selah about it, but she'd have to leave so many things out of the explanation that she didn't bother. She also barely thought about Paul now. Whatever she had felt for him paled in comparison to her feelings for Seth. Why she had let Paul's anger and harsh words bother her so deeply, she had no idea. The pain he had inflicted on her was nothing compared to the ache in her heart for Seth.

None of that stopped her from going to Seth's house now, however. After she arrived at the Yoders', she paid the taxi driver and got out of the car. The progress made in the two weeks since she'd last been here amazed her. Two brand-new barns stood near the dried-out pasture. Without the rain, the fields were blowing dust, but they were clear of burned crops and other debris.

Then she saw him, standing in the far back of the pasture. Seth. Her palms grew damp, but she took a deep breath and went to him.

He was bent over the stubbled grass, running his hand over

the dry, cracked earth that had once been lush with swaying timothy grass. She couldn't stop herself from watching him, his profile no less handsome to her covered in dirt and sweat than it was when he was dressed up for church. Finally, she cleared her throat.

He turned and looked at her. "Hi," he said dully, not getting up.

"Hi." She gripped the envelope in her hand. She had thrust it behind her back before walking over here. "How are you?"

"Fine." His voice was clipped.

"I want to give you something."

"If it's the key, forget it." He stood and faced her, putting his hands on his narrow hips. "I told you to keep it."

"It's not the key." She brought out the envelope and handed it to him. "Here."

He opened it up and saw the thick stack of bills inside. "What's this for?"

"For you and *yer familye*. I know you'll need it for more livestock and seed, and whatever else it can help with."

"This is a lot of money." He held the envelope out to her. "I can't take *yer* paycheck."

She didn't accept it. "It's not *mei* paycheck."

"Then where did you get the money?"

She inhaled, steeling herself for his reaction. "I sold woodcarvings."

He stilled. "You did what?"

"I sold all the woodcarvings. I wanted to help—"

"I told you they weren't for sale!" He looked up at the sky and then back at her, anger flashing in his eyes. "Don't you listen to anyone? Or do you just do whatever you want to do and hope for the best, never thinking about how anyone else will feel?"

"Seth, I—"

"Here." He thrust the envelope toward her. When she wouldn't take it, he shoved it into her hand. "I don't want the money. And I'll take *mei* key back after all. It's obvious I can't trust you. I said *mei* woodcarvings weren't for sale, but you ignored *mei* wishes, just like you ignored everything else."

Martha's throat clogged. She'd expected to have to convince him to take the money. She hadn't expected him to lash out at her like this. Even though she understood why, it didn't hurt any less. "They weren't *yer* carvings, Seth," she choked out. "They were mine."

. . .

Seth's jaw dropped open. "What?"

"I sold *mei* carvings." Tears sprang to Martha's eyes. "*Yers* are still back at the shop. I wouldn't dare sell them without *yer* permission. I . . . I respect you too much for that."

He soaked in what she had said. She had sold her carvings and was giving him the money. Carvings she could have sold for her own benefit. She'd used his scrap wood and borrowed his tools, but she'd made enough money to pay him back for that several times over. He'd known she was good. Evidently other people had recognized it too. He was the biggest jerk on the planet. "Martha, I'm sorry." As though that lame apology would make up for everything.

"You have nothing to be sorry for, because you're right." She wiped her eyes. "I'm not trustworthy. I've been deceptive and untruthful and have caused you a lot of problems, all because I didn't want to hurt anyone's feelings, and because I'm a coward." She sniffed, but lifted her chin, making her look strong despite her tears. "This is *mei* way of making some of that up to you, because I owe you after everything I put you through. That, and because I . . ." She bit her bottom lip so hard he thought she might draw blood. Then she pulled a key out from the pocket of her apron. His key. "Here."

"*Nee*," he said, shaking his head. "Keep it—"

"Here!" She shoved it at him. He refused to accept it, so she dropped it on the ground in front of his dusty work boots. "I'll leave you alone from now on, Seth. You don't have to worry about me making a mess of *yer* life anymore." She turned and started to leave, only to stop and look back at him. "You haven't been able to trust me with much, but you can trust me with this. I will never tell *yer* secret. Ever." Then she hurried away.

He bent to the ground and picked up the key, folding it into his fist. He'd yelled at Martha, but he was being hypocritical about her dishonesty when he wasn't being honest with her. He'd hurt her deeply. He'd seen it in her eyes. He felt it in his heart.

"Was that Martha?" *Daed* said, coming out of the barn, wiping his hands on a rag.

"*Ya*." He shoved the envelope of money into his pocket, unsure what to do with it, not feeling right about taking it since it was really hers.

"She didn't stay long. Is she walking home?"

Seth nodded, still watching as she disappeared around the front of his house.

Daed frowned. "Is everything all right between you two?"

"*Ya*." *Nee*. There was nothing between them. It was all one-sided. He couldn't say that to his father, so he changed the subject, swallowing his pain. "How are *yer* eyes?"

"Been using the new drops every day. Medicine is an amazing

thing, Seth. I can tell I'm seeing a little more clearly. He smiled, although it was a tired one. "The doc seemed confident I wouldn't have to worry about *mei* eyesight for a long while, as long as I keep up with the six-month checkups."

"That's great," Seth said, but his voice sounded flat. He was happy for his father, but still tied up in knots over Martha.

"That means we can slow down. We've all been working hard, and we're all exhausted. Especially you, *sohn*."

"I'm fine." He didn't intend to slow down, not until he'd made up for what he'd let happen. He pushed past his father. "I told Ira and Judah I'd help them with the hay they brought back from the Beilers'—"

"Seth," *Daed* said. "We haven't talked about the fire."

"There's *nix* to talk about."

"There's plenty to talk about." He grabbed Seth's elbow. Not hard, but enough to get his attention.

Seth turned around. "I'm listening."

"I've already talked to Ira and Judah. Ira felt guilty about going fishing that day, but I reassured them both that I don't blame either of them, especially Judah. He made a terrible mistake, but he's learned from it. I shouldn't have mentioned wanting to get rid of the pile in the first place. He was trying to help me out."

"I'm glad you talked to them. I've been worried about Judah."

"Me too. But he'll be okay. He's a strong *bu*. Like his *bruders*." *Daed* put his hands on his waist. "But I'm not here to talk about them. You and I need to discuss a few things."

Steeling himself, Seth prepared for the full brunt of the blame to be put on him. He should have been here, not in the woodshop thinking about Martha and his other problems. "I know what you're going to say."

"I doubt that." Daed looked at him directly. "I know about the woodshop, Seth."

Seth's jaw dropped for a second time. "How?"

"*Yer mamm* found a receipt for some carving tools in *yer* pants pocket, and those tools weren't anywhere on this property. You also kept disappearing on Sunday afternoons for a while, and I was concerned. So I followed you. Not proud to admit that, I gotta say, but when I saw the shed, I put two and two together." He took a step toward Seth. "Were you there the day of the fire?"

Seth swallowed and nodded. "*Ya.* I'm sorry, *Daed.* You don't have to worry about me doing that anymore. I'm giving up woodcarving for *gut.* This farm and our *familye* have *mei* 100 percent attention. I don't want to put our future in jeopardy again."

Sadness passed over his father's eyes. "I appreciate *yer* loyalty."

"It's not just loyalty. You put *yer* faith in me." Seth looked at the ground, his throat thick. "I let you down."

"*Nee, sohn.*" He put his hand on Seth's shoulder. "I let *you* down. When I found out I had glaucoma, I didn't want to worry everyone. I put an undue burden on you. This farm isn't *yer* sole responsibility. It belongs to all of us, equally. Ira and Judah can learn everything I taught you, and they'll have to for us to bounce back. It doesn't matter how many setbacks we have—and we will have setbacks, Seth. That's life. We can't live in fear because we're not in control. We live in peace because of who's in control."

Seth nodded, but didn't look at him. "I want to believe that."

"You will. Sometimes it takes these tough experiences to drive that point home." He smiled. "Listen to me, Seth. If you want to have a hobby, that's all right by me. You should have something that gives you joy."

"But I can't make a living with a hobby," Seth said, lifting his head. "That was the whole reason I started woodcarving . . . because I didn't like farming."

Daed looked dumbfounded. "But you've always worked so hard."

"And I hated every minute of it. But something changed when you and I were working together more closely. I realized that farming is in *mei* blood too. I want to work the farm. I want to make it a success again. I have an appreciation for it now." He shrugged. "I think I'm pretty *gut* at it."

"That you are." *Daed* smiled.

"Better than woodcarving," he muttered.

"There's *nee* reason you can't do both. If woodcarving makes you happy, there's *nix* wrong with that, as long as you take care of *yer* responsibilities. I'm not going to sugarcoat it. We'll have to work harder than ever before. But the work will be equal this time. I told Ira and Judah about *mei* eye condition, and I'll tell *yer schwesters* after church. I should have been up-front with everyone." He shook his head. "Seems like we've all learned some lessons lately."

"Some hard ones," Seth said, thinking about Martha.

"The harder they are, the better they stick. At least in *mei* experience." He glanced up at the sky. The sun beat down relentlessly. "The Lord's taking his time with the rain," *Daed* said, then looked at Seth. "I'm going inside to get a drink. Want to join me?"

He looked in the direction Martha had gone. Like his father said, God was in control of the farm and the future. But in the present he needed to act. "*Nee*," he said. "I've got something to take care of first." He had to set things straight with Martha, once and for all.

. . .

Martha knelt at the edge of the garden, yanking the weeds out through a blur of tears. She couldn't bring herself to go inside once she left Seth's. Her parents were both in the house, and she didn't want to explain what had just happened. She would jerk these dried-up weeds until she gathered her emotions, even if she had to stay out here all day. And night. At the rate she was crying, she might be here all week. She wiped her stinging eyes with the edge of her apron and grabbed another clump.

Gray clouds suddenly gathered, but they'd done that before. She felt the cool relief from the hot sun, but she didn't look up. She wasn't going to anticipate rain again. She'd been fooled too many times this summer.

She sat back on her heels and wiped her eyes again. She had so many regrets about what had happened the past couple of months. But giving Seth the money wasn't one of them.

Despite how things had ended between them, she still cared about his family. She cared about him. She couldn't make her feelings for him go away like she'd let go of Paul. She loved Seth. That wasn't going to change, not for a long time. *If ever.*

A strong breeze kicked up. It was so refreshing she closed her eyes and let it fall over her, cooling her hot skin and bringing a moment of relief. When it passed, she opened her eyes, sensing someone next to her. She looked up, stunned. *Seth.*

He opened his mouth, then closed it again. Then without a word he knelt next to her and started to pull weeds. She didn't have to tell him what weeds to pull. He knew more about crops than she did.

After watching him for a moment, she finally found her voice. "What are you doing here?"

"Weeding, as you can see." He pulled out another tough weed.

"You don't have enough work to do?"

He didn't respond, but instead moved a few feet away from her to a new patch of weeds.

"Seth," she said, unable to hide her confusion. He'd been furious with her, and now he was helping her with the garden? Maybe he was dehydrated after all. She'd heard that dehydration could make people act strangely.

Seth pulled a few more weeds and tossed them to the side. He ran his hands over his pants, then said, "I'm here to apologize."

Surprised, she glanced away. "That's not necessary."

"Oh, *ya*, it is. I said some awful things to you earlier."

"You don't have to apologize for telling the truth." She started to stand up, but he clasped her hand.

"I didn't tell the truth." He squeezed her hand, refusing to let go. "Let me explain, Martha. Please."

She hesitated, then sat down next to him. He released her hand, leaving it tingling. She grabbed a weed as a distraction. "I'm listening."

"I'm sorry I said you were untrustworthy. That's not true. I can trust you. You've proved that by keeping *mei* secret."

She nodded and kept pulling the weeds, unable to look at him. Keeping his secret didn't absolve her from everything else she'd done.

"I also don't want you to stop using the shop."

This time she looked at him, shaking her head. "I'm not

going back there." She couldn't tell him it had nothing to do with the carving and everything to do with her need to forget her feelings for him. She couldn't do that and still work in his shop, even if she was there alone.

"But you have to."

Now she was getting annoyed. "*Nee*, I don't." A drop of rain landed on her cheek, but she ignored it.

"You're talented, Martha. Very talented. I'm not going to have much time for it anyway. I'll be busy with the farm." He shook his head slightly. "Never thought I'd say that. But I've learned a lot recently. Farming is what I'm meant to do. Not woodcarving. That's what you're meant to do."

She looked at him. Was he serious? A warm feeling surged through her. He said she was talented. His respect for her skill meant everything to her. *Too bad it doesn't matter in the long run.* "You've said *yer* piece," she told him as a few more drops fell.

"*Nee*, I haven't." He took her hand again. "I didn't run away from *yer* parents that night because I was angry with you. I ran away because I couldn't lie to them."

"I don't understand."

He looked at their hands clasped together, making no move to separate. "We were supposed to tell them we didn't have feelings for each other."

"I know," she said, bitter.

"But I couldn't tell them that." His gaze met hers, deep and intense. "I couldn't tell them *mei* feelings aren't real, because they are."

The rain came down in a steady shower, but neither of them moved. "What?"

"I *do* care about you, Martha." Water streamed down his

face. "I've been the deceitful one, not you. I was afraid of the truth. Afraid of how much I care about you." It was raining harder now, but he squeezed her hand more tightly. "I didn't want to hear you say you didn't feel the same way about me."

Her *kapp* was drooping and her dress was getting soaked, but Martha couldn't move. She couldn't take her eyes away from his. She opened her mouth to speak, but nothing came out. *Not again.* She tried to form words, but all she could do was squeak like a tiny mouse.

"Martha?" he said, frowning a little. "Are you all right?"

Was she okay? Of course she wasn't. Seth Yoder had just said he cared for her. He was holding her hand in the pouring rain, looking at her with such deep emotion that she couldn't find her breath, much less her words. His frown deepened, and she knew she had to do something to reassure him she hadn't lost all her marbles.

So she did the sensible thing. She threw her arms around him and kissed him.

Seth's hand went to the back of her neck, and he returned the kiss as the rain everyone in Birch Creek had prayed so earnestly for continued to fall.

A sudden jerk of thunder pulled them apart. "We better get inside," he said, grabbing her hand and gently lifting her up. They ran under the patio roof, both soaked to the skin.

"I can't believe this," he said, running his hand through his wet hair.

"I know." She put her hand out and felt the rain. "It's been so long."

"Not that," he said, his voice husky. He cupped her wet cheek in his palm and turned her to face him. "Who cares about a little rain?"

She laughed. "I don't."

He grinned and dropped his hand. "Plan B."

"What?" she said, confused.

Seth put his arms around her waist. "Plan B actually worked."

Her mouth formed an *O* shape. "You're right. It did! But we can't tell Cevilla."

"She'll never let us live it down."

"*Nee* one but us will know Cevilla was right," she said. "*Mei* lips are sealed."

He kissed her again. "Just making sure," he said when they pulled away.

She placed her hand on his shoulder, not caring that they looked like they both had taken a dunk in the pond. "You think I can't keep a secret?" she said, teasing.

He shook his head, pulling her close. "I know you can."

. . .

Two months later

Seth and Martha strolled to their woodshop together. It was a Saturday afternoon, and the leaves were almost all off the trees, the November weather on the chilly side. They opened the door, which they kept unlocked now that they didn't have to keep the shop a secret. Seth still wasn't interested in selling his pieces, and he had settled into farming as if he'd always loved it. Martha still worked for her uncle, but he didn't ask too many questions when she wanted to leave early when business was slow. She spent more time there than Seth did.

Martha went to the scrap-wood bin and picked up a flat piece of oak. "I had *mei* eye on this before *mei* last project," she said, turning around and showing him the wood.

"I have *mei* eyes on you." He went to her and put his arms around her waist.

"We won't get any work done like this," she said, smiling.

"Exactly." Then he kissed her quickly and stepped away. "We might have to start coming here separately, you know. Even on Saturdays. Too much temptation."

"Just focus on *yer* own project."

The shop had two worktables now, and they had purchased more carving tools. Saturday afternoons were designated for them to work in the shop, since both their families knew about their hobbies. *Mamm* had been thrilled with her plaque for her birthday, and she also hadn't been surprised when Martha and Seth told her and her father the truth—they loved each other.

"I knew it," *Mamm* said, after Seth had gone home a few hours later. "I knew it the day of the fire."

"How?"

"I thought I'd have to pin you down to keep you from going to him. If that isn't love, I don't know what is."

It was love, and they had admitted it to each other many times since that day in the garden.

Martha went to work planing the wood, expecting to hear Seth moving behind her while he started on his own new project. When she realized it was too quiet, she turned around. He was looking at her, but instead of the normal mischievous look in his eye, his look was serious. "Is something wrong?" she asked.

"When was the last time you heard from Selah?"

"A couple of weeks ago." Martha frowned. Seth knew she and Selah had written letters to each other ever since her friend had returned to New York. "Why?"

"Tell her something for me in *yer* next letter," he said, moving closer to her.

She set down the plane and leaned against the worktable. "What's that?"

"Ask her to be *yer* bridesmaid, or maid of honor, or whatever you women call it."

Her heart skipped three beats. No, make that four. "Are you asking me to marry you?"

"Are you really that surprised?" He leaned down and kissed her. "Martha Detweiler, would you be this farmer's bride?"

She threw her arms around him with such force he lost his footing. He steadied them both, holding her tightly in his arms. "I would love to be *yer* bride," she said, then kissed him. Once. Twice. Three times . . .

No, they wouldn't get any work done today.

EPILOGUE

Selah Ropp folded Martha's letter and put it back in the envelope. She smiled, happy for her friend. Maid of honor. She'd never been anyone's maid of honor, and to her it really was an honor. Martha's wedding to Seth would take place at the end of November, a little over two weeks away.

Selah put the letter in her side table drawer and looked out the window. Snow had been falling since early this morning, but it was light and airy and wasn't accumulating much. In a few weeks it would cover the ground, and she'd assumed she'd be getting ready for Christmas with her mother and other relatives in her community. But then she'd had a feeling she wouldn't be here for Christmas, and Martha's letter just confirmed that she wouldn't. She'd felt drawn to Birch Creek for a few months now, and she'd brought it up with her counselor last week.

"I don't see why you can't go back for a visit." Her counselor, a kind *English* woman named Sally, had been meeting with Selah for over a year. Selah had learned that clinical depression didn't disappear with a pill and a few talks. It took work and therapy to keep it at bay, which was what Selah had been concerned about.

But Sally thought she'd made enough progress to reduce

their visits to an as-needed basis. "You can always call me," she said as Selah left her last session. "Anytime, day or night."

Glad for the reassurance, Selah started making plans to visit her brother, Christian, and his wife, Ruby. She missed them, even Ruby, despite their rocky start when they first met. Selah had been at one of the lowest, most confusing points of her life then, but Ruby had forgiven her for being difficult. Of course, she also missed Martha, who had become her best friend despite the distance between them.

She was excited to go back to Birch Creek. She wasn't sure how long she'd stay, but she would make it a long visit, at least through Christmas. This time would be different from when she'd moved there with Christian, trying to escape her depression by running away from her home. No, when she boarded the bus to Ohio next week, she would do it with anticipation and a sense of adventure. She couldn't shake the feeling that God was leading her back to Birch Creek, and she was ready to find out why.

ACKNOWLEDGMENTS

A big thanks to my amazing editors, Becky Monds and Jean Bloom. They know almost as much about Birch Creek as I do. My gratitude to you, dear reader. I hope you enjoyed another adventure in Birch Creek.

DISCUSSION QUESTIONS

1. Martha caused a lot of problems for herself and others by not being straightforward. What advice would you give her to help her tell her suitors the truth?

2. Seth's passion is woodworking. What job or hobby do you love to do, and why?

3. How are Cevilla and Delilah similar? In what ways are they different?

4. Nina mentions that comparing others was a problem in her prior community. Why is that kind of comparison a problem?

5. Richard struggles making a decision to join the Amish. What factors would you consider if you had to make the same choice?

6. What lessons did Martha learn from lying? What are some other reasons God wants us to be honest?

7. Freemont was sure that God would turn their tragedy into something good. When has God done something similar for you?

8. Cevilla and Delilah have a tentative friendship by the end of the book. Do you think they'll ever become closer? Or will they always be "frenemies"?

Read more from Kathleen Fuller in her Amish Letters series!

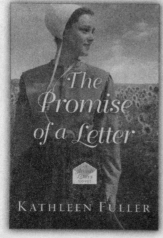

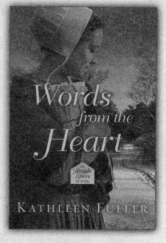

DON'T MISS FOUR SWEET AND FUNNY AMISH LOVE STORIES.

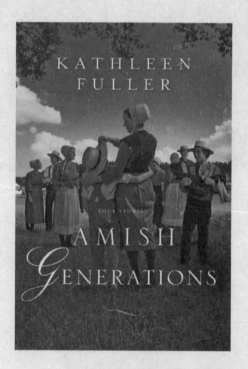

COMING JUNE 2020

AMISH BRIDES
of
BIRCH CREEK

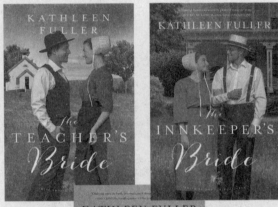

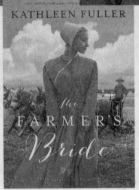

AVAILABLE IN PRINT
AND E-BOOK

Love Kathleen Fuller?
Check out the new
Amish Mail-Order Brides series!

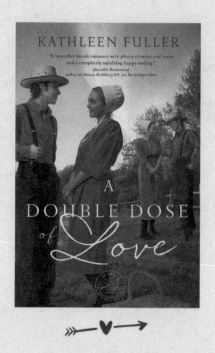

Available in print, e-book, and downloadable audio

ABOUT THE AUTHOR

With over a million copies sold, Kathleen Fuller is the author of several bestselling novels, including the Hearts of Middlefield novels, the Middlefield Family novels, the Amish of Birch Creek series, and the Amish Letters series as well as a middle-grade Amish series, the Mysteries of Middlefield.

Visit her online at KathleenFuller.com
Instagram: @kf_booksandhooks
Facebook: @WriterKathleenFuller
Twitter: @TheKatJam